JUST VENGEANCE

A DETECTIVE NOVEL

ANTHONY D'AUGUSTINE

outskirtspress
DENVER, COLORADO

Just Vengeance
A Detective Novel

v3.0 r2.0

Outskirts Press, Inc.
http://www.outskirtspress.com

Paperback ISBN: 978-1-4787-6307-9
Hardback ISBN: 978-1-4787-6361-1

PRINTED IN THE UNITED STATES OF AMERICA

For my son,
Staff Sergeant Joseph D'Augustine
1982–2012

Prologue

"Cry 'Havoc!' and let slip the dogs of war."

William Shakespeare
Julius Caesar
Act III, Scene i

1/8th Infantry, 4th Infantry Division, Kontum Province, Vietnam, May 20, 1967

It was late afternoon. Captain Nick Polsani made the sign of the cross. He'd been through this chaos before. Only this time, as his UH-1D MEDEVAC chopper approached the eye of the battle, a cold shiver ran down his back. The wall between control and emotion was beginning to break for the aviator who had been in the field for the last eighteen months. His hands began to shake. He had difficulty breathing. Polsani prayed not to lose his nerve, at least not until this mission was over.

Suddenly, stinging enemy fire ripped through the Huey's fuselage. Fighting a hand tremor, Polsani, the lead pilot of the four-man crew, lowered the craft onto the barren hilltop. All the while, his port and lee side gunners fired their .50 caliber machine guns indiscriminately into the triple canapé foliage surrounding the high ground. Dug in along the hill's crest were a smattering of foxholes. Polsani eased his hand down on the stick. With a bead of sweat dripping from his forehead, the young pilot landed the chopper, barely missing the body of a young U.S. soldier lying directly in front of him. He noticed the mangled body was one of many sprawled across the landscape. The .50 caliber gunners fired over the heads of the soldiers in the field as the combatants made a mad rush up the hill to load as many of the wounded onto the helicopter as it could bear. During the scramble, Polsani maintained as steady a hand as he could on the stick. The loud pounding of his heart could not be heard among the whirl of the rotors, the roar of machine-gun fire, the screams and moans of the wounded soldiers, and the shouts of the field commander struggling to gain control over the disorder. Polsani bit his lip, readjusted his headphones, and waited for what seemed an eternity. Then the moment he waited for came: the signal to take off. Polsani immediately pulled up on the stick. As the Huey rose, away from the maelstrom, a loud explosion shook the craft.

On high ground, approximately 750 yards away from the battle, hidden in the heavy brush was a lone sniper, his spotter had been the victim of an earlier battle. As the helicopter was lowering onto the battlefield, the sniper looked through the telescopic lens on his rifle and noticed a North Vietnam Army soldier giving orders to his troops. He focused in on the enemy and pulled the trigger. The weapon recoiled. The soldier took the bullet in the chest and fell to the ground. The sniper then noticed a group of enemy combatants circling under the protection of brush to the right of the helicopter. He took aim. Drawing a bead on a soldier preparing to place a .50 caliber machine gun onto a tripod, the sniper took him out with a head shot. He proceeded to kill two more of the enemy, forcing the rest to fall back and regroup. The sniper then zeroed in on an NVA soldier running at the helicopter from its rear with a grenade in his hand. Just as the chopper was lifting off, the enemy slid across the fuselage and pulled the pin on the grenade. A quick shot from the sniper's rifle to the shoulder of the enemy's throwing arm forced him to drop the grenade before he could toss it into the opened side door. The copter drifted forward and lifted about ten feet when the grenade exploded. The blast caused the aircraft to shutter. With minimal damage from the blast, the bird gained altitude, leaving the area of engagement without further incident.

The battle continued with other Hueys and crews returning to the scene. The sniper changed his position with each returning rescue mission, protecting their flanks and notifying the responding air cover via radio the positions of the enemy. The carnage continued until the last helo left the field. All that could be heard then were the moans and cries of enemy wounded. The battle was over. After several moments, the enemy moved back onto the hill. As they spread out looking for possible wounded American soldiers, the sniper slipped back into the veil of vegetation. He moved silently along the landscape at a quick pace, covering ten miles before stopping to rest by a fast-moving stream. Kneeling by the water's edge, the sniper closed his eyes and braced himself against the soft earth with both hands. After several minutes of heavy breathing, he managed to unscrew the cap of his canteen and take a long swig of water. With some difficulty, he was able to refill it.

Crossing the river, he headed toward its source, toward higher ground. The sun setting over his left shoulder cast a yellowish hue across the landscape. Though vulnerable in open areas, he was able to continue his trek to higher ground. He followed the stream until he came to a mountain pool. There along its sandy shoreline, he sat, leaning against a low, thick tree. The sniper stretched his legs and rested his rifle across his knees. He took out a piece of beef jerky from the breast pocket of his camouflaged shirt and chewed on it. Soon the cover of darkness arrived. That night, in the pitch blackness of the lush forest, with his loaded Browning .45 caliber handgun at his side, he field-stripped his M21 sniper rifle and cleaned it by touch. Chewing on another piece of beef jerky, his thoughts revolved around surviving the night. Tomorrow he would follow the enemy to the next battle site. And on to the next. Resting beneath the tree's cover and within the surrounding brush, Sergeant Donald "Mac" MacPherson swallowed his last piece of jerky and wondered when the battles would end.

I

"Goodness had nothing to do with it."

Mae West
Night After Night
1932

Chapter One

September 9, 2003

Edinburgh is undoubtedly the most beautiful city in all of Scotland. Home to Robert Louis Stevenson, Arthur Conan Doyle, various James Bond actors, and the locally famous Bobby (the dog that never left the gravesite of his master), the city is a classic melding of new and old. North of Prince Street bustles with modern-day shoppers, taxis, and buses. Famously-named retail outlets line the east side streets of New Town, offering all forms of goods, including the finest plaid kilts and tams, bagpipes, and the smoothest malt liquors. South of Prince Street, from Lothian Road in the west to The Palace of Holyrood in the east, lies Edinburgh's treasured past. Scores of buildings erected centuries ago, cobblestoned streets, and historic pubs pull one back to a time when men like Robert the Bruce, William Wallace, and Rob Roy clapped swords and daggers to their hips and walked this proud and beautiful land. Concession stands and store fronts fill this historic area selling items from clothing and jewelry to books, liquor, and legendary videos of knights, castles, dragons, and sea monsters (most notably, the famous Loch Ness denizen affectionately known as Nessie). Moving west up High Street, past the Castle Hill Lawnmarket, one is met by a foreboding edifice known as the Edinburgh Castle. Erected in the early eleventh century, it stands guard over the city to this very day.

The Edinburgh Castle was built on volcanic ash at the highest point in the city. It left Scottish hands only once when it was captured by the English during the Wars of Independence. Shortly after, the Celts, under the cloak of darkness, recaptured it by scaling its high walls. No invading army has since occupied it. Toward the end of the seventeenth century, the castle became a military base, housing a large garrison. Over the last two centuries various renovations have been made to it in appreciation of its historic value. As a result, numerous ceremonies are held on and about the castle's premises in tribute to the great Scottish traditions for which it exemplifies.

Today, a band was practicing just east of the castle in preparation of a celebratory march known as the Edinburgh Military Tattoo. The marching band stopped just outside the front gate and performed musical arrangements in tribute to the Scottish culture. Many visitors rushed to the east gate to view the band. One particular visitor, however, an Austrian in his mid-fifties, slowly moved away from the crowd by the eastside of the castle and walked up the winding road inside the historic stone structure. He made his way to a corner of the stone wall on the western rampart which connected two parapets. The location was in the midsection of the castle. With the vast amount of visitors mounting the east wall or exiting the castle to listen to the music and to see the spectacle, the area in the west where the Austrian stood was now secluded. Blustering winds whistled throughout the castle. As the Austrian took in the view of the scenic lowlands below and the Firth of Forth River which ran to the western horizon, a large husky black man, in his early forties, approached him from the rear. The man removed a .22 caliber pistol with an attached silencer from inside his light jacket and placed the barrel at the top of the Austrian's spine. As the band played loudly below, the killer quickly pumped two rounds into his neck. The bullets pierced the victim's spinal cord, causing immediate paralysis and an inability to breathe. The victim instantly slumped into the stranger's arms. The attacker laid him down along the stone wall, put another .22 round in the victim's head, and returned his weapon to the waistband beneath his jacket. He quickly searched the victim. Finding a sealed white envelope in his inside jacket pocket, the killer removed it. He secured the envelope—which contained information on weapons and funding—in his own jacket pocket. Satisfied the body was concealed well enough for him to make a safe escape, the killer turned to leave. Suddenly he noticed an elderly man at the bottom of the stairs leading to his location. The man had a look of horror in his eyes. The killer quickly removed his gun and fired three rounds. The elderly man dropped to his knees, one hand holding the camera strap around his neck and his other hand clutching his chest. He landed face down onto the hard stone floor. The killer returned the gun to his waistband. He descended the stairs two steps at a time and stepped around the bloodstained body of the elderly man. *No time to conceal the second body*, he thought. Then, at a brisk pace, he made his way to the castle's gate and the crowd below.

The killer wove in and out of the sidewalk stands, dodging the many tourists perusing the variety of Scottish souvenirs. It was then he heard the police sirens. As one patrol unit came down the roadway toward him, the killer quickly turned left onto a side street leading to the river. Crossing over a bridge, he walked to the curb on Prince Street. Within less than a minute, a car pulled up next to him. He got in the front passenger seat. The driver took him to a nearby marina where he boarded his 40-foot Mainship yacht.

The next stage of the killer's plan was to run north to Inverness. With a cruise speed of 15 knots and a range of 3,300 miles, the trip along the northeast coast of the kingdom would take him less than a day. Along the way, he would dispose of the handgun in the North Sea. His destination: to meet Devin Barrow, a courier of his Latin-American contact, Eduardo Melo Ortez. The killer's plan was to give the envelope to the courier in exchange for a large cash bounty. Then he would set a course for the city of Paris, docking his yacht along the Seine River. From there he would board a private jet to Pisa International Airport.

Chapter Two

September 14, 2003

The rain made the cobblestone streets surrounding the baptistery, cathedral, and campanile shiny and slippery. The rock walls of the centuries-old religious structures were set pale against a gray sky. Despite the inclement weather, tourists from around the world crowded the streets, dodging the heavy raindrops. Many of the visitors held a camera in one hand and an umbrella in the other. They moved about in undulating waves of excitement and anticipation, looking for the best locations and angles from which to take their treasured photographs. On this day, however, the otherwise strikingly beautiful vista had been turned quite sadly into one giant monochromatic snapshot.

In the Piazza del Miracoli, also called the Campo del Miracoli (Square of Miracles), which is situated just inside the wall encircling the historic structures, gypsies were working the new tourist groups. Dressed in casual attire, the petty thieves mingled with the groups as they shopped at the stands along the street or turned to take photographs of the "Torre Pendente." At one of the shops, an elderly woman bent over to examine a souvenir statue of the Leaning Tower. As she picked up the piece, a slight man in his late twenties brushed by her, stopping momentarily to reach into her unzipped pocketbook and extract her wallet. In an instant, the gypsy moved through the crowd, then just as quickly disappeared around a corner.

To the rear of the Tower was a street that was uncharacteristic of the Italian culture. It had all the flavor of the Middle East. The street bustled with Muslims. European tourists tended to shy away from this part of town. Nonetheless, it held one major attraction: it housed the only public bathrooms in the immediate area. So, for those weary travelers in need of fast relief, it was an oasis. The bathrooms were tucked away a few hundred feet from the Tower. There were no toilets, just separate compartments with tiled floors. Each compartment was open at one end with a hole in the center of the space. For just one-tenth of a euro and good aim, a lady or gentleman could find instant relief.

In one of the tiled areas a middle-aged Saudi man stood, facing the hole before him. He looked at his wristwatch, noting he had about twenty minutes before meeting his contact by the buses just outside the medieval wall. He knew his Latin-American contact was traveling as a tourist on a bus tour, and that the bus he was on was scheduled to arrive around 11 AM. He didn't like waiting. He knew the gypsies were out in full force this day and he did not want to be separated from the letter he was to deliver to his contact.

As the Saudi began to unzip his pants, a gloved hand quickly came up from behind him and covered his mouth. Before he had a chance to struggle, a seven-inch army knife cut through his back to the left of his spine and pierced his heart. The attacker laid the dead man over the hole and removed the knife from his back. After wiping the blood from the blade with a section of the dead man's shirt, the attacker slid the weapon back into a sheath just inside his jacket. He reached into the dead man's pockets, searching for a small yellow envelope. Locating the envelope—which contained names, addresses, and shipping information—in a pocket of the deceased, the attacker quickly secured the item and made his way to the exit.

Leaving the facility, he nodded and walked past the Muslim woman collecting money by the outside door. She looked back sternly at the husky individual. Moments later, a tourist's scream from one of the bathroom compartments broke her from her trance. She rushed into the bathroom and observed the body sprawled on the floor. She then placed a call to the poliziotti locale. With police and ambulance sirens blaring, and chaos brewing as illegal merchants wrapped their wares in blankets and fled from the streets that surrounded the ancient citadel, the killer made his way down the back streets of Pisa. He tossed the knife into a nearby river before getting on a gray Vespa. He negotiated the tight back roads and alleyways leading to the highway that brought him to the port town of Livorno. There he boarded a private cruising yacht that took him to Porto Vecchio in Corsica where Ortez's courier Barrow awaited the second letter. The killer received another handsome payment. From there, he set a course for Cairo's Port Said, where he piloted the cruising yacht down the Suez Canal, and, ultimately, to his home in Saudi Arabia's port city of Yanbu.

Chapter Three

September 29, 2003

The weather was perfect for the indoor/outdoor party at the palatial Montclair home. The get together was a fundraiser for the next governor of New Jersey. The hosts, John and Martha Thomlin, were well known in political circles. Among some of the guests were the gubernatorial candidate himself, a U.S. Congressman from North Jersey, two county sheriffs, two county police chiefs, four local mayors, several party chairmen, a host of lower echelon police personnel vying for promotions, and an assortment of financial backers. One of the money men, an attorney representing a multinational investment firm that has done some work for John Thomlin, stood by the waterfalls of the kidney-shaped pool eating skewered shrimp and watching the casual networking among the attendees for the exchange of money and favors.

The attorney, Eduardo Melo Ortez, a native of Aruba and an expert in offshore tax shelters, was looking for someone to get him inside New Jersey politics. His company, Global Network International (GNI), had lobbyists throughout the world, influencing government policies. GNI was looking to encourage the Garden State to direct a significant portion of its pension investments to and through one of its clients, a large European investment bank. Ed Ortez had an additional reason for buying his way into New Jersey politics: a more personal, or to be more specific, nefarious one.

"Hi, my name's Wallace Burkner."

Ortez looked up from his cocktail plate. "Aah, Mr. Burkner, John spoke of you. I'm told you are the deputy chief for the City of Newark."

The two shook hands.

"That's right. And our host tells me you're an attorney by trade."

"True, true."

Ed Ortez smiled. "John is a good friend. We've done business together over the past few years. He's very intelligent, an excellent businessman. And his wife, Martha, is a wonderful woman . . . and hostess. Have you known the Thomlins long?"

"Not that long; a little less than a year. I met Martha first. It was at a Christmas party slash fundraiser my department was running for impoverished inner-city kids. She was the one who introduced me to her husband, John, several days later. He and I talked mostly about politics and found common interests. It wasn't long afterwards that we became good friends."

Ortez put his plate down on a table by the pool and picked up a long-stemmed half-empty glass of chilled white wine. He held the glass loosely it in his hand and sipped from it. "Yes, politics; that's right. When John mentioned you'd be at his party today, he said you are considering a run for Essex County Sheriff. That's a noble cause."

"Well, my campaign is still in the early stages, Ed . . . can I call you Ed?" asked Burkner.

"Of course," said Ortez. "And may I call you Wallace?"

"Absolutely." Burkner responded. "As you know, Ed, a campaign is only as good as the people willing to support it. If I can accumulate seed money for my war chest, I won't have to rely so much on party funds. I feel I bring a lot of experience to the job. I'm pretty much at a dead end in the Newark PD. I think the chief is going to be around for quite awhile."

Ortez nodded. "A man has to recognize his obstacles. A successful man finds ways around them. You apparently are one of those men. I know it costs a lot in money and man-hours to run for office in this state. If you need any assistance, my company would be in a position to help. We believe in noble causes, in successful men. Officially, we can help with that seed money. Unofficially, if you need any 'walking-around' money . . . you know the kind to throw around as favors without the government needing to know—which, I'm sure, your opponent has plenty of—we can help you there, too. My company has vested interests in northern New Jersey. We like to give back to the community. What better way than to help people such as yourself compete in a tough market, that market being politics."

Burkner grinned and reached out to shake Ortez's hand a second time. "I truly appreciate anything you can do to help me in this run for office."

"My pleasure," Ortez said, as he spotted a waiter, just beyond Burkner, carrying flutes of champagne. He flagged the waiter down with a wave while finishing off his glass of wine. He then placed his empty wine glass on the waiter's tray, took a glass of champagne, and placed it on the table. He reached for his wallet.

"What are you doing, sir?" asked the waiter.

"Oh, not for you," he said as he pulled out a business card and handed it to Burkner.

"I'm sorry," said the waiter sheepishly. He then turned to Burkner. "Would you like one, sir?"

"No, thank you," he said to the waiter as he held up his half-finished glass of Jack Daniels.

The waiter moved on.

Burkner reached into his pocket and pulled out his business card. He handed it to Ortez.

Ortez held the card in his left hand, and, with his right, he picked up the glass of champagne and drank down three-quarters of its contents.

"Well, it has been a pleasure meeting you, Wallace. You have my number. Please call me. I can be of some help for your campaign."

"Thank you, Ed. I will."

"Sheriff Burkner, I like the sound of that," Ortez replied. He raised his glass and said, "To good friends."

"To good friends." Burkner and Ortez clicked glasses and finished off their drinks.

"Let's keep in touch," Ortez said, before moving off to the buffet table and his second helping of shrimp.

Burkner remained by the waterfall.

Martha Thomlin had been watching the conversation between Burkner and Ortez. As Ortez headed to the buffet table, she saw her opportunity and took it.

"Wallace, may I have a word with you?" she called out.

"Certainly, Martha," he said.

"Over this way," she replied, taking his arm and directing him to a gazebo on the far side of the pool.

"How'd it go with Eduardo?"

"Very well. He offered to provide money for my campaign."

"So I was able to help, again."

"Yes, dear. Your money and his should be all I'll need to sway this election. I owe you."

"And I expect to collect tomorrow night. John will be leaving on business. I'll see you at the Madison Hotel, 6 PM."

"Looking forward to it, Angel."

"Don't be late!" was all Martha said before sharply turning on her heels and strutting back to the party.

Meanwhile, Burkner swirled the remaining ice cubes in his glass. A smile cut deep lines in his cheeks. Putting the glass down on the gazebo's railing, he thought, *Sheriff Burkner. That does have a nice ring to it.*

Chapter Four

November 7, 2003

The Patriot Act was established, in part, to follow money that might be used to finance terrorist activity. The Act, in effect, places high fines on U.S. banks that are involved in the movement of such funds. As a safety precaution, these banks hired attorneys, who, in turn, hired retired police officers to scan all multinational money transactions. Any transactions that appear suspicious, whether amount or location of transfer, the officers would turn those records over to the FBI for further analysis. This way, the U.S. banks avoid paying any huge fines or incurring any bad publicity for failing to make all efforts to combat terrorist financing.

"Here's an interesting one, Paul," said FBI Agent Sara Dillon to Paul Lindstrum, Special Agent in Charge of Counterintelligence, Newark Office. "$150,000 transfer of cash from Paris to Aruba. We have no record of where the money originated. Our liaison in Paris said the signature on the paperwork for the transfer is listed as Eduardo Ortez. Background check on this guy shows that he works for GNI. We've seen other suspicious transfers of money with this investment group, and the name Eduardo Ortez popped up a few times."

"All right, Sara, flag that transaction for Homeland, notify our Caribbean Task Force, and check with Intel on this guy, Ortez. Oh

. . . and see if we can trace this money back to its source."

"I had done a cursory background check on Ortez. It seems he travels rather frequently between Europe, the Mideast, and the Caribbean. He's an attorney by trade. A facilitator in practice. He makes things happen. The transfer of money is his game. Whether it's a merger, leveraged buyout, startup companies, government debt financing, he's the mule GNI uses to move their money."

"Anything to do with terroristic activity?"

"Just suspicions, nothing tangible. His Mideast dealings revolve around oil and currency exchange. The profits from these business dealings are bundled by large European investment companies such as GNI and then dispersed internationally to governments and private profiteers willing to pay higher than standard commercial interest rates. Higher rates, higher risks. It's the risk side that raises the specter of suspicion. Some of the characters GNI—Ortez, in particular—have been known to deal with are involved in shadow governments, weapons and drug trafficking, the sex trade, and money laundering. In these cases, the higher rates far exceed the risk factor. Unfortunately, we have nothing tangible to attach to GNI, or to Ortez specifically. As far as money provided to terrorists, to date no connection has been made."

"Good work," said Lindstrum. "Just stay on top of this. If this guy Ortez is involved in anything the least bit suspect, I want to know."

"I have to say, Ed, your support has been critical to my, or should I say, our success." Burkner looked around from his seat in the far corner of the restaurant. "I'm sure, though, that you didn't ask to meet with me at this very discreet restaurant for just a sumptuous dinner."

Ortez shook his head. "Ah, Wallace. Too bad your wish to be sheriff didn't work out for you. Nonetheless, county chief of detectives is not too shabby a position. A lot of people will be surprised when that nugget is announced. It's good news. Yet, you remain cynical. Driven, but so cynical," said Ortez. "I suspect it's a casualty of your job. Nonetheless, you are to be admired for your ambition, enthusiasm . . . and, yes, your rich propensity for cynicism."

"Thanks for the left-handed compliment. Now, what is it, Ed? 'Payback's always a bitch.' So, my friend, what can I do for you?"

Just then the waiter came over. The two men placed their orders. After the waiter left, Ortez said, "I was hoping to have dinner first, but if you must know, my company doesn't ask for much. We're looking to get into the oil shipping business. A lot of profit in shipping oil. But before committing a large sum of money, we want to eliminate all potential negative variables. Information is synonymous with money, profit, success. One area of information that greatly affects our bottom line is in regard to seaports: entry fees, security, storage locations, capacities, available manpower, and so on."

"Some of that information is readily accessible, but the security issues are classified," said Burkner.

"Why do you think I'm coming to you for it? If I could make some calls, do some Internet checks, I would have. Unfortunately, because of all the paranoia, I'd get a visit from Homeland Security if I ever did research on the Newark Bay area. Now, you know me. I'm a businessman. My company is only interested in getting inside information for the purpose of reducing expenses and raising profits. Besides, if you can do this for us, you will be well compensated." Ortez exhibited a broad smile.

"If I was so disposed to do this, I'd be risking my job. Not a good way to begin my career in the prosecutor's office. I was hoping to parlay my career into a state directorship of some sort; homeland security, transportation, corrections, you know, the alphabet soup of state government agencies. I might even run for elected office. What you're asking me to do could end my career as quickly as it started."

"Not necessarily. Not if you do it right." Ortez leaned closer to Burkner. "That's assuming you have access to the information in the first place."

"Access isn't the problem. Releasing classified information is. Too risky."

The two stopped talking as the waiter placed down the appetizers.

After the waiter left, Ortez leaned back and spread his hands. "Now, Wallace, let me ask you, could you use $100,000? Just think what that money would mean for your war chest. Besides, no one but me and you will know that the documents came from you. And since we'd both profit from it and *not* be implicated by it, there would be no chance of anyone else finding out their origin."

"One guy will, the detective who gives them to me."

"We can deal with that if we have to, but remember, the information will only be used to determine how profitable it would be for GNI to invest in the oil shipping business. Nothing sinister about that."

Ortez went on, like any good salesman would after planting a seed. "Let's meet here for dinner the day after tomorrow, say seven o'clock. That should give you enough time to gather the documents. I'll have one of my men meet you at the public parking lot down the road from here after we have lunch. Once he has the documents, I will let you know where you can pick up the money. Deal?"

Burkner took a sip from the water glass. "There's a lot at stake here. I need time to think. Let me sleep on it."

Adjusting the cloth napkin on his lap, Ortez said, "With all due respect, Wallace, I must know now what your decision is." With a cold stare, Ortez added, "Need I remind you about our past financial dealings? And, of course, that affair with Martha. I don't think your wife would take too kindly knowing that."

Burkner jumped up, "Don't threaten me! And what are you talking about, my affair with Martha?"

"Sit down," Ortez said in a calm voice. "It's your career, your reputation. If you don't give me the information, someone else will. You might as well be the one to benefit from it, financially and politically. And do you think my organization would not do a complete background on you before having me approach you? We know quite a bit about you. But not to worry, we are very discreet. Please, now sit down."

Burkner slowly sat back down.

"Okay. As soon as I get my hands on the documents, I'll call you."

"The day after tomorrow, be here with them, seven o'clock," Ortez reminded him.

"With his eyes locked on Ortez, Burkner dug into the stuffed mushroom cap in from of him. "I'll be here. Just make sure *you* don't forget the money."

Detective James Grossman of the Newark Police Department Intelligence and Homeland Security Squad was on the telephone talking with his FBI liaison, Agent Sara Dillon, when Deputy Chief Burkner walked into his office in the basement of Newark Police headquarters.

"Jimmy, where do we keep the city maps?" he asked.

Detective Grossman looked at the deputy chief. "Problem, boss?"

"No, there's a mayor and council meeting coming up and I just want to be able to lay out for the pols where our community policing problems are most critical."

"The maps are over here, Dep," Grossman said as he pointed to a metal filing cabinet consisting of wide, narrow drawers in the far corner of the room. "Help yourself sir. If you need any help, just let me know."

"I'll be fine, Jim. You can finish what you're doing."

Burkner walked over to the cabinet and opened several drawers until he found the map he was looking for: Port Newark. Burkner took a copy of the map and rolled it up. He then walked over to Detective Grossman's desk.

"Excuse me, Jim," he said. "Where can I find the business files for companies in the high-risk areas?"

Grossman put his hand over the phone. "Over by the water cooler, sir."

Burkner walked over to the filing cabinet by the cooler, pulled open the top drawer and shuffled through the files.

Across the room, Detective Grossman cupped his hand over the telephone. "Sara, I'll have to call you back," he said. "The boss is here going through our files. I'd better see what he needs." Grossman hung up the phone.

"How can I help you, boss?" Grossman blurted out as he approached Burkner.

"To tell you the truth, I don't even know what I'm looking for. For now, I just need information on the security at the Port. The mayor and council will also want information on Liberty International and University Hospital, but that can wait for another day, another meeting. I'm not going to release any of the documents to them. I just want to get some idea on what policies and procedures are being carried out so I'm not caught with my pants down should they throw a curveball at me. I'd also like to have some background on how the Port operates. You know how these politicians can be, always sticking their noses where they don't belong, asking questions with no concern as to who might get hurt. Nonetheless, I'll need some ammo in case they try to sink me or the Chief as being out of touch."

"I'll see what I can do, Dep, but it may take a day or two to put it all together. When's your meeting?"

Burkner hesitated for a moment before saying, "Do what you have to do. The meeting's not 'til next week. Since it involves security issues, it's going to be closed. So, please, James, not a word on this."

"Absolutely, boss."

"Just let me know when you have the information put together and I'll come pick it up."

"I'll get right on it," Grossman said

Chapter Five

November 8, 2003

Father Nick Polsani remembered the time in Vietnam when his hands started to shake and he prayed he would give his life to the Lord if he could safely return the wounded soldiers to base. Then as his helicopter rose several feet from the ground, a powerful explosion rocked the ship. Was it coincidence that his friend, Sergeant Donald MacPherson, was there that day to take out the NVA soldier with the grenade, or did Providence have a hand in allowing him, his fellow crew members, and the handful of wounded soldiers to live yet another day? He wondered about that for many years, as he did another incident that occurred to him after coming home from the war. He remembered a time when he had given a homeless woman, who had been standing by the side of a brick building with her hand out, a ten-dollar bill. "You're lucky I happened down this street," he said to her as he placed the ten spot in the palm of her hand.

"Do you believe in Jesus?" the woman asked.

"Why, yes," he said.

"Then there's no such thing as luck," she replied.

He smiled and walked on, thinking about what she had said. *No such thing as luck.* At that moment, Nick Polsani had an epiphany. *St. Augustine. Predestination. Grace. Spiritual Guidance. Christ in all of us.* It was then he remembered his promise to God. Though not as miraculous as God's revelation to Saul of Tarsus along the road to Damascus, Polsani's intercession with the Almighty occurred with a ten-dollar bill, a homeless woman, and several words about a path laid out for him. Nick Polsani decided, at that moment, he wanted to become a priest.

Now, several years following that fateful, or shall it be said faithful, moment, Father Nick stood on the pulpit about to address the congregation. He turned to Luke 43 - 45 and in a loud voice read:

> "A good tree does not bear rotten fruit, nor does a rotten tree bear good fruit. For every tree is known by its own fruit. For people do not pick figs from thorn bushes, nor do they gather grapes from brambles. A good person out of the store of goodness in his heart produces good, but an evil person out of a store of evil produces evil; for from the fullness of the heart the mouth speaks."

After he read the Gospel verses, Father Nick moved from the pulpit out into the center aisle of the church.

"Jesus speaks here of the things we store up in our lives, be they good or evil. By our fruit, our actions, so are we known. By what we say, how we talk, so are we known. Our time here is short. We can live a life of holiness or of sin, of love or of hate, of forgiveness or of vengeance. It's your call. Your life. How do you wish to be known when your hour is at hand? When you're about to meet our Father on Judgment Day?"

Father Nick continued speaking for another ten minutes. As he ended his sermon, he made the sign of the cross and continued with the mass. When he finished, he waited by the rear door and greeted the parishioners as they left the church.

"Have a nice day, Father," Cheryl Taylor said as she shook his hand. "It was a beautiful sermon, but I think my husband would have a very difficult time with the part of scripture that places forgiveness over vengeance."

"How so?" Father Nick said.

"Mac's had a long military and police career; a lot of skeletons in his closet. He takes his job too serious. Granted, he's had a lot thrust on his shoulders over the years. Maybe someday he'll see things a bit more your way."

"There's always hope, Cheryl, always hope."

As the line behind her began to grow, Cheryl quickly added, "Well, have a good day, Father. You have many well wishers wanting to say goodbye." She then moved on. While Father Polsani shook the hand of the next person in line, he turned his head and watched her as she walked out the door.

Detective Grossman entered Burkner's office located on the second floor of the old city building. Burkner was sitting at his desk mulling over some police reports. "Hi, Dep," Grossman said as he placed the long cardboard tube on the deputy chief's desk. "Here are those documents you wanted."

"Thanks, Jim. I know it was somewhat of an arduous task but you know how these politicians can be."

"Some of this stuff is pretty confidential, boss. I hope they don't expect too much in the way of explanation. Those guys leak information to the press like a sieve. I know smoozing the media is a big part of their reelection campaigns, but there's some pretty delicate info in these files."

"Have no fear, Jim. I won't give them anything they can put out to the public and jeopardize the security of our facilities."

"I was speaking with our FBI liaison, Agent Dillon. She tells me there's been some questionable financial activity lately. You know the feds. They won't give you much. Still, they need our manpower if anything goes down, so I'm in the loop to get a taste of their info. I don't know if there's anything to what she tells me, but I thought you should know in the event the feds call on our services."

"Good," said Burkner. "Keep me informed if there are any

developments. And for security purposes let's keep this and any new information from the feds between the two of us. The fewer people who know, the less chance of a leak."

"I'm with you there, sir." As Grossman left Burkner's office, the deputy chief contemplated whether or not he should make the call. He decided another dinner with Ortez was in order. So he walked down the hall from his office, picked up the receiver from one of the phones, and dialed Ortez's number.

November 9, 2004—7:30 PM

Burkner slid in the booth across from Ortez at the rear of the restaurant. Ortez had just finished eating his salad. Pushing the salad aside, he pulled the charred steak close to him and sliced into it. "You're late," he said, without looking up at Burkner.

"We had a double homicide that just came in," said Burkner. "I had to rally the troops."

"Too bad. I didn't know if you would honor our dinner agreement. After, when I hadn't heard from you, I decided to order the house special: blackened steak with Cajun fries. Excuse me if I eat while you talk."

Just then the waitress approached the table and placed a menu in front of Burkner. He tossed it aside. "I'll have what he's eating."

"How would you like it cooked?"

"Rare."

"Drink?"

"Make it a beer. Whatever you have on tap."

"Thank you, sir," she said as she took the menu and left the table.

Once she was out of earshot, Ortez said, "As I said the last time, my man will meet you in the lot down the road after we finish dinner. He'll ask you if you have plans for the Architect. That's your signal. After you drop off the map and documents, you can pick up your money. It will be at a second location."

"I'm not stupid. I turn over the documents, but come up short on the cash end."

"Trust me, you'll get your money. I've come through for you before, haven't I? The man you will meet handles our exchanges. He will turn those documents over to an operational coordinator. Separation of responsibilities protects not only the company from fraud and manipulation but it also protects every person involved in the plan and transaction by limiting their participation, or as a cynic might say, 'culpability.' That's about as much as I can tell you."

"I still don't see how bringing others into the mix improves our deniability. Seems to me, the more people, the greater chance of leaks and corroboration should the creditability of witnesses ever become an issue."

"Relax, Wallace. That will be taken care of. I trust my man. I suspect the money you get from the transfer will seal your lips."

"Don't worry about me," Burkner said with a hint of anger in his voice. "No one will hear about this transaction from my end."

"I thought you would understand. It would not be good for your political aspirations."

Burkner's jaw tightened a bit, remembering the other veiled threat Ortez made the last time they had dinner together. "My political aspirations are my concern, not yours."

"Whatever you say," Ortez quipped before slipping another piece of steak into his mouth. He then proceeded to tell Burkner the location of the park and where he could access the money.

The waitress soon brought Burkner his steak and beer. The two settled down and finished their meals. They spoke further about the drop-off details. After coffee and a sumptuous dessert, they got up, said their goodbyes, and left the restaurant. Unbeknownst to them, it would be their last goodbye to each other.

Burkner pulled into the lot and parked in the corner under a large pin oak tree. Devin Barrow parked his car alongside and got out.

"Do you have the plans for the Architect?" Barrow asked.

Burkner took the long round tube from the backseat of his car and gave it to Barrow.

"I received a call just as you left the restaurant," Barrow said. "Your package will be at the park. You know which park and where in the park it's to be found. That's my understanding."

"Right, right, I know where it is," Burkner said. At that moment, some old memory popped in his mind. "Do I know you?" he asked.

Barrow turned his head away from Burkner. "You must be mistaken," he said, before quickly heading to his car. He backed out of the space and left the area in a hurry.

Burkner hadn't gotten Barrow's license plate number, but he knew he had seen him before. It finally occurred to him that the courier for Ortez was an old-time hustler and businessman from the streets of Newark. *Small, small world*, he thought, as he put his car in gear and headed to the park in Bayonne.

Chapter Six

November 9, 2003

The air was crisp and the sky black. Devin Barrow approached the railing at the edge of the Palisades. With an eagle's view of the George Washington Bridge, the Hudson River, and Washington Heights, he held a three-foot cardboard tube in his left hand and took a nervous drag on his cigarette with his right. Barrow had a bad feeling about this meet. The rustling he heard in the bushes behind him did little to quell his jitters. The wind suddenly kicked up at the top of the two-hundred-foot cliff where he stood. He quickly leaned the cardboard tube along the railing, tossed his cigarette to the side, and struggled with the zipper on his jacket. After zipping it up to his neck, Barrow looked at his watch: *9:25 PM.*

He lit another cigarette.

He waited. Barrow looked at his watch again. *9:49.* He took a long draw from his third cigarette and looked out over the river from historic Fort Lee, where on November 16, 1776, General George Washington galloped from Hackensack up Fort Lee Road to the garrison where American Revolutionary soldiers were watching helplessly as British soldiers burned down Fort Washington across the river. Three days after the fall of Fort Washington, the American troops abandoned Fort Lee in order to fight another day. Barrow, though, worried about the nature of his meeting, had no intention of abandoning the deal that was about to take place.

Suddenly, he saw two headlights break the darkness. He heard a car pull into the parking lot approximately one hundred feet to his rear. Moments later, a door clicked shut. Barrow only heard footsteps in the quiet evening before an incandescent street lamp along the pathway leading to the lookout point produced the shadow of a man. Out of the shadow emerged a stocky black man wearing a dark trench coat. As the stranger neared, Barrow stepped away from the railing. He took one last drag from his newly lit cigarette before crushing it out underfoot.

"It's you," Barrow said. "I was expecting someone else."

"Who's that?" asked the stocky individual.

"The Architect," he replied.

"That's who I'm here for."

The two men shook hands.

"Have any problem finding the place?" asked Barrow.

"None," said the man. "I actually got here a little early. I had parked a bit away. Had to make sure you came alone. I don't like surprises."

"Was that you I heard in the bushes a few minutes ago?"

"Yeah. I was waiting to hear if you made contact with anyone, cops or otherwise. One can't be too careful in this business, especially when money's involved."

"Well, then let's get this done so we can be on our way."

"Are those the documents?" the man asked pointing to the cardboard tube.

"That's them," Barrow replied as he picked up the tube and held it with his shaking right hand.

The man took the tube, opened it, and pulled out the map of Port Newark. He unrolled the map and took a moment examining it. "This is the map I'm supposed to pick up, but where are the other documents?"

"They're in there."

The man looked down the tube and noticed additional papers rolled up inside. He slid them out of the tube and quickly looked over them. Satisfied, he placed all the items back in the tube.

"The envelopes I had given you in Europe, did they make it to their final destination without a problem?"

"No problem," Barrow said.

Suddenly the man cried out in a hoarse whisper, "Damnit!" as he fumbled with the cap, trying to secure it to the top of the tube.

"Settle down, settle down. It's not that difficult. You just have to catch the threading," Barrow said as he reached out to help.

The man dropped the cap.

Barrow bent over to help pick it up.

Pop! The gut-wrenching sound of metal on bone lasted only an instant. A stinging pain shot through Barrow's left temple, followed by an immediate disconnect with the world around him. Unconsciousness quickly followed. His legs buckled. Falling first to his knees, Barrow landed face down on the pavement.

The man quickly put the small lead-weighted club back into his right rear pocket. He picked up the cap and deftly snapped it onto the tube. With a Herculean effort, he threw Barrow over his shoulder and walked to the railing. In a burst of energy, the stranger heaved him over the divider into the darkness below. He walked back to the cardboard tube, picked it up, and headed back to his car, where he picked up his cell phone and placed a call. "The package is good" was all he said before hanging up.

Burkner drove north on Park Drive. He turned into the northwest lot of Bayonne Park. The area overlooked the Newark Bay. Though the park was drenched in darkness, across the way from where he was parked, hundred-foot-tall mechanical monsters were working feverishly under bright lights plucking large containers from a docked ship. Beyond the dock and containers were the rail lines, the New Jersey Turnpike, and Liberty Newark Airport. Burkner knew the topographical map he had given to Barrow gave better than a bird's-eye view of the Port area and the security documents provided critical information on the operational aspects within the area.

Looking around, Burkner searched for a green Dumpster. He spotted it in the corner of the lot. He drove up to it and got out of his vehicle. He looked around for the presence of any people or vehicles. Not seeing any, he opened the lid of the Dumpster and extracted a large vinyl duffle bag that had been placed on several broken cardboard boxes. Burkner took the duffle bag out and sat back in his car. He unzipped it and counted each stack of hundred-dollar bills. It was all there, all $100K. He thought a moment whether he should pull out of the parking lot and wait nearby to eyeball whoever was to confirm that the money had been picked up, or just leave the area as agreed upon in his last conversation with Ortez. After looking at the duffle bag lying in the passenger seat, he decided to leave well enough alone. He placed his vehicle in drive, pulled out of the lot, and headed south on Park Drive. He turned left on West 40th Street, then made another left onto JFK Boulevard East.

In the northeast wooded area of the park, along the Hackensack River Walkway, the individual, now confident that Burkner left the area, put down his miniature binoculars. He walked through the lot, toward the Dumpster. Upon reaching it, he opened the lid and looked inside. Satisfied the hundred grand was no longer there, he headed back to the northeast wooded area. He continued walking through the woods until he came to the dead end area of West 48th Street. He got into the rear of a black limousine. The vehicle headed east on West 48th Street, before turning southwest on JFK Boulevard.

November 15, 2003

The twin in-board diesel Mainship yacht cruised down the Seine River. After passing through several locks and slipping under the low bridges that spanned the river, Conroy entered the City of Paris and docked at the Port de Grenelle. With a partial view of the Eiffel Tower, Barrow's killer got off the boat and, with suitcase in hand, crossed the Quai de Grenelle and walked briskly to La Rue du Docteur Finlay. He stopped in front of building number 26. Before entering the apartment complex, he checked to see if there were any persons or vehicles in the area watching him. Convinced he wasn't being watched either by the Paris Police, Interpol, or any number of shadowy figures he had dealt with over the years, the killer entered the building and walked up three flights of stairs to the one-bedroom apartment.

"Ahmed!" the beautiful, young Syrian woman cried out as he entered the apartment. "I am so glad you are back. I missed you so much!"

He dropped his suitcase, closed and locked the door. The woman jumped into his arms. Ahmed slid his hand around her back and caressed her bottom. After a long, passionate kiss, he said, "Zeala, Zeala, you can't imagine how much I've missed you. I'm long overdue for a little lovin'."

The two moved to the bedroom where they spent the next hour remembering how much they missed each other. At one point, Ahmed, near sheer exhaustion, rolled over and asked, "Is the money safe?"

"Is that what's on your mind right now?" she asked.

Silence.

"Well, is it?" she asked again.

"Just answer the question. I need to know if the money is safe."

"Yes, of course," she said. "I have deposited it in several banks—I'll show you the slips. And some of the cash is in the other room just like you told me."

"How much is in the other room?"

She kissed him on the shoulder. "Ten thousand euros."

She kissed him again, this time on the cheek. "Forget about the money. Let us play around some more."

Ahmed's attention was suddenly elsewhere. He turned his head toward the bedroom door. "Has anyone been coming around, asking where I've been?" he asked.

Zeala began nibbling on his ear. "No, no one," she said in a mumble. Lifting her head, she asked, "Why? Are you expecting someone who I don't know about?"

"You know my business. You know the type of people I have to deal with. Any one of them can mean trouble."

"You trade currencies for my people. No? Why would they want to hurt you?"

"It's a bit more involved than that. It's best you don't know all the small details. Just like they don't know the small details about you."

"Me? What about me?"

"Well, for starters, that we are lovers. You know how those Sharia Law followers feel about our arrangement. They'd stone you to death. Secondly, if they know you're sitting on a lot of cash, and that you have access to a lot more cash in various bank accounts that can be used to fund their jihad, you probably would live only long enough to withdraw all the money and give it to them. And thirdly, if they wanted to get to me, they just might use you as bait. All-in-all, it's best they don't know *the small details* about you."

"Now you are scaring me, Ahmed. When will you stop doing what you're doing; say you have enough money, so we can marry, live openly as man and wife; so we can travel, see the world?"

"Someday, but not right now." Ahmed turned and kissed Zeala on the neck. He moved down, kissing her on the breast, then stomach. "Forget all that small detail stuff. I agree with you. Let's play around some more," he said. For the next hour, no more words were exchanged between the two.

Meanwhile, the camera hidden across the street from 26 La Rue du Docteur Finlay continued to record all street activity, coming and going.

II

"Ay, now the plot thickens very much upon us."

George Villers
Duke of Buckingham
The Rehearsal
Act III, Scene ii

Chapter Seven

January 6, 2004

Mac and Cheryl Taylor Investigations—or MCT Investigations, as it was officially called—had an office entrance in the rear of a large center-hall colonial situated on a tree-lined street in Bloomfield, New Jersey. After their wedding a year earlier, Mac and Cheryl searched for a place close enough to Newark for him to conduct business, but far enough away to enjoy the quaintness of suburban living.

Over the past year, Mac applied for, and received, a New Jersey Private Investigator's License. There was some squabbling with the NJ State Police Private Investigator Licensing Bureau, but with a clean Newark PD check, dismissed charges in New York State for his part in the LaForge/Parnel case, and recommendations from Detective Lieutenants Martin Presler (Newark PD) and Evan Falco (NY State Police), he was issued his license in six months. It took a little longer for him to get approval to carry a firearm. Nonetheless, with his years of police experience, the approval finally came through before the year was out.

"It looks great!" Cheryl beamed. Holding both hands on the back of her hips, she added, "I've been so busy with the baby's room that I hadn't had the time to see what you've been doing down here."

The twelve-by-fifteen-foot room had one window that

overlooked the wooded backyard to the west. Along the north wall was a four-tier filing cabinet. One file contained business records; another file held research and intelligence documents; a third, closed cases (presently empty); and the last file housed the open cases (presently empty). Next to the cabinet was his desk. Alongside the desk was a leather-cushioned chair. On the desk was a telephone with a split connection. One of the two lines ran into the top right drawer of his desk and was connected to a tape recorder. A calendar blotter, several books, and a see-through plastic paperweight containing a coiled piece of string sat on top of the desk. Along the left inside wall of the desk was a small shelf. On it sat a fully-loaded .45 caliber Glock automatic handgun.

Along the east wall was a combination copy/fax machine. Several feet to the south of the machine were two computer workstations: one for Internet connections and the other for off-line financial and case file records.

"So here's where I'll be doing business?" Cheryl asked while attempting to carefully sit in the chair. As she rolled on casters toward one of the computer terminals, Mac hurried in her direction.

"Take it easy," he said. "You're seven months' pregnant."

"Relax, I work out every day on the treadmill. And I do my yoga. Plus, I'm barely showing. I can do everything I've done before you did this to me," Cheryl said while rubbing her midsection. "Besides, pregnancy is not a sickness. I'm fine . . . and I'm not due for another two months."

"Just take it easy. Okay?"

"All right, all right, dad," she said sarcastically. "Were you like this with your first wife?"

A troubled look crossed Mac's face. Before he could answer, Cheryl said, "Forget I asked that . . . . Listen, I'll be fine. Believe me."

Mac watched as Cheryl twirled in the chair, fiddled with one of the keyboards, and examined the drawers and shelving on the *L*-shaped desk.

He walked back to his desk, reached under the center drawer of it, and grabbed his .45 caliber Glock off the shelf. He removed the magazine and popped the round from the chamber. He racked the slide several times before removing it. Mac proceeded to clean the weapon. When he was finished, he loaded it and placed it back on the shelf under the desk. After that, he took out his Mossberg 12 gauge shotgun from a locked cabinet behind the desk. He jacked the pump several times before loading the weapon and placing it back in the cabinet.

"Are you preparing for something I don't know about?" Cheryl asked.

"One never knows, do one," Mac replied with a smile. "Boy Scout motto, 'Be Prepared.'"

"When you're spending your afternoons cleaning your guns, I know you're looking for things to do. I realize it's hard starting out, but I just hope you get a case soon."

"I will. It takes time getting established," Mac said. "What about you?"

"What do you mean?"

"Well, you seem to be in your own world, waiting for the baby to come."

"I am a bit worried. After all, I'm not a spring chicken, and this is my first child. I'd worked the delivery room for a period of time when I was a nurse, but it's a different story when it's you having the baby."

"Don't worry, I'll drop everything the moment you tell me it's time."

"I'm not concerned about *you*. I'm a big girl. I'll find a way to get to the hospital if you're out somewhere on a case. I'm just worried that the baby will have a problem. It's every mother's concern."

"You'll be fine. The baby will be fine. Think positive."

"You, too. A case *will* come in any day now. I'm sure."

"I know," said Mac.

A dimpled grin came over Cheryl's face. "How many more guns do you have left to clean?"

"Just two," Mac said grinning back. "My .22 caliber Savage scoped rifle and my .9mm Sig Saur handgun. That should take me 'til quitting time."

"Must you leave these guns *loaded* in this room?"

"I know it goes against all the basic retention training I've been taught over the years, but I find comfort in knowing my weapons are not only accessible, but ready for anything."

"Well, don't think for a second you'll be leaving loaded guns around the house once the baby's born."

"When the time comes, I'll get a lockbox for my handguns. Until then, I like having a weapon nearby, always at the ready. "

"I can see we have some issues that have to be ironed out," Cheryl said. "I pray you'll never have need for a gun in the house. Why don't you carry it with you instead of just leaving it lying around?"

"I carry one now. The .45 is a spare."

"Have you always been this paranoid?"

"No, not always. Only since I've been a target starting in Nam and ending two years ago at Mongaup Pond."

Cheryl took a deep breath. "Well, hopefully, that's all in the past and—"

Several sharp knocks on the side door drew Mac and Cheryl's attention away from their conversation.

Chapter Eight

January 6, 2004

The man looked left, then right before pounding on the door.

"Come in," said Mac.

A stout, middle-aged man wearing a collared shirt, casual slacks, and loafers entered the office and looked around.

"Can I help you?"

"I hope so," the man said as they shook hands. "I had a little problem finding you. You're not in the phone book."

"Well, I've just opened shop. Been in the business of investigations, one way or another, for quite some time. It's only been recently, though, that I decided to hang a shingle. This is my wife, Cheryl."

The man looked her up and down. "Pleased to meet you."

"Same here. Well, let me let you two talk. I have to check on several matters."

The man bowed his head as Cheryl left the room.

"I've heard about your exploits," said the man, a slight grin cutting across his face. "My name is Lamar Darcy."

"Glad to meet you, Mr. Darcy. Why don't you have a seat and tell me how I can help you." Mac directed Darcy to the leather-cushioned chair. He then slid into the low-back swivel chair behind his desk.

"I need you to find the man who murdered my good friend two

months ago. The police believe it's an accident, but I don't believe that to be the case."

Mac leaned forward and scratched his forehead. "The police are usually pretty good at handling death investigations. They have quite a bit of forensic support. I'm sure they've had good reason to classify your friend's death as accidental." Mac sat back in his chair. "However, I suspect you *too* have good reasons *not* to believe it's an accident. Or should I say *to* believe it's a homicide. Otherwise, you wouldn't be here. So, please, Mr. Darcy, explain what are those reasons."

As Darcy began to tell his story, Mac silently recorded his impressions of the man. Darcy was no more than five-eight inches in height and weighed approximately one hundred ninety pounds. He had light hair and piercing blue eyes, a square jaw that jutted out considerably, a gray-laced mustache, and the soft hands of a concert pianist. The eyeglasses he wore were steel-rimmed and fashionable. Though the man before him was dressed casually, his wardrobe cried out money. *Good for business.*

"The police say my friend fell from the Palisades. I know he didn't fall . . . . He was pushed or thrown off those cliffs."

The old Humpty Dumpty dilemma, Mac thought. "Sounds tragic. Just so you're aware, before we go into the nuts and bolts of all this, I have to first tell you that one of the hardest cases to prove is a push or fall homicide. Unless there's a confession, a witness, or extenuating circumstances—such as injuries not consistent with a fall—it's a bear to prove homicide."

"Well, that's why I'm here," Darcy replied. "I heard you might be able to prove it."

"Why is that?" asked Mac.

"Well, for starters, you know my friend. His name was Devin Barrow."

"Silky?! . . . I always check the obits. I'm surprised I didn't read anything about his death in the papers."

Darcy lowered his head and pulled at his shirt cuffs. "Devin moved into Bergen County several years ago. Bought one of those monster homes in Alpine. His obituary was in the local newspaper up there. Nothing here in Essex County. The cops in Bergen are checking it out. Judging from newspaper reports in Bergen County it looks like they're leaning toward either an accidental fall or a suicide. Apparently, according to one detective, Frank Arnet, quoted in the newspaper article on page four of the Local section, 'Unfortunately, the Palisades and the George Washington Bridge attract quite a few individuals each year who are intent on killing themselves. This might not be the case with Mr. Barrow's death, but at this time we have no indications of foul play.'"

"Hmm," said Mac. "Strange way to put it. Usually, the PR guy would simply say, 'The matter is under investigation. At this time we cannot rule out suicide or accidental fall.' Case closed." He placed both hands on the desk. "Why are you so sure Silky was murdered?"

Darcy leaned forward and looked directly into Mac's eyes. "Let's just say we were friends . . . and I'm concerned that his killer will go free. If you can find out who killed him, I'm willing to pay whatever the going rate is . . . and then some."

Mac sat back in his chair and folded his hands across his stomach. After several moments he said, "I know Silky was involved in many underhanded operations, but is there any evidence you can give me to support your claim that he was murdered?"

"That's why I came to you. Hopefully, you can find something." After a moment's thought, Darcy said, "I realize you need something tangible to go on. I'll tell you what I can, which isn't much. So, where do you want me to start?"

"You tell me."

Darcy brushed an imaginary piece of lint off his pants. "He wasn't your model citizen, as I'm sure you well know . . . but Devin was a good friend to me."

"How good?" Mac interjected.

"What do you mean?"

"You know what I mean."

"Well, yeah, Devin and I had a good relationship. If you know him, as you say you do, you know he was gay. We were partners for the last two years. He had money, lots of money, but few friends and no living relatives. I'm basically it. I know he's had his run-ins with the law but regarding his death, there's a lot of stuff here that they're not seeing."

Mac scratched his head. "Why didn't you give the detectives investigating the case this so-called 'stuff' that would help them find the killer . . . that is, of course, since you think he was murdered."

"Without a doubt he was murdered. Unfortunately I can't tell the police because all my dealings will be put on the table, and I can't afford that."

"I'm sure you're aware I can't be party to illegal activity. I can lose my investigator's license, worse yet I could go to jail. Although Silky never busted my chops when I was working the street, he was not the kind of guy I'd be willing to do time for."

"You don't have to worry about me or where the money for you is coming from. We'll keep it a 'don't ask, don't tell' policy. You can feed the information to the police as you see fit. Just leave me out of the picture."

"Will do, but remember, if this gets too borderline, I might have to pull out of this case."

"You won't," said Darcy.

"What makes you say that?" Mac replied.

"Do you think I happened upon you by chance? No way. Devin and I were very impressed with what you did at Mongaup Pond. You surely caused a big stir with that case. A lot of people took notice. I like how you operate. And I suspect you have a lot of connections on both sides of the fence."

"Don't be so sure about that."

"Anyway, here's the story. Devin kept his dealings pretty much to himself. However, before he was found at the base of the Palisades in Edgewater, he had a map with him. I noticed it to be a map of transportation routes and what looked like storage facilities."

"How did you become aware of all that?"

"Like I said, I saw the map in his possession."

"Did you ask him about it?"

"No, because he always had something brewing . . . and I never got involved in his business affairs."

"Do you recall any contacts that he made just prior to his death: letters, emails, phone calls?"

"Just one call, about two nights before he died. He seemed a little uneasy about it. He wouldn't say who it was, only that he was getting tired of the game. 'The money just isn't worth it anymore,' he said."

"That could mean he was despondent and was going to kill himself. No?"

"No. He had talked at times about selling his home and businesses, and moving south. He had enough in net assets to pay off all his bills, buy a nice home down south, and live his remaining years in comfort."

"Well, suicides don't usually think rationally."

"Look, I'm telling you he didn't kill himself. It wasn't in his nature. Besides, he left with the map that night. Why would he do that?"

"You know that as a fact?" asked Mac.

"I saw him stuff it in a cardboard tube along with other papers. Why would he have brought the map and other documents with him the night he was killed? That doesn't add up. The police didn't mention anything about finding the map on him or in his car."

"Did you tell the police that he took the map with him?"

"No, I didn't." Darcy began fidgeting with a loose thread on his pants. "See here's my dilemma: I didn't know what Devin was involved in. He dealt with some pretty unsavory characters. I wouldn't doubt for a minute they would cut my throat if they thought I had some information that could implicate them. As for the police, they'd hang me out to dry in a courtroom just so some prosecutor or investigator could get a feather in his cap or a premature promotion. That's why I came to you. I need somebody who's going to act in my best interest."

"Well, if I take this case, I have to advise you I don't come cheap."

Actually, he was hoping to start out with a case simpler than a mystery homicide; a theft, a cheating husband, a night or two of house sitting, or doing some bodyguard work, that'd be the way to start. But a dead body that the police feel is an accident or suicide. *Well, I'll set a high price on this one.*

"Two thousand dollars as a retainer."

Darcy reached into his pocket and pulled out a wad of bills. "I'd like to keep this between the two of us, if that's okay with you? I don't want anyone to know I'm hiring you . . . just in case this leads to something that might put me in danger. So I hope you don't mind dealing in cash." He peeled off two thousand dollars in hundreds and handed them to Mac. "Here, you go." Then, handing Mac another thousand, he said, "This should take care of immediate expenses. Here's my card. Let me know if you need another payment. Oh, and I'd like to be apprised of any developments at least once a week."

Mac looked at the plastic card Darcy had given to him. It was aqua blue and had a thin gold trim around its edges. It's lettering in gold read:

LAMAR DARCY
Arbitrageur
Navesco Corp.
New York / London / Paris

His card also listed in gold two telephone numbers, a fax number, and an email address.

"Here, give me that card back for a minute," said Darcy. He took it and wrote down another telephone number. "This is my private number. It's not a cell phone, so leave a message for me to call you if you get the machine recording. Don't leave any information other than to call back." He returned the card.

Mac looked at the hand written telephone number, then at the money he held in his other hand. *Something's not right here*, he thought. *Nevertheless, though the client appears a little shaky, he hadn't asked me to do anything illegal . . . yet . . . and the money looks good.* "I suspect you don't want a receipt?"

"That won't be necessary," said Darcy as he got up and reached across the desk to shake Mac's hand. "The fewer records of this transaction the better. Oh, and don't bother to write a report, either. Just let me know what's going on. If any of your work can help prove that Devin was murdered—as I believe it to be the case —I've done my job for a friend."

Mac rose from behind his desk. "Give me a day or two to get a handle on this, and I'll give you a call," he said as he walked Darcy to the door.

"Good. And, as I said, please keep all conversations and my identity in this matter confidential. Shall I say, 'Just between the two of us'?"

"Of course, you've made your point perfectly clear," replied Mac.

Lamar Darcy got up and went to the door. "Let's stay in touch," he said as he walked out.

A moment later a black limousine pulled up to the curb. Darcy got into the backseat. Mac watched from his living room window and was able to jot down the license plate number as the limousine began to drive off.

Chapter Nine

January 7, 2004

Mac met Homicide Detective Frank Arnet by the front desk of the Bergen County Prosecutor's Office in Hackensack. Arnet, at 32 years of age was the youngest investigator in the homicide squad. He fit the image of the modern detective—tailored suit, heavy-starched white shirt, silk tie, leather slip-on shoes, and a gold watch. Mac immediately suspected that this guy had good connections. *How else could he have worked his way into the premier squad in such a short time?*

"So you're Mac Taylor," Arnet said. "I've read about your exploits. It seems guys like us, in this business, can never retire. I hope the PI world is a little more relaxing."

"That depends," said Mac, "on the client and the agencies one has to deal with."

"Well, I assure you I'll try to provide you with any information I'm allowed to regarding the matter of Devin Barrow. As I told you on the phone, we've got nothing here to indicate anything other than a suicide."

"Yeah, I read about that in the papers. I take it you have a motive—debt, cheating lover, business going under, substance abuse."

"Still no motive, but in order to log the case as a homicide, we need evidence that would rule out suicide. You know the game. First prove homicide, then look for suspects."

"How about undetermined or suspicious. Don't you follow up on those cases?"

"Not if the Medical Examiner determines the death to be accidental or suicidal."

"Could I see the ME's report?" Mac asked.

"Sure." Detective Arnet brought Mac into the Homicide Squad. He pulled the case file for Devin Barrow out of his desk drawer.

"Here's the ME's report," he said as he handed it to Mac.

Looking through the report, Mac noticed the cause of death to be blunt force injuries. The injuries were as follows: multiple skull fractures, compound neck fracture, dislocated and fractured right shoulder, five fractured ribs, fractured sternum, fractured upper spinal cord, fractured right tibia, and multiple lacerations and contusions to face, torso and lower extremities. The ME listed the mode of death as a suicide. Mac looked at the naked photographs of the deceased.

"That's odd," he said.

"What's odd?"

"The injuries."

"How's that?"

"It's my understanding that jumpers jump. They don't dive. Which means they usually land feet, back, or chest first. The vast majority of the injuries Barrow sustained were to his head, neck, and upper torso. You'd think if he jumped, there would be broken ankles, broken shin bones, lower spinal injuries. And there's a greater degree of bruising about his head, torso, and arms than there is on his back and lower extremities. And how about interviews? What did family, friends, creditors have to say about him? About his demeanor prior to his death?"

Arnet smiled and closed the file. "Let's take a walk."

The two men left the courthouse and turned off Hudson Street onto Main. "Look. I couldn't show you our investigative reports without permission of the Prosecutor or Chief, or without a subpoena. Not my rules. It's office policy. The ME's report is public record. Different story. What I will do is tell you what I know. If you need to look at our investigation records afterwards, you'll have to call or send a letter to the Chief. I wish I could be more helpful with that, but you can appreciate office rules. What I can do is to verbally tell you what we know about Barrow. As you might have known, he had a large home in Alpine, probably the most exclusive town in Bergen County. He owned a check-cashing business and a construction company in Essex County. From what I gathered during the investigation, he owed quite a bit of money to lenders, employees, in taxes, etcetera. Seems he had a drinking problem and things were beginning to slip away."

"Sounds like a possible motive for murder, too."

"Not the way we see it. Why kill the golden goose. With him dead, no one gets a dime. Sure the legit ones can go after his estate, but it would take years to collect assuming they win their case. Besides, with him alive they can always file suit. Listen, if there was a shred of evidence that would indicate murder I would have jumped on it."

"I just gave you one back at your office. Mode of death."

"Listen, my friend. Without any evidence to support a claim of murder, other than routine injuries as a result of a long fall, the ME won't signal a need for a full-scale homicide investigation. Who knows how Barrow fell? Why he fell? His leg could have hit a branch on the way down and flipped him over, head first. It's anybody's guess what happened during the fall. But one thing seems apparent, he might have been depressed knowing he owed a lot of people money and he was a drinker; two motives for suicide. Plus, if you're looking at murder as a mode of death, killing him wouldn't have gotten any of his creditors their money back. There's a motive *not* to kill him, but to keep him alive.

"Now I have a more important question for you, Mac. Who

hired you to look into this as a murder? That might give me reason to reopen this case."

"Actually, I'm the interested party. Silky operated out of Newark for years when I was a detective down there. He owned and operated several coin-operated laundry services and an auto repair shop. I'm sure your criminal background check showed that he was arrested and convicted some twenty years ago for chop-shop violations at his garage. Unfortunately, we couldn't prove that the laundry service money was used for elicit gains. That's a tough business to track receipts.

"Anyway, I'm interested because I know his past and suspect there's more to this than a mere suicide. He had too many enemies on both sides of the aisle."

"So, what you're telling me is that this is simply a matter of curiosity for you?"

"Basically."

"Well, I'll tell you what I'll do. I'm free tomorrow morning. What say I meet you at the Fort Lee park where Barrow took a swan dive? If you can give me an indication that this case is anything but a suicide, I'll reopen it. Sound fair? I'll meet you at 10, after rush hour."

Mac nodded. "10 it is."As he turned to leave, Arnet said, "Oh, and just so you know, right now I'm not buying the *curiosity* line."

Cheryl entered the office. "How goes it, pard'ner?" she said, walking to where Mac sat and kissing him on the back of his neck.

"It's going," he replied.

"Well, you're first case sounds like a doozy. A possible murder in Bergen County with a tight-lipped gay lover as a client."

"You know me, nothing's ever easy."

"Isn't that the truth," she said while leaning on the edge of the desk in front of Mac. "How'd you make out with the Prosecutor's detective?"

"Not as well as I had hoped. Seems Detective Arnet wants to write Barrow's death off as a suicide. I'm not seeing it. Not right now at least."

"So what are you going to do about it?"

"What any good detective would do: return to the scene, interview people, research Barrow's recent contacts and acquisitions. Plus, I'm curious about his relationship with Darcy. My instincts tell me Darcy might have an ulterior motive."

"Remember, he's your client. Don't bite the hand that feeds you. You're working for him now, not the State of New Jersey."

A quick smile crossed Mac's face. "Don't I know it. Still, I have to get to the bottom of all this. I don't like loose ends. And I don't like people playing me. I know he's my client, but I've dealt with many people like him in my career. They like to control everything. Tell you only what they want you to know, no more. And see how much info they could squeeze out of you. They're one-way streets."

"Well, let's just say Mr. Darcy is not being totally honest or forthright with you about his reason for wanting to find out if Barrow was murdered, and, if so, by whom. What are the possibilities?"

Mac hesitated for a moment. "Only God knows. It could be just as he says. He's concerned about the loss of a friend. Or, he could have been a creditor of his. That's not a stretch. Darcy appears to be a wealthy man. Then again, maybe he could be afraid that if Barrow *was* murdered, he might be next. Another possibility, he simply wants information on what led to Barrow's murder, or suicide. And, of course—hard as it might be to believe—there's always the chance it's something I haven't yet considered. One thing's for sure, though, as I get closer to the truth, I'll get closer to his motive in pursuing this matter. As it stands, there's something missing here that I can't put my finger on right now."

Cheryl rubbed Mac's shoulders. "Well, I'm sure you'll figure it out. After all, it's not like Mr. Darcy had Barrow killed."

Mac quickly turned to face her. "Interesting, very interesting.

I hadn't thought of that. Granted, on its face it doesn't make sense why Darcy would want me to look into this as a homicide, if he did it or contracted it, when the police ruled it a suicide. But, again, there's definitely more to this matter than meets the eye."

Cheryl smiled and made her way toward the living room. "Whatever the reason, I'm sure it'll all make sense at some point." As she walked out of the office, Mac remained seated, his elbows on the desk with his chin resting on his crossed hands. Lost in thought, he continued to ponder all the possibilities.

Chapter Ten

January 8, 2004

Using an online PI records account, Mac ran the license plate for the limo Lamar Darcy had gotten into outside his house after their first meeting. The vehicle came back to Navesco Leasing with a corporate address in New York City. A further public records check indicated that Navesco Corp. was a subsidiary of GNI, an international investment and holding company. *Well, at least Darcy seems truthful about the company he works for.*

Mac left his office and hopped into his pickup truck. He drove to the Fort Lee Lookout car lot, punched his stick shift into 'park,' and looked at his watch: *9:59 AM. No Detective Arnet.*

About ten minutes later an unmarked police car pulled into the upper lot of the Fort Lee park. Detective Arnet got out. He met Mac by the pathway leading to the George Washington Bridge overlook.

"Sorry I'm late. I got caught up at work. One of our regulars stopped in, a Mr. Jensen. He thinks his wife is trying to kill him. Last week he thought she was trying to gas him to death. Turns out it was a gas leak by the curb. Two weeks before that he woke up with a pillow on his head. She wasn't even in the room but he believed she tried to smother him. This morning, it was poisoning. According to him, her eggplant parm tasted lousy. Let me tell ya . . . his wife's a saint. The crap he puts her through. I wouldn't blame her if she did try to kill him."

Mac laughed. "You know the old saying, 'Even the paranoid are sometimes being followed.'"

"Well, this guy is certifiable. He does lighten up the day for us though," Arnet said. "Now, to business. Follow me."

They walked along a winding tree and brush-lined path for less than a minute before arriving at a guardrail by the edge of the cliff.

"What a view," Mac said as he watched the cars, trucks, and buses cross the tall, battleship gray-colored bridge.

"It sure is. And this is the spot where Mr. Barrow drew his last breath before taking the big dive."

Mac surveyed the area, looking for any clue. "I remember reading in the post report that toxicology came back negative. No signs of illness, terminal or otherwise. A residual amount of alcohol in his blood and organs, but no drugs in his system. Isn't that odd? Barrow was reportedly a big drinker, a man who reportedly committed suicide, but he only had residual amounts of alcohol in his system. I'd suspect he'd be loaded before taking the plunge."

"Point well taken," Detective Arnet replied. "As you know, suicidals do the strangest things. Maybe he just wanted to experience death with a clear head and a clear conscience."

Mac chuckled. "And you believe that?"

"Stranger things have happened."

Mac gave Arnet a look of disbelief, then peered over the side of the guardrail. "What did he have on him when he was found below?" he asked.

"A button-down shirt, casual beige slacks, a Rolex watch, a pair of dock shoes, brown leather belt, and a wallet containing identifications, credit cards, and $135 in small bills—fives, tens, a couple of twenties. If you're still thinking murder I guess you can safely rule out robbery, what with the Rolex watch and the cash. Oh, and he had a half pack of menthol cigarettes in his shirt pocket. We found a crushed one, same brand by this area where he went over."

"What about car keys?"

"Yep. One set, which we needed, since he had locked his doors. We searched the vehicle. It was spotless. Nothing of interest. Registration, insurance card, vehicle maintenance book in the glove box, eyeglasses and change in the center console, oh and a scrap piece of paper in the driver-side visor. Nothing in the trunk. The guy was a metro, natty dresser, car neat as a pin."

"Interesting," Mac muttered below his breath.

"What's that?" asked Arnet.

"The scrap of paper in the visor. Anything written on it?"

"Yeah. It made no sense. It just said, 'The Architect'. Why, does that mean anything to you?"

"No," Mac replied. "I was just thinking, why would someone as fastidious as Silky—you know his nickname is Silky—would leave a piece of scrap paper in his visor, especially if he was going to check out? I'd be interested in knowing what the Architect meant."

"Yeah, I was told he was called Silky, but I still don't see how any of this would lead to homicide."

"Well, in general, based on what you've told me, I could see where robbery can be ruled out as a motive. On the other hand, though, if there was a perp involved, he could have robbed Barrow of something other than money. But suicide, with all due respect, might be a bit of a stretch. I've never been a big proponent of the negative corpus method for making a determination. Ruling it a suicide simply because you can't prove homicide or accidental leaves me wondering. The facts, as I see them, are these: no suicide note, an expensive watch and cash in pocket although there are indications that he was in dire financial straits. He lives in Alpine. If he wanted to jump, why not the Alpine Lookout? Or, for that matter, the Rockerfeller Lookout? Or several other jump-offs closer to where he lives? There were no drugs and only a trace amount of alcohol in his system . . . and he was well dressed. Plus the fact that he didn't leave the keys in the car. It could just be force of habit to put the keys in his pocket, but I'd suspect someone about to kill himself, someone as meticulous as Silky, would leave the keys in the car with the doors unlocked. Then the scrap of paper with the words 'The Architect'. What the hell does that mean?"

"All speculation. You know the story as well as me. You don't have to go to court to prove a suicide. Proving a homicide with no hard evidence and a mystery suspect is a waste of time and destined to go nowhere. Speculation doesn't translate into probable cause."

"Well, that's why we in law enforcement get the big bucks . . . to get to the truth, no matter the cost."

Arnet laughed. "Yeah, the big bucks."

Mac looked out onto the Hudson River. "What about his house? You find anything there worthwhile?"

"Well, he was living on and off with a fella by the name of Darcy, Lamar Darcy. He wasn't much help. So we ran a basic search on the premises. We didn't find anything of use for our investigation."

"You mean you didn't find anything to help support the claim of suicide?"

Arnet stiffened with that comment. "Listen, I've been doing this for several years. I know how this game works. If I found anything, I mean *anything* that would have led me to believe this case was anything more than a suicide, I would have jumped on it. I don't know what your interest is in turning this into something it ain't. I really don't know where you're going with this, but if you have any information indicating that this is a homicide, let me know; otherwise, if you need any further information from me or my office, you'll have to submit a letter to my chief requesting such information."

Arnet turned to walk back to his car. He stopped in his tracks when he heard Mac say, "Barrow left his house with a map and several other documents. When he was found, the map and the documents were gone. Any idea what happened to them?"

"What?!" said Arnet. "Where the hell did you get that information? And why didn't you tell me sooner?

"Frank," said Mac. "I don't know if he had a map and other papers with him or not. I just thought it would complement 'The Architect' note. Sounds good, don't it? It's possible he had something on him worth stealing that we don't know about. Hindsight is 20-20, but foresight can have zero visibility. I don't know what could be possible in the case. I do know one thing, though. Silky was always a survivor. Suicide doesn't fit the bill for him. "

Detective Arnet shook his head and smiled. "I'm not buying it. You know something you're not telling me. I've been around long enough to know bullshit when I hear it. What's going on here?"

Mac looked out and watched as the cars zipped back and forth across the bridge, heading into Washington Heights. "Normally, a case is determined by the evidence, facts showing, not the lack thereof. I'm hesitant to draw any conclusion based on what *wasn't* found, be it a note, a fresh witness or eyewitness, or even a stolen item of which we are not aware. I had searched Barrow's house and found that he was gathering information on homes he was interested in buying. 'The Architect' note seemed to fit the bill. If he were to meet someone with that handle, what better than a plot map to drop off. I know it's a stretch, but, Frank, call it intuition, it makes about as much sense as a street survivor committing suicide. It's worth looking into further. Believe me, I'm not questioning how the investigation was handled. I'm sure you've done a superb job, but I've known Silky for quite some time and unless something drastic happened to his mental state, I'm not ready to accept that he killed himself. All I'm asking is to leave the case open a little while longer as 'undetermined,' 'suspicious,' 'under investigation,' however you guys list these kinds of cases."

Arnet shook his head. "Tell you what I'll do. Out of respect for the fact that you're a former cop—because I have no obligation, otherwise—I'll leave the case open until the end of the month. That will give you three weeks. If either of us can't come up with any info to warrant a reevaluation of the cause or mode of death within that time frame, I'm closing it out. I need something to convince my lieutenant this case should remain open. What can we do . . . try to get an ME to amend his report from suicide to homicide, then present that case to a judge and jury? . . . and that's if you can even find a perp, motive, or evidence to support the charge. Good luck with that one."

"I know, it's a tough one. I'd appreciate anything you can do."

"Three weeks, that's it," Detective Arnet said as he walked back to his car.

Mac felt the case was going nowhere. Still, he knew there were several leads he could work on to please his client, flimsy as those leads may be: the missing map and documents, the conflicting facts within the ME's report, the odd location for the reported 'suicide', and, now, the latest piece of evidence—the so-called 'Architect'.

Chapter Eleven

January 10, 2004

Martha Thomlin at 45 years of age was still somewhat of a looker. Her long and brightly painted fingernails matched her fiery red hair. Though a bit plump, her shapely legs and short skirt shouted out that she was still in play.

"I was raped," she said rather nonchalantly to Essex County Detective Ed Birch seated across from her.

"When did this occur?" asked Detective Birch.

Ms. Thomlin let out a deep sigh and said, "Two days ago . . . and several times prior to that."

Detective Birch had heard these multiple rape charges many times before. The *I wouldn't have had sex with him if I knew he wouldn't call again rape,* or, the *I said yes but I really didn't want to have intercourse with him rape,* or, the *I'm pissed off at the way he treated me rape,* to name a few. "Okay," said Birch, "let's start at the beginning."

Stretching her long fingers across the table between them, Ms. Thomlin looked at the large diamond ring and wedding band on her left hand. "Well, for starters, my husband is Jack Thomlin. He is part owner of the Newark Bengals baseball team. He also owns several companies: communications, transportation, manufacturing. I, myself, own several businesses: a realty agency, a travel agency, and a company that manufactures novelty items for card and gift stores.

"Needless to say, my husband and I are financially well off. As such, with money comes the desire for power. And trust me, we are politically powerful. We are one of the largest fundraisers in New Jersey. We like to stay under the radar, however. But by what I'm about to tell you, this may no longer be an option."

Detective Birch slid the yellow legal pad in front of him and clicked his pen. "We'll see," he said as he began to document the interview.

"This may sound odd to you but my husband and I have an open marriage. He keeps his dalliances to himself and I keep mine to myself. Several years ago I met a Newark Police detective lieutenant who was trying to raise money for the Policemen's Athletic League. A relationship blossomed between us. My husband didn't care, but the detective wanted to keep our relationship secret for the sake of his wife and kids."

Detective Birch didn't like where this was going. A cop was involved. That always resulted in hard feelings between the local police departments and prosecutor's office. "Who's the detective?"

"I'll get to that, but first I'd like to lay out the situation and get your opinion on whether or not I have a case before I name the cop. Please don't take this the wrong way, but I know you police officers have a tendency to protect your own. I'd just like an honest opinion before I tell you who it is. That's why I came to your office, instead of going to the Newark Police Department."

Detective Birch nodded. *Newark Police Department?* "That's fine Ms. Thomlin."

"Well, we met several times at the Liberty Motel and at several fund raisers my husband and I held at our house. Back then I had my husband write a check for the PAL in the amount of $5,000, and for my detective friend, I slipped him $1,000 in cash, as a personal gift. I mean, how much do they pay you cops? After all, he was a good lover. I told him to go spend the money on himself."

"Go on," said Birch, starting to sense where this conversation was going. *Another eccentric rich broad who now wants this dopey bastard to pay her back. A threatened rape is a nice card to hold over his head, especially since it puts his marriage and job in jeopardy.*

"Well, several years ago, my husband and I raised money for Republican Josh Mansfield for Essex County Sheriff. He was a good candidate. He was the former chief of the county police department. He picked Maggie Ellis, a former Newark police detective and fellow Republican as his Under Sheriff. When Mansfield retired, Ellis moved up to Sheriff. That's when . . . ."

Detective Birch dropped his pen. "Where are we going with this, Ms. Thomlin? What does any of this have to do with a rape charge?"

"I'll get to that, detective. I want to lay out the background first."

"I understand there are things you wish to tell me related to sexual assault, but we need to get to the point. Who are we talking about? Who's the person who raped you?" said Detective Birch as he picked up his pen.

"Wallace Burkner."

"Who?"

"Wallace Burkner."

"Deputy Chief Wallace Burkner of the Newark Police Department. Is that who we're talking about?"

"One and the same."

Detective Birch sat for a moment and looked past Ms. Thomlin at the painted cinderblock wall. All the walls were bare except for the wall behind him which contained a two-way mirror. *I hope the LT is hearing this.*

Newark PD Lieutenant Martin Presler, along with Essex County Detective Janice Miller, did in fact hear what Ms. Thomlin said as the two officers stood in the adjacent conference room peering through the two-way mirror and listening to the interview over the intercom. Detective Miller was Detective Birch's cover. Lieutenant Presler, recently assigned to the NPD Sex Crimes Squad, was there just to get a feel for the new assignment. He was there simply for observation and interest. Now, however, that his deputy chief was named as a suspect in a rape, Presler was involved in the investigation, big time.

"All right, you left off where Ellis became Sheriff."

Ms. Thomlin stared at Birch, trying to get a read on him, any reaction. She saw none.

Birch had been a detective long enough to have developed the classic poker face.

"Well, that creep Burkner approached me and said he wanted to become sheriff. The problem was, Ellis and Burkner were in the same political party. Besides, they were "reportedly good friends". That was a joke. Burkner wanted me to finance Bill Connerly to the tune of $50,000 as a third-party candidate. All, of course, which he, Burkner, officially knew nothing about. The reason for supporting Connerly was to split the vote and let the Democrat opponent win. Which is what happened."

"And did you provide the money?" asked Birch.

"Yes, I did. And Burkner's plan worked. James Arsnault, the Democrat, won the election and became the next Essex County Sheriff. Jerry Goodwin, an Irvington cop, was picked to be his Under Sheriff. That's when Burkner began his fundraising for a run against Arsnault. I, of course, being his major contributor. Well, things accelerated when, as you well know, Arsnault was indicted by a federal court on corruption charges. So, Under Sheriff Goodwin became acting Sheriff. A year or two later, US Congressman Tyler stepped down. He's in a black district. Goodwin is black. The Democrats wanted to keep the seat so they filled it with Goodwin.

"A secret deal was made with Newark Police Chief Matson and Burkner. Burkner would run for sheriff on the Republican ticket and Matson on the Democrat ticket. In the deal about one month before the election, Burkner would drop out claiming personal problems, which he wouldn't discuss with anyone. Since it was too late for the

Republicans to put together a good candidate or campaign at that point, Matson became the next Sheriff."

Birch was becoming less interested in finding out about the rape charge and more interested in the political maneuvering. "And what did Deputy Chief Burkner get in return?"

"You'll find out soon enough," she said. "This, however, was when I was raped. Burkner called me shortly after the election and asked if he could stop by, that he 'had a present for me.' I told him 'fine,' my husband was out of town. Shortly afterwards, my doorbell rings. I opened it and there stood Burkner with another guy. I met the guy at one of my fundraisers. He had done some work for my husband regarding some offshore investment business. He represented some big money that wanted some influence in Jersey politics. I forgot his name, but my husband later reminded me. His name is Ed, Ed Ortez. Anyway, I looked at Burkner and asked, 'Where's my present?' 'Right here,' he said pointing to Ortez. I didn't want any part of that, but they walked me upstairs, into my bedroom, and both of them had sex with me."

"Did you verbally tell them 'no,' that you didn't want to have sex with them?

"Yes."

"Did you physically resist?"

"No, I was too afraid to."

"It's been, what, a month since the election. Did you have any visible bruises? Did you document them, location, photos, anything?"

"None that I noticed, and no, no documentation."

Birch tapped his pen on the pad. "Had you contacted him since and expressed your feelings of what happened?"

"Yes, I called him and told him never to contact me again. That he and his friend raped me."

"What did he say?"

"He said it never happened. It was all in my mind."

Burkner was in the business long enough to know the phone call might have been tapped.

"Did you tell anyone about the situation immediately afterwards?" *The fresh witness.*

"No, I was too embarrassed. That's why it took me so long to report it."

"Why did you report it now?" asked Birch.

"I finally had the courage to tell my husband last night. He was very supportive. He told me I should report it. That it would make me feel better."

"Going back to something you said just before discussing the nature of the rape, you said I will find out soon enough. Soon enough about what?"

"Well, this will make your investigation a little more difficult. You know we have a Democrat governor. And that the governor picks the county prosecutors. And each county prosecutor picks his chief of detectives."

"Are you saying . . . ."

"Yes, I am. Burkner's going to be your boss next month."

"Are you kidding me, Marty? This Thomlin woman wants to charge Burkner and a friend of his with rape?" Mac whispered across the desk.

"Swear to God."

"What's the friend's name?"

"Ortez, Eduardo Ortez."

"Never heard of him. Well, sorry for the woman, but it's about time the law caught up with Burkner".

Presler sat back in his chair and nodded. "Don't get your hopes up. I think the prosecutor's office is going to deep six the case. The woman sounds a bit unstable. I just thought you'd like to know, considering his part in Internal Affairs, forcing your early retirement. Just keep it under your hat."

"Marty, you've always been good to me over the years. I wouldn't do anything to jeopardize your job. This stuff about Burkner is between you, me, and the rest of your staff. I know that kind of info flies around like camel shit in a sandstorm, but have no fear, not a word about it will exit my lips. Though, you know me, Marty, I'd love to see him go down, big time. There ain't an honest, loyal, descent bone in that slug's body. He's a blight on law enforcement."

"You're right about him. I always felt bad about what he did to you. You loved this job. Well, thankful you can still do PI work. Speaking of which, you're obviously here to find out more on Barrow."

Mac smiled. "Actually, I stopped by to say hello, but since you brought it up, I've got a question for you."

"Let it rip, my friend."

"Do you know anyone in any of the neighborhoods referred to as 'The Architect'?"

Presler put his left hand to his head and looked down to his right. After a moment of thought, he looked up at Mac. "No, can't say I have. The Architect. You know the characters around here all have 'down low' aliases. The Architect has that upscale sound to it. If I were you, I'd be looking for a top ender. If the perp was from around here, I'd focus in on the Heights or downtown, at least for starters."

"Thanks, Marty. I know it's not much to go on, but you and I have solved our share of cases with less evidence. When given the chance, we've always worked well together. I miss those times. You're one of the good guys. I'll just have to see where this case takes me. If you hear anything, I'd appreciate it if you'd let me know."

"Will do, Mac."

"Stay well, my brother."

Chapter Twelve

January 14, 2004

The four fifteen-year-old boys headed to the ball field of Bayonne Park. The larger one carried the old scarred, leathery football. The others carried four orange traffic cones that they picked up from behind the nearby road department. It was a blustery Saturday afternoon, but now that the recreational football all-star games were over, Big Mikey, the ball holder, wanted to hone his passing skills from atop the rock-infested pitcher's mound. Many a black eye and swollen nose were attributed to the routine bad hops off that mound. Now, though, late in the winter, both the infield and outfield were hard and rough as concrete.

When the boys reached the field, Big Mikey threw a bomb, deep to the northeast corner of the park. "Go ahead, Louie," he said to the fastest of the four youths. "See if you can locate that missile."

Louie took off toward the wooded area, as Pete and Sammy went to place the cones in the four corners that would determine the boundaries of their two-man touch football game.

Beyond the northeast section of the ball field was a stretch of woods. A routine double or triple, in baseball season, easily turned into a four-bagger once a ball rolled into the woods. A football, though a lot larger than a hard ball, could just as easily disappear in the wooded area. Such was the case with Big Mikey's rocket pass.

"Find it yet?" he yelled out to Louie.

"Not yet!"

The other two boys ran over to where Louie was, to help look for the ball.

"I wish I had a nickel for every baseball we lost in these damn woods," Sammy said. "And I can't believe that idiot Mikey threw the freakin' ball before we even got out here. We should make him pay for it if we can't find it."

"Any luck?" shouted Big Mikey.

"Why don't you get your ass out here and look," said Pete just loud enough for Louie and Sammy to hear. "Nope! Nothing yet!" he shouted back to Mikey.

Just then Sammy noticed a cardboard box about two feet wide and two feet high lying in the dead weeds by a tall oak tree. "Hey, guys, look at this."

Pete and Louie came to where Sammy was standing. "Why don't we open it up," said Pete.

"By 'we,' you mean Sammy or me," said Louie.

"Chicken?"

"I ain't chicken. How 'bout you?" said Louie.

"What the hell are you guys doing out here?" said Big Mikey, as he ran up to meet the others.

"Sammy found this box," replied Pete, "but these guys are too afraid to open it."

"Sounds like you don't have the stones, either," Mikey said as he pulled back the top flap of the cardboard box.

"Oh God, it's a foot!" yelled Mikey.

Underneath the unclad foot was an assortment of neatly-stacked, butcher-cut body parts.

The boys looked back and forth at each other several times without saying a word. Then, as if on cue, they ran out of the park as fast as their feet could take them . . . leaving behind the old leathery pigskin.

January 17, 2004

It was a hot and lazy day the *Orgullo* eased out of Puerto Cabello, the main commercial port of Venezuela. The temperature was in the 90s and the water was calm as the 680-foot Venezuelan oil tanker headed north toward Puerto de Altamira, Mexico. The coastal class tanker, ladened with product petroleum, also tucked away 10,000 pounds of granular chlorine in fifty-pound containers. In addition to the cargo, thirty passengers accompanied the crew of the tanker. The thirty men were a mix of Saudi, Yemeni, Irani, and Syrian nationals.

"Troppo caldo, el capitan, no?"

"Si, si. Your Spanish is good, Qutaybah, but remember we are to speak English. It is the best way for you to get by where you are going."

"Get by where?" Qutaybah asked.

"It's just an expression. It means that you will need to know what to say and understand what is said to you once you get into the land of Satan."

"I 'get by' very good when I get there. You do not have to worry yourself about that. You just have to get us there. After that, you can do what you have to do with this boat."

"Ship."

"What?"

"Ship. It's a ship. Not a boat," Captain Ramos said.

"Ship, boat; no one cares. Just get us to where we need to go, pronto. And don't you concern yourself with me or my men. I will worry about what we will do or say once we get there."

"I can see you live up to your name, Qutaybah."

"What do you mean by that, Capitan?"

"If I'm not mistaken, your name means 'impatient' in Arabic."

"Impatience gets thing done. You would not understand. In my country, a man must always be, how would you say, 'alert,' 'on guard.' If you don't kill, you will be killed. What would you know about that, Capitan? You drive this big stupid boat, yes boat, back and forth, from port to port. There is no one behind you waiting with a sword to slice your head off. We, my men and me, live with that threat every day. So we fight and we kill . . . and we will die for Allah. Who will you die for . . . the Venezuelan Oil Company?"

"You surprise me, Qutaybah. Isn't oil the life blood of *your* country, too? You will fight and kill, but it's not Allah you'll be dying for. It's for some rich Saudi prince who will fuel his jet with your blood."

"So, in your eyes, we are not so different. You believe we will both die for oil; you for your socialist president and his quest for oil domination in the region, me for some Saudi prince so he can fly around in his jet. I do not agree. You *will* die for money and oil. I will not. It is for the caliphate that I die. Ali Akbar!"

Chapter Thirteen

January 19, 2004

"Are you serious? Thomlin's a suicide?"

"Somehow, I knew you would have an issue with this call."

"But really, Marty, a suicide?"

"That's what the ME said."

"It's just another bogus autopsy report. Why are they paying these guys?"

"The ME felt he had enough evidence to make that call."

"Well, the ME is wrong. What is it with these guys lately? I've always had great respect for the majority of them, but this is ridiculous. First Barrow. I guess that could be a tough one. But Martha Thomlin? You said she shot herself. How many female suicides did you get where a gun was used as the weapon of choice? Women usually take a more nonviolent approach to killing themselves. Granted some are jumpers or cutters, but I suspect the majority of female suicides are the result of drug overdoses, gas inhalations, or poisonings. In my 25 years on the job, I can't remember even one female suicide the result of a gunshot to the head."

Presler nodded his head in agreement. "That's true, Mac, but you know in this business, there's a first time for everything. Besides, if the facts fit, the call should be made. The ME felt the facts fit."

"What were the facts, Marty?"

"First off, the victim was a flake; what with her open marriage, and the fact that she was seeing a shrink for depression at the time of her death. Plus, the gun was registered to her husband." Presler threw up his right hand. "I know what you're thinking. No, the hubby had a solid alibi. He was out of town in the company of several friends at a basketball game when she died. And there was no indication of marital problems or financial issues. He squared out in the interview and volunteered to take a polygraph, which by the way he passed. In addition, family and friends said the victim was despondent lately and she was acting irrationally, constantly arguing with herself aloud. Oh, and one other thing that comes to mind. The only prints found on the gun and shell casings were partials of hers and her husband's."

"What about cadaveric reaction?" asked Mac.

"What about it?"

"Cadaveric reaction. You know, when someone shoots themself, a spasm can result in the trigger finger leaving a permanent indentation. Did she have that indentation?"

"Mac, I know what cadaveric spasms are. I thought you were referring to whether the body was moved and the cadaveric *lividity* and rigor mortis didn't match up with the final position of the body. That didn't happen. The short answer to your question of whether or not her trigger finger, in particular, showed signs of CR, is 'no'. But, as you well know, that doesn't occur in every incident of self-inflicted gunshot deaths."

"Yeah, but if it was present, that sure would help to prove the ME's case. And the fact that only the victim and the victim's husband's partial prints were on the gun and casings doesn't prove she or he was the shooter. An assailant would have worn gloves if he or she intended to make it look like a suicide. As for her despondency and irrational behavior, that could have been attributed to the fact that she suspected she was a marked woman after calling out Burkner, a very powerful and influential man."

"Listen, Mac. I agree there are some unresolved issues in this case, all of which I addressed to the prosecutor and pathologist, but barring any evidence—not just supposition—the case is closed. That's what the upper brass wants. Besides, what is your interest in this case? What's Martha Thomlin to you? Is this a personal matter? "

"It seems like every place I turn there are loose ends. I hate loose ends. As for why I'm interested in Martha Thomlin, I'm interested in her because she was in a circle of friends that just had another suspicious death ruled a possible suicide: our boy Barrow. Coincidence? And what about that reported rape that went nowhere. Another coincidence? You know us cops don't believe in coincidences. So, humor me, Marty. Just a few more questions."

"Shoot."

Mac scratched his head. "Any luck IDing the guy who supposedly was with Burkner when this woman was reportedly raped?"

"When we spoke with Burkner concerning the incident, he did say he met with the woman at her house, but only to bring her a gift, some plaque which he produced, thanking her for her support for his campaign. He said she was very shaky, a real fatal attraction–type bimbo, who seemed to want more from him than a plaque. Burkner added that since he was afraid to be alone with her for the very reason he was brought in for questioning, he brought a friend to drop off the plaque. That friend being, as I told you before, Eduardo Ortez.

Mac's head popped up. "I knew I heard that name before."

"Yeah, what about it?" Presler asked, giving Mac a hard stare.

"The body of a guy named Ed Ortez was found just last week in a ball field in Hudson County. He was cut up, all in nice, neat pieces. It took until this morning to identify the body. He had no U.S. prints, dental or surgery records on file, so Hudson County had to solve the case in long hand—interviews, foreign records, FBI distinguishing characteristics checks . . . you know the routine. "

Presler put both his hands on the desk in front of him. "This is starting to get crazy. If Burkner is involved in all of this, he's surely making some bad decisions. Rape is bad enough, but a premeditated double, perhaps triple homicide. Why would he draw so much attention to himself, even if he was psychotic enough to commit or be involved in these atrocities?"

"I don't know, Marty, but I'm going to find out. Meanwhile, could you check with the prosecutor and medical examiner to see if that suicide case can be reopened? Meanwhile, I'll be working on our old friend Silky Barrow's case. I suspect he didn't exactly throw himself off the Palisades up in Bergen."

Chapter Fourteen

January 21, 2004

"Nothing new. Our overseas contacts have little information as to suspicious transactions on the part of GNI," said Agent Dillon.

"What, if anything, *do* they have?" asked Special Agent in Charge Lindstrum.

"First off, as we discussed, GNI is a large investment company that transacts huge monetary transfers across international borders. With that volume of transfers, some funds can conceivably be routed to terrorist activities. The company had not been red-flagged by us because there are no known ties to terrorist organizations, no informant reporting such connections, and no direct money trails that can be traced from GNI to illicit activity. Now that doesn't mean no such connection exists, only that none can be made at this time."

"How about Ortez?"

"Now, he turned out to be a great lead. Eduardo Ortez had an interesting career. He came from an impoverished town in Haiti. Somehow he was able to rise above his poverty level and go to law school in Mexico. That part of his life is sketchy. He then got into the banking business working his way into GNI as a junior loan officer. He eventually became a regional investment manager with a large portfolio of investors from Aruba, the Cayman Islands, and several South American nations."

"Which South American nations?" Lindstrum asked.

"Brazil, Peru, Ecuador, Colombia, Venezula..."

"Colombia, Venezuela. That should send up red flags."

"Well, yes," Dillon replied, "but apparently most, if not all of the money invested went into Colombia tobacco and coffee beans, and the Venezuelan funds went to, what else, oil."

"I don't get it. Why then is he such 'a great lead'?"

Agent Dillon tightened her lips. "Because he was just found eight days ago in a Bayonne ball field . . . dead . . . cut up in pieces and stuffed in a box." Dillon then proceeded to give SAC Lindstrum all the details surrounding the discovery of the body.

Lindstrum blew air into his cheeks. *Now we're getting somewhere,* he thought. *But where?* "Get on this, Sara. Check with the locals and see if they have any leads on the killer or Ortez's involvement with any illegal activity. Run all the checks you haven't already. DEA, ATF, NJ State Police, SEC, our embassy people. You know the list. I suspect you've already checked with Homeland. Nobody gets murdered, cut up, and left in a field unless their death is a warning for others to keep quiet. Just a thought, but what's the name of the place where the body was found?"

"The ball field is called Bayonne Park."

"Hmmm. Interesting location to drop a body. I don't know what it means but it's as good a place as any to start."

Mac Taylor needed to see Darcy in person so he could study his reactions to some of his questions. Darcy initially objected to the face-to-face meeting at Mac's office, but eventually gave in to his demand.

"I told you I did not want any more personal meetings between us. You'd better have some good information for me."

"Oh, I have some good information. But, more importantly, I have some serious questions that need to be answered by you."

"Me? I'm paying you for answers, not questions."

"Well, you answer some of my questions and I'll give you all the answers you want."

"Okay, Investigator Taylor, what answers do you want from me?"

"For starters, what do you know about a company named GNI?" Mac asked.

Darcy shot a quick glance at him. "Are *they* involved in this?"

"You tell me. What do you know about it?"

"I've done business with GNI in the past. It's a fairly large corporation. How did its name pop up?"

"Let's just say one of its employees was found chopped up in a Bayonne ball field. I don't know if there is any connection with GNI, this fellow in the park, and our friend Silky, but I have my reasons to be suspicious." Mac wasn't quite ready to let on that Darcy, who worked for a subsidiary of GNI, was possibly the key to this connection.

Rubbing the back of his neck, Darcy noted, "GNI is an international investment corporation. It deals only with large investors, $100 million or more. Some GNI investors have notorious reputations. Those wielding that kind of money many times have a sordid past—drugs, guns, stock swindlers. Not all, mind you. Just some. And some of the big money people might also be involved in terrorism or—"

"Terrorism?" Mac interjected.

"I'm just speculating. There's a large amount of money filtered to terrorists from state-sponsored regimes as well as wealthy Mideast oil and shipping barons. Where do you think a lot of hijacking, drug, and other organized crime dollars originate, or end up? Ever wonder what Afghan poppy fields, Somali pirates, Colombian cocaine, and Iran oil money have in common? Granted, a lot of it stays in the pockets of the criminal enterprises, but some of the money filters into terrorist activity."

"So you think GNI is involved in terrorist activity?"

"I don't know. The company could either be in bed with terrorists or turning a blind eye to them. I'm just speculating, though." Darcy looked down with a hard stare. "Now, you mentioned some guy who worked for GNI was found cut up in a box."

"That's right," said Mac. "His name was Eduardo Melo Ortez. Ever heard of him?"

Darcy's eyes grew wide and his hands began to shake. "Ortez, uh . . . No, no," he stammered. "The name doesn't ring a bell."

Bullshit! First he talks about GNI as if he barely heard of it even though his company is a subsidiary of it. Then he shakes like a leaf at the mention of the name Ortez. Mac leaned toward Darcy. "Well, he might have made some telephone calls before his death. The Essex County Prosecutor's detective will undoubtedly get a warrant for his phone records. Check your phone bill for last month and see what calls were made to Barrow within a day or two of his death. There might be some phone numbers I can work with to pin down a relationship between the two."

"I told you about that one call where Devin said, 'The money ain't worth it anymore.' I don't know who that was, but Devin might have made the call and not the other party. It could be on the bill."

Maybe it was Ortez, Mac noted to himself. Then, aloud, said, "Well, I'll try my best to find out who that person is. So, it'd make my job a lot easier if you could get me that bill."

"I'll have a copy of the last phone record dropped off at your office," said Darcy.

"Good. Oh, and one other thing. I know you're a businessman. See what you can learn about GNI. If this case turns into an international problem, I might have to bring Homeland Security into the matter. Don't worry, though. I'll sanitize the investigation enough to leave you out of the picture."

"And how do you plan on doing that?!" Darcy said somewhat alarmed.

"I have someone else who's supplying me info on GNI and on some of the players. Half of a detective's workload is corroborating information. Unsubstantiated, uncorroborated information, in many cases, leads to bad intelligence and faulty casework. I don't want to leave my flanks unprotected. I don't like surprises."

Darcy stared out the window of Mac's office and asked, "Who is this other source? After all, I am paying you for your services."

Mac smiled. "That's true, Mr. Darcy, and, in due time, I will tell you. Right now, however, I've got to get a good handle on this case before any moves are made to lock in a killer or killers. Your friend Devin Barrow and one possible acquaintance of his are dead. Let's not make it three. For all parties concerned, especially for you as my client, maintaining anonymity must be the first order of business. That's how I operate. If you have a problem with that, let me know and we can square up now. "

Darcy shook his head and stood up. "No, I don't have a problem with that. Just as long as you can prove that Devin was murdered, and his killer brought to justice."

The two then shook hands and left the office. Mac walked him to the waiting limo. As Darcy got in the rear seat of the vehicle, Mac took note of the middle-aged dog walker a block away. The black man was quite large, wearing tinted glasses, a baseball cap, and a heavy coat with the hood up. Just then the man and his dog turned away from him and headed up the street. Mac hadn't seen that person or dog in the neighborhood before.

January 25, 2004

"I've got some good news, Paul," said Agent Dillon.

"I could use some," Lindstrum replied.

"I got a call from a Bergen County Homicide Detective named Frank Arnet. He thought we might be interested in a suicide case."

"Why's that?"

"The victim's name is Devin Barrow. He's reported to be a

jumper, but there are extenuating circumstances. He might have been involved in some kind of a deal, a transfer of something. I was about to tell him we really have no interest in a case like that when he said the victim's roommate was a man named Lamar Darcy, who was an arbitrageur for Navesco Corp., which happens to be an international company and a subsidiary of GNI. That name keeps popping up. That can't just be a coincidence. Anyway, Arnet thought this might have international implications beyond his scope of investigation. He thought it might be something we'd be interested in."

"Forgetting Navesco and GNI for a moment, you said it was death by suicide?"

"Yes, but Arnet had his doubts. He said the medical report was ambiguous and there was a lack of normal suicide behavior."

"That's not unusual. Not all suicides are textbook."

Agent Dillon nodded repeatedly. "Yes, yes, that's true, but he said there was one other thing about this case that didn't seem right to him."

"Go on."

"Actually, the main reason why he's calling us is because there's a private investigator nosing around, trying to turn this suicide investigation into a homicide. He doesn't know who the PI's client is, but he suspects it might be someone connected to one of these companies. Why would they be interested in Barrow's death? He thinks there's more to this case and this PI than meets the eye, and he thinks it might have something to do with Navesco or GNI."

"Well, GNI surely falls into our chum bucket," said SAC Lindstrum. "What's the PI's name? Do we know him?"

"His name is Mac Taylor. I don't know him. You might."

"Yes, I've heard of him. He's new in the PI field, but he has a wealth of experience in police work. Not long ago he was embroiled in a shootout in New York State. I remember reading the bulletin on him; 25 years in the Newark PD, served 2 tours honorably in Vietnam, divorced, daughter killed. He had a rough couple of years.

Well, let's hope he'll be helpful."

"So, you want me to reach out to him? How about Darcy?"

"Yes, when you get a chance see what Taylor knows, or what he's willing to tell us. We do have leverage with the PI's. Hold off on Darcy for the time being. Taylor might just give us leverage we can use against him. Who knows—" Lindstrum suddenly stopped what he was saying. After a moment of silence, he continued, "No, no, wait, I've got a better idea, can both interviews. Get paper for a 30-day tap on their phone lines. Let's go fishing first." Lindstrum grinned, then added, "Don't tell the judge I said that when he signs the warrant."

Just as Dillon was about to leave the office, Lindstrum called to her, "Sara, again, good job. Don't forget to thank Detective Arnet for the information. We could use another agent like him around here."

January 26, 2004

Bergen County Homicide Detective Arnet picked up the receiver and dialed Mac's number. Mac answered after three rings. "Hello."

"Hey Mac, it's Frank Arnet."

"Frank. What's up?"

"I was going to call to tell you we hadn't come up with any additional info on the Barrow case and the bosses wanted it closed out. Then this morning, an FBI agent named Dillon stopped in my office and asked to see the case. Seems like there might be a larger issue here with Homeland. Dillon requested copies of the file. You know them. They don't give back a hell of a lot, but she did say they want to confirm whether or not Barrow was murdered in 'a money or information exchange.' So, we will be keeping the case open."

"Good. Thanks for not shutting down the investigation. If I hear anything, I'll let you know. I'd appreciate it if you'd keep me in the loop."

"I'll tell you what I can, but you know we're pretty tight-lipped here, too."

"Well, here's a big tip. You might want to consider dropping off a subpoena at a company named GNI for any and all transaction records conducted by an individual named Eduardo Melo Ortez."

Arnet grabbed a pen and pad. Scribbling the information down, he asked, "What's that all about?"

"All I know at this time is that a global company named GNI had a guy in its employ named Ortez who might have authorized an exchange between Barrow and another party. Ortez was the guy found cut up in the Bayonne ballpark. That's all I know now." Mac was hedging. "Oh, and be prepared that if you start getting close to anybody, the feds might just come and scoop up your case."

"You seem to know an awful lot you're not telling me, Mac. Why don't you come in and we'll talk, lay out the whole scenario?"

"I'd love to, but at the moment I'm working some other leads. I'll keep you posted if I learn anything else." *Best to keep Arnet guessing,* Mac reasoned. *Maybe he'll learn something through a subpoena. The feds aren't going to give me anything. Working both ends toward the middle might get a bit tricky, but the more angles worked on this case, the better. Information to an investigator is like gold to a prospector.*

February 3, 2004

Four trucks rolled up to Pier 22 and parked by the dock as the general-purpose tanker slip into its berth in the bustling Mexican petro port of Altamira located in the Gulf. Shortly after, the petroleum extraction began. As the product oil was being emptied, the ship's ballast filled with sea water to maintain proper trim. Then, 100 fifty-gallon containers of granular chlorine that were stored in the machinery space located behind the cargo tanks and pump room of the ship were brought on deck and loaded onto two of the awaiting trucks. The other two trucks were already carrying large amounts of isopropyl alcohol. One of the two trucks carrying the large containers of isopropyl alcohol unloaded its entire contents onto the ship's deck. The cargo was stored below in a hull section, away from the remaining 5,000 pounds of granular chlorine.

Fifteen men disembarked. Four of the men were assigned to drive the vehicles. The remaining eleven men piled into the back of the empty truck which was supplied with weapons. Once the transfer was complete, the four trucks headed west, to the border town of Juarez. The terrorists were to meet up with other fighters at the border, enter the U.S. through a tunnel run by the cartel, and remain at a safe house in Texas. The trucks containing the alcohol and chlorine were to cross the border, then head directly to the safe house to reconnect with the fighters.

Qutaybah was not one of the men to disembark with the fifteen. He and fourteen other terrorists remained with the ship. Their focus was to the east, to the Newark Bay area. If all went as planned, their mission would be the greatest terrorist attack since 9-11. At least that's what Qutaybah hoped would happen.

Chapter Fifteen

1/8th Infantry, 4th Infantry Division Army Base, Kontum Province, Vietnam, May 27, 1967

After a week in the field, Sgt. MacPherson arrived back at base where he met his bunkmate, Staff Sergeant Joseph Taylor. The men shook hands. Mac dropped his gear by his assigned cot as Taylor brought him up to date on the latest news in the country and in the States. Shortly after, Mac took a much needed shower before working his way down to the chow hall to fill up on beef and biscuits. He then headed back to his barracks and laid in bed for a long, restful sleep. It wasn't to be. Mac found himself heading to the bathroom with a bad case of diarrhea. The beef and biscuits hadn't sat very well with him after a week of living off jerky and ground water.

The next day, Mac was sent to sick bay with a case of extreme dehydration. SSgt. Taylor was assigned to replace him on an upcoming mission. Taylor and two soldiers MacPherson knew from Newark, Camin LaForge and Mike Parnel, were to conduct surveillance on a village infiltrated with Viet Cong soldiers suspected of buying military secrets from American soldiers. During the surveillance, the three soldiers were separated. The mission was a failure. Only LaForge and Parnel returned. They advised that they were unable to learn who was leaking U.S. secrets to the Viet Cong. Taylor's body was discovered shortly after their return from the field. MacPherson never trusted LaForge and Parnel from that day on. He later changed his name from MacPherson to Taylor, to honor the man whose life was taken in his place. Mac swore someday LaForge and Parnel would pay for Taylor's death. That debt was paid in full years later at Mongaup Pond.

February 4, 2004

At 8:00 PM, the sweeper pushed past the two window shoppers and made his way to the bookstore on the main floor inside the Skylar Mall. He had reached the store just in time to see the senator gathering up his belongings and preparing to leave. Colorado Senator Vince Tremore had just completed his first East Coast book signing. As the senator shook the hand of the store manager, the sweeper reversed his position and walked to the mall entrance located on the south side of the complex. Exiting, he lifted his baseball cap and scratched the top of his head.

Approximately one hundred yards away, the husky black male in his early forties was sitting in a late-model Ford sedan with its engine running. With his hands clad in latex, the man reached over and grabbed a scoped rifle. He sat and waited for the second signal.

In the bookstore, Senator Tremore was conversing with two young men.

"Hopefully, we can make a difference with my new senate bill. We have to start somewhere. This problem has to be dealt with now, before these militia groups get too powerful."

"Absolutely," said one of the young men. "I hear where their numbers are growing, particularly in the prisons."

"Well, my bill provides for tighter controls over domestic terrorist groups, stiffer sentencing for militants and it provides more money and manpower for surveillance, infiltration, and disruption of these groups. In addition, it offers real solutions to the border control issue. We desperately need tighter controls over all of our borders, land and sea, as well as air. "

"I wish you the best of luck, Senator, but do you have enough co-sponsors for your bill?"

"I'm almost there," he said.

Just then the senator noticed one of his aides walking toward him. The sharply dressed man in his thirties whispered in his ear.

Tremore quickly looked up at the two young men. "I'm sorry, guys, but I must go. I have to be in New York in 45 minutes for a television spot on just the issue we've been talking about. I hope you fellas have a good evening. Thank you for your time . . . and, of course, for purchasing several of my books."

The senator scooped up his briefcase and made his way out of the bookstore, heading into the mall's main corridor. He walked quickly toward the exit.

Heads turned as he entered the south lobby, then pushed through one of the glass exit doors. Stopping just outside the mall to meet with another one of his aides, the senator was greeted several times by well-wishers. As he spoke to an older gentleman who asked him what he was going to do about reducing federal spending, a short, rather muscularly built man brushed past him. He was wearing a blue shirt, faded jeans, and sneakers. He pushed his way into the mall, ducked into an isolated alcove, and pulled a small portable transmitter/receiver from his pocket. "Now" was all he said into the hand held transmitter.

After hearing two clicks on his receiver, the man in the blue shirt headed down an escalator by the alcove. He passed several food concessions and went into the main center of the mall. He continued walking north, swiftly blending into the crowd of shoppers.

Outside in the far corner of the parking lot adjacent to the south mall exit, the man in a late model Ford put his handheld transmitter/receiver back in his pocket, picked up a rifle from the passenger seat, and got out of his car. He placed a small beanbag on the roof of the car next to his. He brought the weapon up and rested the fore section of the barrel on it. Zeroing in on the small group of people by the southside revolving door, the shooter held his position with quiet anticipation.

The shooter cursed as shoppers continued to block a clear shot at his target.

Stepping quickly to his right, Senator Tremore suddenly bumped into an inattentive shopper. At that moment, a high-powered bullet ripped through the air.

The sound of the blast stopped everyone in their tracks. Screams and shouts went up everywhere as patrons of the mall scrambled for cover. Tremore's aide, Jack Anderson, just kept yelling, "The senator is shot! The senator is shot!"

The shooter threw the rifle and bean bag into the late model Ford, got in, and pulled the door shut. He slapped the shift stick into *reverse* and quickly backed out of the space. He then put the car in *forward* and drove against the flow of traffic to a marginal-access road cutting through the westside mall parking lot.

Meanwhile, on the north side of the mall, the short, muscular individual had just reached his silver mini-van. He jumped in, spun the vehicle around, and traveled west along an access road. After several more evasive twists and turns, he pulled into an industrial park. He drove his car into the rear of a paper-processing plant, passed a large Dumpster, and parked alongside a nearby river. There he waited.

Chapter Sixteen

February 4, 2004

"7-0-3, 7-0-4."

"3 'by."

"4 'by."

"Respond to the south entrance of the Skylar Mall. Report of a shooting. Man is down. Repeat, Man is down. His condition is unknown at this time. Ambulance, paramedics, and detectives are on the way."

"3 received."

"4 received."

"3 to H-Q. Any info on the suspects."

"All Paramus units prepare to copy," said the dispatcher. "Initial reports indicate that the shot was fired from a distance as the victim was exiting the south side entrance of the mall. No description yet on the suspect or suspects. All surrounding agencies, as well as county and state police notified over SPEN.*"

"3, I'm at Broad and Fifth. ETA under a minute."

"4 to headquarters. I'm pulling up to the scene now. It's a little crazy here. They dragged the victim back into the building. I'll need assistance asap. 7-0-3, enter from the south. Make sure there are no perps in that area."

"3 received."

* State Police Enforcement Network

"Base to 0-7. Assist on the north perimeter. 7-1-1, cover the west side. Maywood PD could you assist us by covering the south and east sides?"

"Maywood H-Q received. 4-2-8 and 4-3-0 acknowledge."

"2-8 received."

"3-0 received."

"7-10 to Base."

"Go ahead Captain."

"Contact the FBI and our Attorney General's Office. The confirmed victim is Senator Tremore."

"Received."

The shooter pulled the late-model Ford behind the paper plant and parked next to the mini-van. He got out of the vehicle, rifle in hand. He walked to a bulkhead and peered down into the murky, dark brownish-green water. With a powerful swing of his arm, he threw the rifle out approximately twenty yards into the river. He then threw the bean bag out in that direction.

"Don't forget the gloves," the man in the mini-van called out.

With that, the shooter removed the latex gloves. "I'm not going to give them any shot at DNA evidence," he said as he stuffed them into his back pocket.

"Your call, Ahmed. . . . How'd the shooting go?"

"Good, good. I know I hit him. Hopefully, it's fatal."

"What do you mean, *hopefully*?" asked the man in the blue shirt.

"Well, just as I pulled the trigger, Tremore hit into someone. The bullet might not have hit him directly in the heart."

"We'll find out shortly. I hope Kas will be okay back there. Meanwhile, let's get the hell outta here."

With that, the shooter got into the mini-van. Leaving the stolen late-model Ford behind the plant, the two murder conspirators made their way west on Route 4.

"Move back!" Patrolman Arnie Carroll yelled to the crowd that was hovering around the fallen senator.

He pushed through the group of voyeurs to where Tremore was lying flat on his back, blood soaked through his once impeccably tailored white shirt. A man wearing a blue hat was holding the senator's hand and stroking his head.

"Hang in there," the man said while Patrolman Carroll bent over his shoulder and peered at the fallen statesman.

"0-3 to H-Q."

"Go ahead 0-3."

Carroll keyed his handheld portable radio again and said, "Have the rig run up a trauma pack, body board, and stretcher. Injury to the victim appears to be confined to the chest area. Victim is presently conscious."

As Tremore looked blankly toward the lone cloud in the nighttime sky, Carroll heard a strong wheezing sound. The bullet that ripped through the senator's chest had punctured his left lung. Subsequently, air from outside his body was being sucked directly through the hole in his chest as he struggled to expand the air level in his lungs.

"Received 0-3. A-2 receive?"

"2 Received."

Carroll knelt over the senator and tore open his shirt. He looked around at the surrounding people.

"Gimme that," he said to a young girl who was holding a newly purchased calendar, replete with monthly photographs of Labrador puppies. The girl handed him the 12-inch square, flat cardboard item.

Carroll quickly broke the plastic seal and removed it from the calendar. He threw the calendar on the floor. He placed the cellophane tightly over the wound, preventing any oxygen from seeping in through the new, bloodied airway.

"Don't worry Senator," he said. "The ambulance will be here any moment."

As Carroll continued to reassure Tremore, the proprietor of the jewelry store brought out a towel that he had in the back room. Carroll propped up the senator's head while the store owner placed the towel under it.

Meanwhile, Kas stayed among the crowd, watching for any traces of evidence and listening for any bits of information that would help the police in their investigation into the shooting. Unlike the police, though, his job as sweeper was to make sure, whenever possible, to conceal or contaminate any discoverable items and to forward to his co-conspirators any witness reports, thereby aiding them in their quest to avoid detection.

Chapter Seventeen

February 4, 2004

"Any word yet?"

"I just heard on the news that Tremore was shot. Nothing yet on his condition," said the young man sitting cross legged on the living room floor.

"Well, Abu is a pretty resourceful soldier. And Ahmed is the consummate mercenary. This should slow Tremore down a bit if he pulls out of this," said the stocky little man pacing along the apron of the fireplace.

"What about Kasmir, sir?" asked the young man.

"Don't worry about him. He's been through this before. He knows how to clean up a scene without getting caught," said Mohammed al-Satir, the older, pocked-faced individual. "And if anyone *had* seen anything, we'll soon know about it."

As al-Satir rubbed his eyes, the young recruit pushed himself up from the floor and walked toward the kitchen.

"Make sure you stay online," ordered Satir. "I want to know the second you receive any message."

"As you wish," said the recruit as he excused himself from the room.

Approximately one hour later, the young man reentered the living room. Approaching al-Satir, he said, "I just received an email from Abu."

"Let me see it," ordered the elder.

The email read:

TO: MYCAL1. . . .
FROM: SPEEDBALL9. . . .
SUBJECT: NYC VACATION
THE CITY IS ALIVE WITH ACTIVITY. WE HAVEN'T MET ANYONE WHO OFFERED AN UNKIND WORD TO US. I LOVE THE SCENERY. THE STREETS AND BUILDINGS ARE CLEAN AND BEAUTIFUL. WE'RE ALL SAFE AND HAPPY. WISH YOU WERE HERE.

"Mixed news," al-Satir blurted out.

"It looks pretty good to me."

"Yeah, it's good no one saw anything and no evidence was left at the scene, but it isn't good news that that infidel Tremore is still alive."

"Well, like you said, sir, it'll confuse them a bit."

"I know, but I really wanted him dead. I wanted him as a martyr for his bill. Nonetheless, with him being wounded there still might be enough sympathy to pass that bill of his. The Left will accuse the Right for the shooting. They will push for more gun laws. We cannot control these people if they are armed. Don't forget that. The Americans will think they are protecting themselves against further attacks if they pass this bill. Quite the contrary. We will be armed. We will find the breeches in their borders. We will use their laws and liberties against them. There will be martyrs on our side, be assured. That is the unfortunate consequence of war. But remember, we have time on our side. Be patient. Battles are fought on many fronts. This one will take time. Before we are able to force Sharia Law on these infidels, we must first destroy their dollar and prevent them from defending themselves. Then we attack again and again, in every city. As our numbers and force against these enemies of Allah increase, their resolve weakens. At that point, we will have won."

Al-Satir gazed out onto the Newark Bay from his Bayonne Society Hill condo. Several moments later, he turned and said to his young assistant, "Tell Ahmed I want to see him at my retreat."

February 5, 2004

Mac leaned across his desk and stared intently at Darcy. "This is getting out of hand. The murders are piling up. And now a sitting senator was shot. You better start being square with me before *you're* found floating in the Hudson River. There's a big gap here that needs to be filled."

Darcy looked around the room. "How am I involved in all this, these so-called murders? And why would I be a threat to anyone? I hired you so no one would know I was questioning the death of my friend Devin."

"Well, let's play your game of Hide and Seek. First off, your pal and partner Barrow had a map with him when you last saw him. You didn't question him about it. Shortly after he left the house with it, he ends up dead and the map ends up missing. Suicide they say. In comes Eduardo Melo Ortez. He worked for GNI, the parent company of *your* company, Navesco. And what happens to Ortez? He's found in a box, cut up into little pieces. You said you didn't know him, but your body language told me a whole different story. Finally, we have Martha Thomlin, a friend or associate of Ortez. What happens to her? Dead. Again, suicide they say. I'm not buying it. And I'm not buying your cover story. . . . I have one question for you, Mr. Darcy, and I expect an honest answer this time. Why did you hire me?"

"I hired you, I hired you . . . because . . . because you're supposed to find out what's going on, and to protect me and my interests."

"If you want me to protect you and represent your interests, you need to tell me the whole story, particularly your involvement in this fiasco. So, let's go back to square one. Let's start with names. Who are you working for?"

Darcy lowered his head and picked at one of his fingernails. "What do you mean?"

"I'm not stupid, Mr. Darcy. I'm not buying your concern for Silky's death. There's a larger picture here. As I said, if I'm to continue working on this case, I need answers from you. You are my client. You need to be honest and open with me. Now, tell me, who are you working for?"

"I was hoping I wouldn't have to do this. I thought you would be able to find the killer without me being involved in any way. That's why I've been paying you a large sum of money."

"A name. You want my help? I need a name."

"All right." Darcy leaned forward and pushed Mac's pen holder aside. "His name is Mohammed al-Satir."

"Who the hell is he and how do you know him?"

"I don't really know him," said Darcy. "I was contacted by him through a mutual business associate."

"And who might that associate be?"

"You know who it is."

"I want to hear it from you."

"Eduardo Ortez from GNI."

Mac sat back in his chair and crossed his fingers. "Ah yes. The man you denied knowing the last time we spoke. Now we're starting to get somewhere. What did Ortez say to you?"

"He said al-Satir needed bank documents and information on cash transfers. I would make a lot of money. Not to worry."

"Then what happened?"

"Ortez said for me to have 'my man' meet this guy at a ball field in Bayonne. I asked him, 'What for?'"

"Wait a minute," Mac broke in. "Who's 'your man'?"

"Devin."

"Silky?"

"Yes."

"Go on."

Ortez handed me a satchel of money. He told me to have the satchel placed in the Dumpster, and immediately leave the area. Later, another meet was to be set up whereby Devin would take the cardboard tube containing documents and meet an individual for a second exchange. This exchange would also entail money for documents, only this time, Devin would get three grand for his efforts and the documents would go to the other party."

"Let me guess, the second exchange was the one in Fort Lee where he was killed."

Darcy looked away from Mac. "Yes," he said.

"Where did Barrow get the cardboard tube containing the map and documents?"

"From Ortez."

"Why couldn't Ortez do the exchange in Fort Lee, instead of Barrow?"

"I think he knew Devin was going to be killed after the map and documents were turned over. He might have even set up the killing."

"To eliminate the middle man?"

"I suspect that was the reason. Devin did do two other exchanges for Ortez."

"What two exchanges?"

"One he made in Scotland and one in Italy."

"When did they take place?"

"Back in September of last year."

"And your money drop in Bayonne and the document exchange in Fort Lee?"

"I can't remember the dates but I believe they both took place on the same day in early November."

"Devin's prior exchanges took place as planned without any hitches. I guess he thought the one in Fort Lee one would also go without a problem."

"Well, not exactly. For some reason, he seemed edgy before going out on that one. He kept telling me he didn't want to go, but he needed the money. I encouraged him to do the exchange. I thought that would help him clear up some of his bills. I thought it would be simple, just like the exchanges overseas and the money drop in the Bayonne park."

Darcy leaned an elbow on the corner of Mac's desk. "Call it instinct or just a gut feeling, but Devin didn't like the time or location for the exchange. Still, he couldn't turn down the money he thought he was going to receive. He should have listened to his gut. I guess it doesn't matter, though. If they wanted him dead, they could always find another time and place."

Mac put both hands on the desk and looked directly into Darcy's eyes. "'They' being Ortez and this guy al-Satir."

"I suppose," said Darcy, sheepishly.

"This whole set of exchanges doesn't make any sense to me," said Mac. "Why couldn't the documents be turned over to Satir directly or to his go-between? Why bother with Silky on all these exchanges? Then have him killed?"

"I guess to sanitize the transaction. It's better to have two buffers between the top guys, than one. And killing them probably cauterizes the deals and ensures deniability. That's just my guess."

"Why not have Silky make a drop instead of a hand-off? That seems like the logical avenue of approach. Then he wouldn't have had to be murdered. And why, for that matter," asked Mac, "would GNI bring you, instead of Ortez, in the exchange process? Ortez could have handled the drop-off himself. I suspect he had other dealings with the contact."

"As for Silky being killed, I guess an example was being made to all parties involved. What's the old saying, 'The best kept secret is when only two people know and one of them is dead.' In regards to Ortez not making the exchange, I have to believe GNI thought it was in their best interest to keep him out of that loop. Maybe to protect him. He appeared to be a valuable asset to the company over the years."

"Well, he couldn't be that valuable," said Mac. "He was found three weeks ago cut up in pieces in a Bayonne park. I'd suspect it's the same park where you made one of the exchanges. Why have Ortez killed and cut up? Is that part of the cauterization process? I thought, as you said, he was a key player in the organization."

"He is, or was," said Darcy. "When I first heard of his death, I though it must have had something to do with the rape. He apparently had gotten too chummy with his contact."

"What? What rape?" Mac knew, all-to-well, what rape.

"Some woman in Montclair."

Wanting to see Darcy's knowledge of the incident, Mac asked, "When was this?"

"I don't remember. You're the detective. You want the particulars, check with the county prosecutor's office. All I know is that he was bringing attention to the corporation. Not good. I guess he was considered expendable. I don't think they wanted to kill the contact because of his connections."

"Who is the contact, a big shot?"

"Well, the guy involved in the rape allegation with Ortez is reported to be a Newark cop. A guy by the name of Burkner."

"Wallace Burkner?"

"Yeah, I think that's his name."

Mac stretched back and shook his head. "Well, that confirms it," he said.

"Confirms what?" asked Darcy.

"Never mind. So you think Ortez was murdered to prevent any connection that might lead to Satir, GNI, you, Silky, and whoever else might be involved in this master plan. And Burkner was the contact, the supplier of the documents, and co-conspirator in a rape."

"And one more thing. The most important thing . . . to me, that is."

"What's that?" asked Mac.

"Ortez's death was to scare me into keeping my mouth shut. I know too much already. I'm now expendable. That was a miscalculation on their part. I have no choice now but to exchange information for protection."

"I guess you kind of knew it might come to this when you first walked into my office. Now it's all making some sense." Mac got up and walked around his desk. "There still might be a bit of truth in your initial story," he said, pointing a finger at Darcy. "You *did* want to know why Silky was killed. But—and it's a big but—your main reason for hiring me was out of fear, fear that *you* would be targeted for elimination. That was slick convincing your handlers that you wanted to hire a PI to spy on the police, see what was up their sleeves. And you knew from Silky that I wasn't the squeamish type, that I don't always go by the book in my methods, and I wouldn't hesitate to pull the trigger should the need arise."

Darcy sat silent for a moment. He looked down at the desk and brushed the fingers of his right hand across it. "True," he finally said. "But I still thought I was an asset to GNI and Navesco, and that the chances were slim I would be killed. Now that Ortez was murdered, I see I really have no options here but to be totally honest with you."

Mac still wasn't sure of the game his client was playing. After several moments of contemplation, he returned to his chair, pulled his notebook in front of him and took a pen out of the holder on his desk. "All right. Let's start all over. Now, you mentioned a code name the courier was to use when he met with Silky."

"I believe the name used was 'The Architect.'" Darcy then added, "When Devin didn't return, I began to worry. Later that night I got a phone call from an unknown caller. He said 'Your man won't be coming back.' He went on to tell me to keep my mouth shut and I'd be fine. I could even make a lot of money when everything 'shakes out.' He said his boss felt badly about what had happened to 'my man' so he would give me a heads up before anything went down."

"What'd he mean by that?"

"He meant I could trade off dollars for euros or pounds before whatever was going to happen. I could make a bundle on the exchange. But being the philanthropist his boss is, the caller said he would only charge me 50% of the profits for the information."

"And you say his boss is this guy Satir?"

"Yes, but I don't think he's the big money or the financial brains behind all of this. I've not heard of him in the network of arbitrageurs, or anywhere else for that matter; not before or after Ortez introduced him to me. He's not a name to know in my business, so I suspect there's bigger money behind him. But that's just speculation."

"Any guesses on who?"

"Well, if Ortez is involved—which he was—it could even be someone from within GNI. I don't know that to be a fact, but it's within the scope of probability."

"Is that when you came to me?"

"I thought about it all night. I originally decided to remain quiet and go along with the program, only because I did not want to end up, as you would say, floating belly up in the Hudson River. Then a hiker found Devin's body at the foot of the Palisades. It wasn't until after the police did their preliminary investigation and told me they believed it was a suicide that I decided to look for a private detective. I knew it wasn't a suicide."

"How did you find me?"

"I know I told you it was because of your exploits in New York State, but that's only a part of it. Devin told me if I ever needed a square-shooting cop to help me out of a jam, you'd be the man. He had a high regard for you. He'd say, 'Taylor's a straight cop with an unorthodox, but effective way of always getting at the truth and taking care of business.'"

"Why didn't you just continue to go along with the program?"

"Because I realized I was dead meat to Ortez anyway. Since I would be a threat to him—knowing what I know—I suspected there would be a good chance he might have me killed, after the payoffs were made."

"Why not deal with the police? Tell them what you just told me?"

"Because I don't want to go into any witness protection program, not if I have other options. That would be my worst-case scenario. I would have to plead out to some kind of conspiracy charge. I'd kiss my career and life style good-bye, and I'd be looking over my shoulder for the rest of my life. I was hoping you'd have a better option for me. I mean, you guys are like priests and attorneys, aren't you? You can keep a confidence and advise a course of action that might be as you said, 'not by the book.'"

"Well, that's not exactly true. To get anything done in this business, one needs the cooperation of the police on a daily basis. And the state police have to approve my PI license every time it comes up for renewal. Not a small matter."

"Nonetheless, I still thought it was the most prudent thing to do under the circumstances."

"Well, now that you're going to be straight up with me, hopefully I can protect you." Mac tapped his pen on the pad. "So tell me who'd gotten you the banking information?"

"I sent Devin to Inverness, Scotland for those documents. He then went to Corsica to pick up some other paperwork. From there, he made a side trip to Capri to meet with Ortez and a Saudi prince docked off the coast. The prince wanted to speak with Devin about establishing a bank account in his, Devin's, name in order to transfer cash . . . I suspect for Satir's operation. Devin was clean—relatively speaking. You're not going to get a Mother Theresa in this business—and Capri was a good place to finally meet so as not to set off a trigger."

"Trigger?"

"Yes, I don't know the scope of the operation al-Satir is planning, but I'm sure the nature of it has something to do with supporting terror cells in the U.S. I know the domestics and international groups have been trying to work together for years. Homeland Security has many ways to track these groups. The terrorists are aware of some red flags that trigger investigations. One of those red flags or triggers is by tracking, through passports, those individuals entering and exiting countries known to have ties with terrorist groups. Italy is one of the least vigilant countries in that regard. And, as I said, Devin's was pretty clean on that account. He wasn't on any watch list as far as I know."

"Makes sense, but what's the story with the other paperwork Devin picked up in Corsica? Was that also banking information?"

"I believe it was, only I don't know that to be a fact. All the envelopes turned over to Devin were sealed; stamped across each seal were the words, 'Security Confidential.'"

"Did you or Devin open those envelopes?"

"I'm not crazy, nor was Devin."

"So the answer's no?"

"Yes . . . I mean, no, we didn't open them."

Mac tapped his pen several times on the desk. After a moment of reflection, he said, "Getting back to Devin's meeting in Capri, you said he agreed to open an account in his name at that time. I suspect that was to launder money to Satir from a Saudi prince or from one of the prince's dummy corporations. Is that what I'm hearing from you?"

"Yes, for a price. A hefty sum of money, I might add. Unfortunately, Devin and I should have seen it coming. Once the money was transferred to Satir's operation—the satchel of cash—Devin's death warrant was not long behind. They needed one more exchange from him: the map and the other documents in the tube. Only there was no money waiting for him in that last exchange, only a long drop off the Palisades."

Mac stood up again and leaned forward, casting a menacing look at Darcy. "I've been patient with you," he said. "I've protected you this far, but I don't have any sympathy for traitors, and that's what I see sitting across from me right now. The only reason you've come out of the woodwork is to protect your own ass, while not too long ago you were ready to help finance an act of terrorism on your own country. And the only reason I don't kill you right here and now for your treason is fourfold. One, I took this case and accepted your money. I have an obligation here and I always pay off all my obligations. Two, there are two deaths misreported as suicides. They need to be reclassified as homicides. Three: there's another dead body, left cut-up in a ball field. The psychopathic killer who did that needs to be found a-sap and put out of his or her misery. And four, most importantly, you're going to help me put an end to this impending assault on our country. So, let the games begin. Where do I find this guy al-Satir?"

Darcy got up and stepped toward the door. Mac came around from the back of his desk and blocked Darcy from moving closer to it.

"I don't know," he said. "I was approached to do business with him from Ortez. I've spoken with him by phone, but never met him in person."

Mac stared at him with cold eyes. "You are fortunate of one thing, Mr. Darcy. We made a deal and I honor all deals I make. I am going to save your sorry ass, but in order to do that I need to know where I can find this miscreant, al-Satir. And you're the man who's going to help me."

Chapter Eighteen

February 7, 2004

The thirty men who were escorting the four trucks that carried the granular chlorine were dropped off at an old factory near the Mexican border town of Juarez. Beneath the factory was a tunnel that ran under the border and into a building owned and operated by a Mexican drug cartel. The thirty men along with their weapons passed into the United States without notice. At the same time, the four trucks passed through the U.S. customs checkpoint with fraudulent documentation for a major pool supply distributor in Arizona.

Agents Sara Dillon and Brad Klein entered SAC Lindstrum's office.

"How're we making out?" asked Lindstrum.

"Pretty damn good, Paul," replied Agent Dillon. "The shooter's vehicle was reported stolen several days ago. The suspect, though, must've scoped out the parking lot of the commuter train station in Waldwick because he changed license plates with a similar make, model, and color there. The victim hadn't even been aware of the plate switch until we stopped by his house.

"What about the gun you guys found in the river?"

"NCIC traced the Winchester to a store in Cascadia, Washington."

"Who do we have as the purchaser?" inquired Lindstrum.

"We don't have a purchaser. The Winchester was stolen with several other guns and ammo in a nighttime break-in. Our bureau in Spokane is just now getting all the paperwork from the Washington State Police on the burglary and theft."

"Any initial info?"

"The shop owner told one of our agents that he suspects a group of survivalists that had lived in and around the area for several years."

"Did he give him a name?"

"*Jally* something. He couldn't be more specific. The Spokane Bureau is running all kinds of partial checks as well as backgrounds on all survivalist groups and known players in each of them. It sounds like our group Jalil ul-Anmar."

"How about the car? Any prints?"

"Only the owner—who, at this time, is not a suspect."

"What about interviews?"

"A guy who saw the shooter was able to give a decent description of him: tall, burly, black male. But here's the best part. We don't need a personal ID. A hidden mall security camera on the roof that covers the entire parking lot area was able to capture a photo of the shooter. We've run computer facial recognition checks against out databases for a match. It looks like we hit pay dirt with a guy named Dirk Conroy. We're doing a background check on him as we speak. Our counterintel boys tell us Conroy's been out of the country recently and that we've had a long history with him. They had given Interpol a heads up on him. He's now a suspect in two relatively new murders in Europe."

"Great! Keep me apprised of any new developments. We'll have a roundtable meeting in about an hour."

Lindstrum turned to Agent Klein.

"Brad, what's the word on the senator?"

"Still in the intensive care unit, but he's stable. Looks like he's going to make it. The bullet missed his heart and major arteries. Still, he lost a lot of blood. The quick action of Patrolman Carroll and the paramedics probably saved his life. I'm sure once he's up and running again, he'll put them in for some kind of commendation."

"Did you send that bullet to ballistics?"

"Yep. It matches up with the Winchester. That's the weapon, no doubt about it."

"Good. Now that we know *how* and *who*, are we making any progress on *why*?"

"With the senator's consent, we've been going through all his public snail mail, email, telephone records, visitor logs, scheduled appointments, and so on."

Klein shuffled through several papers, then added, "We also have a couple of agents interviewing his friends, family, office personnel; checking interoffice memos, legislative bills either sponsored, co-sponsored, or voted on by Tremore. We should have several good leads soon."

"I'd trade in several good leads for one *solid* lead," Lindstrum said. "In any event, I want you, Sara, and the rest of the team, who are not currently out in the field, to meet in the conference room in about forty-five minutes. Bring everything you have with you. We've got new developments coming in and I want everyone brought up to date."

"10-4," said Agent Klein.

Lindstrum faced the group of agents gathered in the conference room. "According to one of our confidential informants, backed up by the NSA guys, there's been chatter recently on a terrorist attack that's going to happen. No specifics on anything—time, location, target, you name it. Not even as to the group planning this action. Well, maybe one. I'll deal with that in a moment. There have been increases in phone calls, emails, and person-to-person contacts with outside sources.

"We've been looking into survivalist and terrorist groups in the shooting of Senator Tremore because he has introduced a bill that would greatly increase law enforcement's ability to disarm and take down these groups.

"Our main target right now is a man named Dirk Conroy. His history is as follows: He's a former Passaic police detective who was drummed off the job over several internal investigations. For one, he was involved in a suspicious police shooting. A stolen revolver taken off the victim had Conroy's partial prints on the barrel and on two of the spent shell casings. When questioned about it, Conroy said he emptied the weapon to see if there were any live rounds left in it. He said he placed the bullets back, each in their own cylinder, so as not to spoil the evidence, which in fact is what he did. That didn't sit well with the committee, but it apparently wasn't enough evidence to prove the gun was placed on the victim by Conroy. Once he cleared that investigation, another one popped up. This one actually put him out of commission. A drug dealer told county investigators that he was paying off Conroy to leave him alone. They wired-up the dealer. His taped conversations with Conroy resulted in Conroy's guilty plea for a five-year prison term on charges of official misconduct and extortion. After prison, he worked for a local loan shark and was soon convicted again, this time on several aggravated assault charges. He served another five years. After that, he was a suspect in several organized crime hits, but the cases against him couldn't be proven for lack of evidence. He disappeared for awhile, then surfaced with a new name . . . Ahmed Sal Mohammed. It's suspected he joined up with a group known as Jalil ul-Anmar. Many of you are familiar with the group. For those who are not, ul-Anmar is a paramilitary organization consisting mostly of African-American Muslims based primarily in Pakistan and here in the U.S. They also operate out of Canada and the Caribbean. It's a terrorist group, although our illustrious leaders and those in the EU have not felt it necessary to list the group as such, even though its members have been suspect in various assassinations, most notably that of Isam Al-Temiyat in 1983 and Mansur Saleh in 1990. We have questioned the group's leader, Fadi Abou Hamed, in connection with the abduction of Daniel Pearl. The group also has been investigated for possible involvement in bombings. Conroy slash Ahmed was probably introduced to this organization during his time in jail. Lately, he's been suspected of using fake IDs to get in and out of the country, though that could not be confirmed. Interpol believes he's responsible for several murders in Europe, notably one in Scotland and one in Italy. He's extremely dangerous, so be very careful if you get close to him. And one or more of us will get close to him. Once he's found, I want him brought in for the attempted murder of Senator Tremore and for questioning in the death of Devin Barrow. So far, what we've got is this: Conroy's been heavily involved in communications with an individual known only by the code name, 'The Architect.'" Found in Barrow's car was a scrap of paper with 'The Architect' written on it. His death was reported to be a suicide by the medical examiner; a very questionable determination, at best. The physical evidence can go both ways, but not the circumstances surrounding that evidence. There appears to be an apparent nexus between Barrow and Conroy, and where Conroy's involved, someone usually dies an untimely death. There are too many unconnected dots here; Barrow's death and the Architect, Barrow's relationship with a guy named Lamar Darcy, Darcy's relationship with GNI, and GNI's involvement with Ortez and possibly ul-Anmar, and Conroy. It all smacks of trouble. There's a good chance Conroy's involved in something big, even bigger than the shooting of a U.S. senator, if you can believe that.

"Let's move on this. Brad check with our European liaison to see what they have on the murders in Scotland and Italy. Run a complete background check on Conroy, see if there's a connection with GNI, Ortez, or Barrow. We should have enough PC from the Tremore shooting to get an arrest warrant out on him by tomorrow. Sara, you're not going to believe this but our office just received a call from Investigator Taylor. He wants to provide us with some information concerning an impending terrorist attack. He won't talk over the phone, so set up an appointment with him as soon as you can. You'll have to meet him at his office or preferably a neutral location. It looks like he's going to cooperate with us. If he does, we can shut down that wire on him. Now, we don't know how much time is left before this ticking bomb explodes. So let's move it!"

Al-Satir's summer cottage in the Pocono Mountains of Pennsylvania held a breathtaking view of the valley below. He liked the property because it was far enough away from the hustle and bustle of Bayonne, New Jersey, yet close enough to oversee the operation set to unfold in the Newark Bay Area.

Stepping out onto his front balcony, he observed the Mercedes Benz L500 wind its way up the hill leading to his summer retreat. The vehicle stopped short of the front entryway and a large black man got out.

"Ah, my good friend Ahmed!" shouted al-Satir. "Come inside. I'll meet you downstairs." Satir went down to meet his guest.

"How was your trip here?" he asked.

"Uneventful," said Ahmed, aka Dirk Conroy. "You wanted to see me?"

"Ah, right to the point. I have a lot to learn of the ways of Americans. I am used to the hospitality of casual conversation before settling into discussions of business. Come, let's talk in my office." Conroy followed Satir down the hallway, past the stairway leading to the second floor on the left, the living room on the right, and on into the office.

"Would you like a drink?" Satir asked. "Nothing alcoholic, of course. Sorry but you are aware of our, how would you say, religious prohibitions."

"No thanks on the drink, but I will have a smoke," Conroy said with a smile.

Satir laughed. "Ah, you are the jokester, Ahmed. You expose the weaknesses of our hospitality, or shall I say strengths."

"I've been called many things, but jokester hasn't been one of them," said Conroy. "Let's put the pleasantries aside for now. Why did you want to meet with me? I thought we agreed to keep our distance from each other. For security purposes."

"Yes, we had agreed to that. Since that agreement, though, you have been paid to kill five people, and you are beginning to draw a lot of attention from a lot of agencies."

"Six."

"Six what?"

"I've been paid to kill six people: the couriers in Scotland and Italy, the courier in Fort Lee, the broad who cried rape, Ortez from GNI, and the senator."

Satir grinned. "The collateral death in Scotland was not part of our plan. And the senator is not dead. Should we ask for a refund?"

"With all due respect, do you think it wise to ask a hired professional serial killer for money back?"

"Have no fear, Ahmed. I'm only joking with you. See, I can be a jokester also." A smile drained from his face. "Let me assure you, though, I do not take threats lightly. I do have the means to extract money owed to me from, as you would say, 'a hired professional serial killer.' The infidels don't call us radical Islamists for nothing."

"So much for hospitality. Why don't we get to the reason I was asked to meet you here."

"Very well. You've been doing business with Lamar Darcy since I've put you two in contact with each other. You know Darcy convinced me to let him hire a private investigator in order to gather information for us. That's when he picked a man by the name Mac Taylor. I thought that was a good idea at first. The last I spoke with Darcy, though, he seemed very nervous. He wanted out. He said Taylor is probing too deeply into matters that can hurt us. He wouldn't be specific but I began to have second thoughts about Taylor's usefulness. That's when I had you check out where he lived and worked just in case he had to be eliminated. Correct, so far?"

"Your point being?"

"My point being that I think it's time to kill Mr. Taylor. And the reason I want to talk with you here is that I don't want Darcy to know about it."

"And why is that?"

"Because I want you to kill Darcy after Taylor's dead."

"I thought he was an asset to you and the money behind this operation."

"Ah, Ahmed. Haven't you learned yet how my people are? Everyone is expendable for the greater cause. Whatever it takes to defeat the infidels. Now, let's discuss price."

Chapter Nineteen

February 8, 2004—Late AM

The water was choppy from the brisk wind that blew across the channel. The fiberglass sixteen-foot Starcraft pitched and yawed, kicking salt spray off all sides. Being a cold, wintery day, it was the only boat on the water. Mac watched it bang back and forth on the frost-tipped water as he stepped down from the hilly, wooded area along the Hudson River just south of the George Washington Bridge. He turned and took several more photographs of the steep cliff leading to the lookout point. He then headed back to his truck parked under the bridge.

"Find anything yet?" Cheryl yelled out from the passenger seat as Mac broke from the small clearing to her right.

"No, nothing. The area had been swept clean by the BCI Unit."

"Too bad."

"Not a problem. I didn't expect to find anything. I just wanted to document the scene from top to bottom. Force of habit. It's said, 'One photo's worth a thousand words.' Very true. These pics can always be used to re-create the scene, without having to explain what it looked like in 20 pages."

"I'm sure the police and BCI have photos, too. I could have called them for copies and saved us a trip up here."

"I'm sure they do have photos. A good investigator should

always photograph the scene, or have it done, in this case, by the Sheriff's Department, Bureau of Criminal Identification. All investigators should follow several procedures: protect the scene first and establish a log listing everyone wanting access to it. Their next steps should be to photograph and diagram the scene, then and only then, collect evidence. I'm a PI now, so, unfortunately I don't have access or the advantage to perform all the 'should do' procedures. You could have called Detective Arnet or the Sheriff's Department, Criminal Identification Unit, but I doubt very much you were going to get copies of the scene photos from them. Besides, an investigator should always visit the scene, at least once. So, at least I'll have some shots for my client and for my memory of this place."

"Is that my first lesson in Criminal Investigations 101, Crime Scene Analysis?" Cheryl said with a smirk.

"There will be a quiz later today on the subject," Mac said jokingly.

As he handed her the camera, he noticed Cheryl staring at the sideview mirror of the truck.

"What's up?" he said.

She poked her head out the window and pointed back to a gray Chevy Caprice parked approximately one hundred feet down the road. "I wonder who's in that car? It showed up while you were up on the hill taking photos. It hasn't moved since."

At that moment, the Caprice began to roll slowly toward them.

"It's fine, honey," Mac said to Cheryl as the car got closer. "I called the feds last night. An Agent Dillon and Agent Klein are supposed to meet me this morning."

"Then why are we here?" Cheryl asked. "Why not meet at the office?"

"I spoke with Dillon. She preferred not to meet at our office, for whatever reason. They live in a world of paranoia. It comes with the job."

"So, why here?"

"It's as good a place as any," Mac replied. "I wanted to see where Barrow's body ended up, and since the feds always like to remain inconspicuous, what better place to meet than under the GW Bridge?" *They show up in a Caprice. Inconspicuous, yeah, right,* he thought.

The big, gray sedan came to a stop about ten feet from where Mac was standing. There were two occupants in the vehicle. The driver's door opened and a woman got out. She was, by Mac's estimation, approximately thirty-five years old. She was wearing black jeans, a light blue sweater, and a dark blue windbreaker. Her blond hair was cut short; her blue eyes, bright and clear. Exiting the passenger seat was a younger looking male, in his late twenties, wearing a white shirt, black trousers, and a windbreaker similar to the one the woman was wearing. *No doubting who they are,* he concluded.

The woman reached into her back pocket. She pulled out a black wallet, flipped it open and said, "I'm Special Agent Sara Dillon, FBI. We spoke on the phone. This is my partner, Agent Brad Klein."

Mac reached out with his right hand and lifted the ID closer to the woman's face. He took a good long look—sizing up the photograph with the person standing in front of him as well as examining the authorizing signatures and the FBI seal. "Glad to meet you, Agent Dillon, Agent Klein," he said with a smile.

"Everything okay?" asked Cheryl.

"Fine," said Mac.

"This is where you want to talk?" said Dillon.

"As I told my wife, 'it's as good a place as any,'" replied Mac. "Haven't you ever heard the expression, 'The best place to hide is out in the open'?"

"No, but if that's what you want, I'm game. I was hoping we could go somewhere *not* so open to public scrutiny. Much of what we're to talk about is classified."

"How if I take a seat in your car? Would that make you feel less paranoid? My wife can head home in the truck and you can give me a lift to my house when we're finished talking."

"Deal."

Mac kissed Cheryl and rubbed her arm. "Honey, head home. I'll be by in a little while. I've a feeling this is going to take some time."

"What about the photos?"

"Download them onto the computer. I'll print them out when I get back and put them in the case jacket."

Cheryl got out of the truck, walked around, and got into the driver's seat. She started up the vehicle, put it in gear, and pulled away.

Mac, accompanied by the two feds, walked to the Caprice and got in the passenger side front seat, Klein got in the back.

Mac looked over at Dillon sitting in the driver's seat and said, "I suspect if you and Brad back there want to give me classified information, you'd want something from me in exchange."

"Let me see if I get this straight," Dillon said. "*You* called us. So why don't you start?"

"I will, but I first have to say, I've never known a federal agent to give out information except to those on a 'need to know basis.' As one ex-cop, private detective, to an active brother, excuse me, sister in the field, I have a proposition for you. I will tell you what I know about a planned terrorist attack. In turn, though, I want a part in the investigation."

"You know I can have your license if you don't cooperate, and there can possibly be criminal charges for withholding information on an inchoate crime. I'm sure an Assistant AG can come up with a few other code violations."

"Boy did you get up on the wrong side of bed this morning," Mac said. Turning to face Klein in the back seat, he added, "Is she always this ornery?"

Mac looked back at Agent Dillon. "Look, here's the scoop. I started investigating the death of an old acquaintance, Devin, aka Silky, Barrow."

"The suicide here in Fort Lee?" Dillon asked rhetorically.

"One and the same. Why do you think I wanted to meet you right here?"

"The photos."

"What?"

"The photos," said Agent Dillon. "I heard you say to your wife to download the photos onto your computer. This must be the area where Barrow landed. I knew it was somewhere close to the George Washington Bridge. I suspect you were photographing the area before we arrived. I did notice the camera in your hand when you approached your truck."

"Very good, Agent Dillon. This is, in fact, where my case begins. I thought the location would provide some perspective, a starting point. I thought you might want to see where Devin 'Silky' Barrow actually died. He deserved at least that attention."

"Well, here's a piece of information: we are very interested in this death investigation."

"You are? What are the odds? I'm curious, what could be your interest in the reported suicide of a local businessman?"

"You, you're our interest. We want to know why *you're* so curious about his death. Why you're interested in a reported suicide. So interested, that you want to review the case file and visit the scene. So interested, that you don't believe it's a suicide. You believe he was murdered. I suspect it has something to do with your newly founded detective agency . . . and newly found client."

"I see Detective Arnet filled you in on our conversations and visits."

Dillon leaned toward Mac. "Now, Mr. Taylor, let's get down to business. What, if anything, did you learn in investigating Barrow's death?"

"First, it's not a suicide. Two, Barrow was killed during an exchange of sorts—money for a map and documents. Three, a company named Global Network International, GNI, is somehow involved, possibly providing financing for the attack. I'll give you four, five, and six but you have to give me something in return."

"I can do that," said Agent Dillon. "Ever hear the name Dirk Conroy?"

"Yes. What about him?" said Mac.

"He was released from prison four years ago."

"And?"

"And we suspect he may be involved in the attempted murder of Senator Tremore and two other murders abroad."

"Would those murders be in Scotland and Italy?"

"Bingo. I see you do know quite a bit of what's going on."

"Here're four and five: the killings were the result of document and money exchanges, part of which Barrow was involved."

Dillon thought for a moment before blurting out, "So we have Barrow and Conroy in the exchanges, and two other couriers dead. Conroy has to have killed Barrow along with the other two. That'd be my guess."

Mac turned back to face Klein. "Feel free to join in anytime you want," he said.

Klein smiled. "This is Sara's show, not mine."

"I see," said Mac. "You're the corroborating witness in case I'm to be charged with anything. We wouldn't want it to just be Agent Dillon's word against mine." Mac looked back at Dillon, "Sara. I like that name. May I call you Sara?"

"Call me what you want, just give me something I—we—can work with."

"Sure thing, here's number six. In Barrow's car was a piece of paper. On the paper was written 'The Architect'. I've since learned the Architect is a man named al-Satir."

Sara kept a straight face. She did not want Mac to know that he had just given her a big piece to the puzzle. *Al-Satir, The Architect!* "Do you know where he can be found?" she asked.

"That's why I called you guys. I could find him, but it could take me some time. I don't have any information on him other than his last name. Meanwhile, something big is supposed to go down. Something you people should be made aware of."

"Well, we'll add al-Satir to our list of primary suspects right alongside Conroy. What could you tell us about him?"

"Satir?"

"No, Conroy. You said you didn't know anything about Satir."

"Just checking," Mac said with a wide grin. "Conroy was a dirty cop, but attempting to murder a senator, that's a real heavy rap. I'm sure you have your reasons to believe that. Only, if you had hard evidence, he'd be in custody as we speak." He thought for a moment, then added, "Unless, of course, you can't find him."

Mac put his head down and was quiet for what seemed a long time. Looking up and turning toward Agent Dillon, he said, "I know some things about Conroy that might not be in any report. Since he was a Passaic cop at one time, I might be able to help you."

"Well, could you, Mr. Taylor?"

"Mr. Taylor. That sounds very formal. Mac, you can call me Mac."

"Very well, *Mac*," Dillon said. "Now, enough with the cordial chitchat. Do you know where we might find him?"

"The short answer, 'No.'"

"And the long answer."

"The long answer is this: I knew some cops from Passaic PD back in the day. And I knew Conroy was a loose cannon. Guys were afraid to work with him. They didn't trust him. I also know that the OC boys were hot on him ever since he began running with one of the local crime families. I sat on a few surveillances in Newark when he was providing police info to drug dealers for a piece of their drug money. He was dropped for that and sent away to prison. Since that time, I lost track of him. He began operating out of my area and my CIs who knew him well began drying up. As you know, I started having problems with two guys named LaForge and Parnel. That's when Conroy fell off my radar screen. If you can give me a little more history on the guy, I might be more helpful."

Dillon hesitated a moment, then said, "Well, for starters, while in prison, Conroy joined an Islamic terrorist group called Jalil ul-Anmar. It has cells throughout the U.S. and continues to do some heavy recruiting in the prisons. According to classified records, Conroy became active with ul-Anmar last year. Since hooking up with that group, one of the names he uses is Ahmed Sal Mohammed."

"The questions 'why' and 'how' jump to mind," said Mac

"The 'why' is obvious, isn't it? We arrested him and put him away for several years. Islamic terrorism is the perfect fallback position for these losers; a chance to get even. Payback's a bitch. And the bennies are terrific. Money, power, and women they'd never get on their own. As for the 'how,' our money guys followed a large amount of cash going from South America to a target bank in the Caribbean. That transfer of funds was suspected to be Conroy's initiation into the group."

"Can you be more specific?"

"Sorry, Mac. I wish I could be, but all specifics are on a need-to-know basis. Since you won't be involved in the money trail, there's no need for you to know. Don't blame me. It's department policy."

"I can appreciate your security procedures, Agent Dillon." A smile suddenly cut across Mac's face. He then added wryly, "What *can* you tell me that won't violate department policy?"

"Well, we suspect the local contact for Conroy is a white male about 35 years old, who goes by the name Darcy." Dillon looked Mac directly in the eyes and said, "I believe you know him. He was an associate of the deceased, Mr. Devin Barrow.'"

"So that's it," Mac said. "I'd ask you how you came across that piece of info, but I suspect that would require a 'need to know.' No matter, I'm familiar with the routine . . . surveillances, wire taps, confidential informants. Here I am reaching out for you, but I suspect you were on me from the get-go."

"Look, we ran all the checks, criminal and otherwise, on Darcy;

and we ran through everything we could find on Barrow and Conroy. That's not the issue. We need to know all of what you know. I don't think it was a coincidence that you called our office yesterday wanting to discuss an impending terrorist attack. You know something's not right about Darcy and about Barrow's death."

"I know the due diligence checks you're talking about," said Mac. "But the written reports don't tell the whole story. Opinions, suppositions, hunches, knowledge irrelevant to the crimes charged but relevant to the character of the perp aren't generally found in the police reports. They're sterilized for judges, attorneys, and jurors. What's in a cop's head goes far beyond his written report. So I'll be square with you. I intended to from the start.

"My client has given me a wealth of information on the upcoming attack. Still there's a lot missing. I know your capabilities for interdiction. I respect client–PI privilege, but this is bigger than solving a local homicide case. As much as a reprobate my client might be, I'd like to afford him some protection. He has been cooperative with me, to a degree. Plus, I've taken his money. That's a contractual agreement I intend to honor."

"That client would be Mr. Darcy, correct?" asked Dillon.

"Very good, Sara. You figured that out all by yourself. Brad didn't even need to help you. Just kidding. Yes, yes, Darcy is my client, although he wants to remain anonymous. I'll help you where I can, but the favor I ask is that he not be compromised, at least not until this investigation is over. National security comes first, I understand that, but let's not burn him unless there is no other way. Since you seem to know my client, maybe you can answer a few questions I've been having about the company he works for and the friends he's been keeping. As you know I'm new at this game of bureaucratic box ball, being cooperative with the law and being loyal to my client. Maybe we can help each other on that point."

"That might be a little difficult. I'll check with the higher ups. You know results many times take a back seat to liability concerns and image. We agents come and go, but the Bureau lives on. What did Reagan say? 'Bureaucracy is the closest thing to eternal life.'"

"How true," said Mac.

You do have one other strike against you."

"What's that?" Mac asked.

"You were a Newark Police detective. SAC is aware of your past record of vigilantism. That style doesn't work with us."

"Hey, whatever floats your boat," Mac said. "I know you guys, er gals, have to be politically correct. That's why you drive these Caprices and wear matching jackets. That's just not my thing. Still, I respect what you do. You're the good guys, gals. You're doing God's work." Mac slapped his knees. "Tell you what," he continued, "I'm sure you know where I live, Sara. Why don't we go back to your office and discuss this further? Afterwards, you can drop me off at home."

"You could have met us there in the first place and you could have driven yourself home."

"Yeah, but then you would have missed an opportunity to see where Silky took his last breath. Besides, here we could spend some quality time together away from my office, your office, and your bosses."

Agent Dillon shook her head and gave Mac a hard stare.

"What?" he asked.

"Nothing," she said as she put the car in gear and headed back to her office.

Chapter Twenty

February 8, 2004—PM

"What I can tell you about Conroy is that he's a ruthless whack job."

"You think?" Dillon said sarcastically.

Mac eased back in the conference room chair. "He was caught paying bums down by the Passaic River a buck to punch them in the face and see if he could knock them out."

"Yes. We know he's quite an unsavory character. Would you recognize him if you saw him again?"

Mac tapped his fingers on the long mahogany table in front of him. "It's been a long time," he said. "I'm pretty good with faces. Names tend to escape me, though. If he hasn't changed his appearance too much, I should be able to ID him again."

Agent Dillon pulled out several photos of Conroy and slid them across the table to Mac. Some were earlier prison photos, but the more recent ones were surveillance telephoto shots. "Have you seen him with your boy Darcy?"

Mac looked intently at the photographs. "Nope, can't say as I have. It looks like he's put on some weight in these surveillance shots. And that looks like a nice boat. I'd like to know where they were taken. And who took them."

"Not important," replied Agent Dillon. "What's important are the connections: Conroy, Darcy, and a person you might have heard of in your conversations with Darcy, a Señor Eduardo Ortez."

Mac was only half listening. "What? Ortez, yes I have. But now that I think of it, Conroy just might be in the area."

"You're jumping around on me, Mac. We're back on Conroy?"

"Yeah. A few weeks ago, I came out of my house and saw a heavy-set black male walking a dog up the block from there. I hadn't seen him or his dog before nor have I seen them since. It could just be paranoia, but now seeing that Conroy put on some pounds, and your interest in connecting Conroy to Darcy, it could have been him tailing Darcy."

"Or eyeballing you."

"I don't see that unless Darcy is playing me and Conroy is working for him," Mac said.

"That's what I'm thinking. Darcy and Ortez are suspects number three and four," said Dillon. "But why would Darcy hire you, only to set you up?"

"If your theory is right, it's got to be for information. Information to protect Darcy, and probably Ortez, too. I'd be his sweeper, his mole without knowing it. He gets whatever inside info I can uncover. There's just one problem."

"What's that?" said Dillon.

"Ortez is dead, cut to pieces. So, I haven't a clue what Darcy's going to do now. What side of the fence he wants to fall on. This might be one big charade. Darcy could be the brains behind this whole thing. He may have started out wanting to play me, but now learned the brutal facts that Conroy has no loyalties and someone else, al-Satir, for example, is pulling the strings. That's why he gave up his name to me. I might now actually be his best chance for staying alive. I need to get into this guy's head. Flush him out. I need to find out his game plan. He's still my client, though. He's paying me. Can I legally accept money from a client and set him up at the same time. Isn't that some kind of a PI ethical violation?" Mac shook his head and laughed. "And this is my first PI case. What a way to start a business."

"Here's the flip side. If you're being used for information and you're not part of the team, you're expendable, Mac. I don't know how far along you are with Darcy, but I suspect once you stop being useful, whoever is running this operation might just decide to take you out of the equation."

"Valid point. I can take care of myself, though."

"Maybe so, but what about your family?" Dillon asked. "Keep us in the loop on Darcy and we'll provide cover for you *and* your wife."

"Thanks for the offer. The more I think about Conroy running around in my area, the more paranoid I get. I should call my wife to make sure all is well on the home front." Mac pulled out his cell phone and called Cheryl. It went right to voice mail.

Cheryl was about to call Mac. She wanted to know when he'd be home for dinner so she could put the fish in the oven. But just as she was about to hit 'send', the washing machine buzzer went off. She looked at the keypad on the phone, then quickly snapped the flip top of the cell phone shut. She decided the call could wait. Cheryl walked down the basement stairs to the utility room. She took the clothes out of the washing machine and began placing them in the dryer. It was then she heard a click coming from upstairs in the vicinity of the back door. As she tepidly continued to load the dryer, she heard footsteps overhead.

"Hello. Mac. Is that you?" she called out.

Not getting an answer, she began to get that queasy feeling one gets from uncertainty that carries with it danger of the deadliest kind.

"Mac!" she yelled again, this time louder with a quiver in her voice.

Again no response.

Cheryl took the cell phone from her pocket and hit 9-1-1 on

speed dial.

"Bloomfield Police. What's the emergency?"

"Intruder, help," Cheryl whispered in her phone before giving her street address and house number. She left the phone open and placed it next to some laundry on the washing machine. Cheryl quickly looked around for a weapon, anything, a bat, lamp, hammer, a knife. She noticed the poker by the fireplace in the finished section of the basement. She quickly grabbed it and ran back into the utility room. She slid behind the hot water heater located opposite the dryer. Cheryl closed her eyes as she felt her baby kick. Tears came to her eyes as she tried desperately not to panic. She heard muffled background sounds coming from the phone as several police units were being dispatched to the scene.

Footsteps could be heard coming down the basement stairs.

"Ma'am, stay on the line, stay calm, police units are on their way," could now be heard clearly over the phone.

With eyes wide and a pounding heart, Cheryl stood in silence behind the water heater. Suddenly, Conroy—holding a handgun equipped with a silencer—moved slowly past the washer and dryer.

"Ma,am, are you still there?" came over the phone.

Conroy quickly turned toward the phone lying on top of the washing machine.

With Conroy facing away from her, Cheryl stepped out from behind water heater. In that split second she was able to bring the poker forcefully down upon his arm, causing him to drop the weapon. Before he could recover from the blow, she swung the poker upward, catching him on the chin, rendering him momentarily senseless.

Cheryl kicked the gun between the washer and dryer and ran past Conroy toward the basement stairs. As she struggled to get hold of the railing, she inadvertently dropped the poker. Reaching the top, she slammed the basement door shut and quickly slipped the bolt lock into its catch. Then she ran toward the office.

At the onset of the assault, the sound of distant sirens could be heard. Now they were getting closer. Suddenly, Conroy broke through the basement door, poker in hand. Cheryl made it to the office desk just as he entered the room. She reached under the desk and pulled out the .45 cal. Glock. Gripping it with two hands, she pointed it at Conroy. Time appeared to have stopped in that brief moment. She pulled the trigger. Conroy dropped to the floor just as the bullet creased his left ear. A second shot rang out. That bullet passed over his head. He broke fast toward the office door. A third shot hit the door jam, sending splinters in every direction and missing him by millimeters. He ran out into the backyard, toward the next block where his car was parked. Conroy knew he screwed up on this one. Realizing that he, a professional killer, was outdone by a pregnant woman, that he was now in danger of losing his own life, and that the police were closing in on the house and the immediate area, he knew he was running short on time.

"Police! Police! Police!" was all Cheryl remembered hearing before she slumped down on the desk chair, clutched her stomach, and closed her eyes.

Conroy continued to move with lightning speed for a man his size and age. Even at that, he barely made it to his car and through the police net that was quickly forming around the neighborhood. He weaved through several side streets before turning onto the highway. As he left the city of Bloomfield, he thought, *Hopefully, I'll get a second shot at Mac Taylor . . . and anyone else who gets in the way."*

Chapter Twenty-One

February 8, 2004

Cheryl sat up in the hospital bed while Mac cupped her hand in his. She looked at him with incredulity. "How did this happen? Thank God the police came in time. I guess they reached out to you."

"Actually, *I* called them. I called you first, but when you didn't answer—which you always do—, I got a bit worried. So, I contacted them. I asked if they could have a car pass by the house to see if everything was okay. I started telling them I was getting a ride home, that it would take me about twenty minutes, but I never got the words out. I was stopped in mid sentence. It was then I was told about your 9-1-1 call, and that they were rushing you to the hospital. My God, Cheryl, I don't know what I'd do if I lost you. I'll find this dirtbag. He'll wish he never set foot in our house."

"Who is he? And what made you think I was in trouble, that you'd want a police car pass our house just because I didn't answer the phone? What's going on here? What aren't you telling me?"

"I just found out this afternoon that a sleaze ball by the name of Dirk Conroy probably had me on his hit list. I knew our truck was in the driveway and if he was planning on going after me, he would think I was home and that it might be a good time for him to act. So I called the PD. The dispatcher knows who I am. "

"Where were you?"

"I was still with those federal agents. We started to put two and two together. That's when we figured I could be next on the list. If, for some reason, I wasn't home, he probably planned on breaking into the rear of our house, kill you if you were home—which you were—and wait for me. Figuring he'd have the element of surprise, he'd be able to take me out without much of an effort.

"My gut told me to call you, then the Bloomfield Police. After that, I beat a quick path here to the hospital. Fortunately the locals got to our house before Conroy could, well . . . you know. I was told you handled yourself unbelievably. You just missed killing *him*. It's a good thing the .45 was loaded and ready. Beating out a professional killer who has the element of surprise and a gun on his side, I'm just amazed. Simply amazed. And you being pregnant."

"Yes, what about that? I know I've been traumatized. Look at me, I'm still shaking. But the doctors haven't said a word about the baby. I pray it's going to be healthy." Cheryl struggled to sit up. "Mac, why won't anyone tell me anything about my baby?!"

"Relax, honey. The doctors seem to believe there wasn't any physical injury to you or our child. They won't know definitely, though, until all the tests come back."

"How long will that take?"

"They'll know sometime today. Please, try to relax. I'll be here. You've been through a lot. I can't image what it must have been like for you to go through that trauma, especially in your condition. You are one hellava woman, Cheryl. That's what you are." Mac leaned over and kissed her.

Her lips quivered and her eyebrows turned down. Her free hand covered her forehead. Then the tears came. "Oh, Mac, I was frightened out of my mind. Not just for me, but for the baby. Why can't you just find a normal job like most people, where killers are not your typical occupational hazard? I just want to have a normal life. Is that possible?"

"Yes, it is. And we'll talk about making the transition after I finish this job."

"Finish this job. What do you have to do? Why can't you just close it out? Didn't you tell me your client's friend was murdered? If so, let the police handle it from here on out."

"Several reasons I have to finish this job. I have a client to deal with. For another, there's something major going on here that could result in the death of hundreds, if not thousands of people. But most importantly, Conroy tried to kill you and our baby. I won't rest until I find him and take care of business."

"You mean kill him," Cheryl said. "When does it end, Mac?"

"When Conroy's dead. It may look to you as just vengeance, but you will never feel safe as long as this animal is out there. He will haunt your dreams."

"Okay, okay. But remember, you agreed to change professions when this is all over."

"Yes, dear. I agreed to *talk* about it."

"Mac, what made me think I could change you? Or want to change you?" she said, a weary grin on her face. "Now I know what your first wife must have gone through."

Mac stiffened. "Don't say that."

"You know, you remind me of the frog and scorpion story. I should have seen that when we started going together."

Mac looked perplexed. "What's the frog and scorpion story?"

"Well, the scorpion wanted to cross the river but it knew it couldn't swim. So it asked the frog to allow it to ride across the river on its back. The frog said, 'Why would I do that? You'll sting me and I'll drown.' The scorpion said, 'And why would I do *that*? If I sting you, we'll both drown.' Well, the frog thought about it and it made sense to him. So he let the scorpion get on his back and they headed across the river. Halfway across the river, the scorpion stung the frog. The frog yelled out, 'Why did you sting me?! Now we'll both drown.' The scorpion said, 'I couldn't help it. It's in my nature.'

"Get it, Mac? It's in your nature to be a cop. You can't help yourself. You'd never be happy doing anything else."

Just then an arm reached around the opened door and knocked three times. "May I come in?"

Without waiting approval, Father Polsani entered the room.

Cheryl smiled. "Hello, Father. Thank you for coming."

Father Nick—as the newer parishioners called him—put his right hand on Mac's shoulder and with his left gently grasped Cheryl's right hand. "How are you feeling?" he asked her.

"Grateful I'm still alive . . . and that my baby is still alive."

"What an ordeal you've been through. Thank God you got through it all, and that you and the baby are going to be fine."

"Thank God?" Mac replied. "Is that who we should be thanking, Father? How about the PD, my .45 cal. Glock, and Cheryl's ability to outsmart her assassin? That's where I'd place my thanks."

"Mac, don't you dare talk to Father Polsani like that! He came all the way here out of concern for us, and you talk to him like that. You can't talk to a man of the cloth like that. Apologize! Now!'

Before Mac could open his mouth, Father Polsani quickly raised his right hand and said, "No, no, that's all right, Cheryl. Your husband and I go way back together. I understand where he's coming from. I understand all too well."

Looking at Mac, the priest continued, "There are many things to be thankful for, many things. And they are not mutually exclusive. When good things happen, like the safety and health of your wife and child, I like to think God had a part in it, Mac. Grant me that indulgence, please."

Mac took a step back from Father Polsani. "For Cheryl's sake, I'll apologize," he said. "But you're right, Nick. We go way back. In your case, as you would say, 'You're in this world, but not *of* this world.' Me, on the other hand, I'm in it *and of* it. It's the only world I know. It's dangerous, mean, and nasty. I will probably die by the sword, but it's a choice I'm prepared to make. Why? Because I'm not going to let the bad guys win under any circumstance. Not if I can help it. That's just how I'm wired. Turning the other cheek doesn't register with me."

"Well, I'm not ready to go to your funeral. I'm too young for that," Cheryl chimed in. "Plus, soon you'll have a baby to take care of, besides me. So, stop trying to save the world."

Father Polsani raised both hands, palms out. "Well, I didn't come here to cause any trouble. I just wanted to see how you were doing, and to offer prayers or any other assistance."

"Thank you, Father," said Cheryl. "Would you pray the Rosary with me?"

"Of course."

Cheryl proceeded to remove a set of Rosary beads from the night table drawer. Father Polsani took a similar set of beads from his pants pocket. They each held the cross of their beads between their thumb and index finger, and began to recite the Apostle's Creed.

Mac Taylor slowly got up from his chair and quietly left the room.

Mac dialed the private number Darcy had given him. After three rings, the party at the other end picked up.

"Hello."

"Darcy," Mac said with an edge to his voice. "Mac Taylor here."

"Yes, yes. Go ahead."

"I have to meet with you. I've found out some information that explains why Silky was killed, about what's going to happen next. I don't have all the players' names yet but I'm getting close."

"Terrific! Sounds like you struck gold. Do the police have this information? Can they act on it yet? Remember to keep me out of this. That's our deal. I don't want any of these people coming after me."

"Whoa, slow down," Mac advised. "No one knows anything yet. That's why I want to meet with you. So we can go over this information."

"What are we talking about? What kind of information are you referring to?"

"I don't want to discuss it over the phone. Only God knows if either of our phones is being bugged."

"Fine. Where do you want to meet?"

"You're in Bergen County and I'm in Essex, so why don't we split the difference. I could come up Route 21 to 3. The Route 3 Service Road runs off it, just west of the N.J. Turnpike. If you come south on 17, jump off at Route 3 East and take it for about a quarter of a mile to the Service Road on the right. I'll meet you there in the Meadowlands. I'll be driving my red pickup truck."

"That sounds secluded enough. Just keep me out of this. Since our last talk, I've hired a security man. I'll send him to meet with you. He's a pretty loyal guy. I'll tell him to pick up an envelope for me and to drop one off for you, your payment up to this point for a job well done. If you can write down the info and seal it in an envelope, that should keep it between you and me."

"I'll write it down, but remember, putting information in writing is as bad as talking freely over an unsecured telephone line. I believe the first time we met you said you didn't want any written reports."

"I know. Don't worry, Mac. After I study what you have for me, I'll destroy it. Then I'll decide if the matter is worth continuing. Now, when do you want to meet?"

"How's 8 o'clock tomorrow night?"

"Fine with me."

February 9, 2004—AM

Mac entered the confessional and eased himself down on the padded kneeler. "It's me, Nick," he said.

"Mac?"

"Yup."

"You know this is a confessional. Do you wish to confess something?"

"Yes, I do."

"Go ahead."

"Bless me, Father, for I have sinned. It's been a long, long time since my last confession."

Father Polsani leaned toward the opaque confessional screen. "The Lord is patient. Now, brother, what are your sins?"

"I've murdered people. Legitimate killings, Father. In war, self-defense, police actions. Still it's a lot of weight to carry. You know all the circumstances I had been under . . . and still am. Nonetheless, I have a good wife who is pregnant with my child. Both she and the baby are in danger, unless I find the person who is trying to kill them and me. "

There was silence.

"Father, did you hear what I just said?"

"Yes, I did, Mac." Silence again. "It sounds like your immediate problem has to be handled by the police. Your responsibility is to your family. You're right, I don't know the nature of your circumstances, why anyone is after you, or why anyone would want to kill your wife and child, but I can't say this strongly enough: you must go to the police. Let justice, not vengeance, be your guide."

"You don't understand, Father. I'm working with the police. They know the situation. I'm here to atone for any of my past misdeeds if that means my wife and child are protected. I've never been a man of faith, but my wife is. Cheryl believes in you and she believes in God. I'm here to ask for spiritual protection for my wife Cheryl and our unborn child. So, I'm asking that my sins be forgiven, that they do not fall on the heads of my wife and child. Will you do that?"

"Your sins are forgiven. That I am allowed by God to do. Your sins would never fall on the heads of your wife and child. Every one of us is responsible for our own actions, and those actions alone. As for Cheryl and the baby, I will pray for their safety and their souls. But as for your contrition, you must do three things. One, say ten Our Fathers; two, say ten Hail Marys."

There was silence.

"You're hesitating, Nick. What's number three?"

Father Polsani leaned closer to the screen that separated them. "You say you're not a man of faith. That's sad. So many tragic moments in your life and nowhere to rest your soul."

"Father, you're in the business of faith. I have little, if any, faith. My job has been and remains in the business of cynicism. I've got a tough time believing in anything outside of my family and friends. I've seen misery. I've seen cruelty. To be blunt, the only justice I've ever seen in my life came at the muzzle of my gun. Hope and faith never quite seemed to fit into the equation. Vengeance seems to be the driving force in my life. What's to gain in wishful thinking?"

"For starters, salvation. Secondly, peace of mind. I suspect that's why you're here. And another reason is that faith is the invisible hand that guides and supports you through the tough times in your life. You say you are guided by vengeance. You also say you've been involved in police actions, so you are a man of justice. Justice is not vengeance, and vengeance is not just. Scripture tell us that vengeance belongs solely to the Lord."

"I admire your commitment to peace and forgiveness, Father, but I heard somewhere that no sin is greater than God's mercy. I believe there are just vengeances in this world and, if believing that is a great sin, I hope to be judged fairly and mercifully by the Infinity Power on my action when my day of reckoning comes."

Father Polsani looked down at the Holy Bible in his hand and opened it. He skimmed through the pages until he came to a passage in *The Book of Wisdom*. He said to Mac, "You may not have faith in God, but as a disciple of the Lord, I can only try to open your heart to His ways. May I read a passage to you?"

"If you wish."

"It's from the Old Testament. Let me paraphrase. 'Court not death by your erring way of life, nor draw yourself destruction by the works of your hands. Because God did not make death, nor does he rejoice in the destruction of the living. . . . For justice is undying.' I agree with you that there is much cruelty and misery out there, but its justice in fighting the good fight that overcomes the evil in this world, not vengeance which merely adds to it."

"Whatever the intention, Father, the outcome's the same."

"In God's world, intentions matter as much as actions, as much as 'the works of your hands.'"

"I'll keep that in mind. In the meantime, what's the third thing you want me to do?"

Father Polsani closed the Bible he was holding and said, "Your penitence is to seek justice, not vengeance . . . if you wish God's blessing."

There was silence as Mac left the confessional.

Father Polsani made the sign of the cross and awaited the next confessor.

Chapter Twenty-Two

February 9, 2004

Mac checked the magazine on the .22 bolt action rifle, snapped it into the port entry, and racked one round into the chamber. He placed the rifle behind the front seat of his truck. Before turning the key in the ignition, he reached along the left side of his body and felt for his .45 cal. Glock. Satisfied that the weapon was securely in place, Mac started the truck and headed out to meet up with Darcy's courier, whom he expected to be a large black male known on the street as Dirk Conroy. At least that's who he was hoping to meet up with.

It was a little after 7:00 PM. The winter sun began to fade in the western sky. Mac wanted to arrive at the meet location early in order to scope out the area and to avoid the possibility of an ambush. He drove along Route 3 to the Service Road and parked his vehicle among the sedge weeds about a half mile east of the meet location. He hadn't seen any vehicles along the roadway in that quarter-mile area. He removed the rifle from behind the seat and got out of his pickup truck. He closed the door ever so softly, leaving only the sound of a light click in the air. He then moved through the tall reeds slowly, silently toward the meet location.

About three-quarters of the way there, Mac heard the sound of a vehicle running along the dirt road ahead of him. As he reached the area where he heard the noise, Mac observed a white Mercedes L500 idling with no one in the vehicle. *It's got to be Conroy,* Mac thought. *He's checking out the area, familiarizing himself with it. Probably looking for a good place to dump my body.*

Mac waited in the reeds while the sun went down and the area slowly turned black. With no Conroy in sight, he surmised the idling car was a trap, a form of hunter's bait. He drew the conclusion that Conroy left the car idling as an enticement to flush him out if he showed up early, which he had done. *He might have been in the brush not far from me, waiting for me to pop my head out and approach his car.*

Slowly and deliberately Mac eased his way from the cover of the high reeds and worked his way back to his truck. He got in it, started it up, and headed west to the meet location. On the way there, he put the .22 rifle down on the passenger side floor and removed the Glock from its holster. He quickly turned left onto the dirt road, jamming on the brakes. Mac immediately turned the ignition off. He slid out the vehicle and into the nearby reeds. By now the sky had turned charcoal black. Mac could barely see his truck ten to twenty feet away. The darkness brought back memories of those days long ago when he was hunting and being hunted in Vietnam. He remembered, though, that as his vision became obscure, his hearing became more acute. It was then he heard movement in the brush just south of him and across the road.

"Do you have something for me?" the voice across the road called out.

"Yes, I do, Conroy, and it's a bullet to the head."

"My, my, Mr. Mac Taylor. So you figured out I'd be coming for you. I thought this would be an easy job. Hell, I thought taking your wife out would be easy. You're a tough family. I'll give you that. But my kill rate is pretty good and your chances of making it out of here are not good. I'll let you in on a little secret. I'm not alone this time."

"Neither am I," said Mac as he fired two rounds into the area where he heard the voice. He heard a moan, after which the muffled sound of gunfire buzzed around him. Mac edged back into the reeds, farther from his truck, and circled to his right. He saw movement ahead. He fired one round. In the flash of his round, a man fell into the reeds. Mac covered the distance between the two in short order. The man laid dead, a scoped rifle with an attached silencer in his hand.

Mac picked up the rifle, quickly checked the chamber and the magazine to see how many rounds were left. Comfortable that there were over twenty rounds left, Mac headed back to his original position in the reeds across from his truck. As he ran toward the rear of his vehicle, several more muffled rounds cracked past him. He rolled back into the reeds just west of his truck. He closed his eyes and listened. About 45 degrees to his left he heard a reed snap. With speed and accuracy, Mac let loose a burst from the rifle. A second body could be heard dropping.

Mac decided it was time to take a big chance. He rushed over to his truck and opened the driver's side door. He quickly turned on his headlights before rolling into the reeds to the east. As he looked down the road he saw Conroy holding his left shoulder as blood dripped from the wound. He was making a break for the Mercedes. Mac tried to get a bead on him but as Conroy opened his car door another bullet zipped past Mac's head. He rushed the shot but was able to connect with a glancing hit to Conroy's left thigh as he got into his car. Conroy let out a wail. With the door of his car banging against his injured leg, Conroy drove his vehicle south at a rapid pace, disappearing in a dust cloud.

Just then another bullet coming from the north missed Mac's head by inches. In response, he fired several rounds in that direction. He moved several feet and fired another round. Several more feet, another round. And so on. An instant before he reached the area from which he believed the shot at him originated, he heard a vehicle screeching east down the Plank.

Mac worked his way back to the first body. He was a young-looking

Mideastern male, approximately 20 to 25 years old. Mac shook his head. *Lucky shot*, he thought looking at the gaping bullet hole in the victim's chest left by his .45 caliber 230 grain bullet. He rolled the victim over and reached into his back pocket looking for a wallet. Nothing. He checked the other pockets, no ID found. He walked to his truck, got in, started the engine, and backed up to where the second body was found.

The air was still. Mac could hear the dirt and stones crunch beneath his truck tires. When he reached the second body, he shut the ignition, pulled a flashlight from the glove box and got out of the truck. Snapping on the light, he trudged into the high reeds. After several minutes, he located the second body, another young Mideastern male, approximately the same age as the first victim. Mac checked his pockets and again nothing, no ID.

Before leaving the area, Mac drove around looking for a second vehicle. Finding none, he assumed the two victims were driven to the scene by either Conroy in his Mercedes or the third accomplice who fired the shot at Mac's head, then took off. *The two dead Mideastern males apparently were dropped off and told to keep an eyeball on the idling vehicle, while Conroy searched the area for my red truck,* he concluded. With that thought, he got back in his vehicle and drove down the dirt road, hoping to find Conroy hanging out the side of his car, bleeding to death. It was not to be. After several hundred feet, the dirt road curved east. It ran for a half mile or so before turning north and exiting again onto Route 3, only closer to the New Jersey Turnpike. "Damn it!" Mac pounded the dashboard of his truck once, realizing Conroy was not to be killed this night.

Chapter Twenty-Three

February 9, 2004—PM

"Well, Darcy. It's come to the point in our relationship where you're going to stop with all the bullshit and be completely honest with me."

"What do you mean?" Darcy said nervously, fingering the arm of the leather upholstered chair in his den.

"I want to know everything," Mac said. "I want to know the entire plan of attack and the rest of the cast of characters you're involved with."

Darcy flushed a bright red. "What the hell are you talking about? I hired *you* to find out who killed my friend. Have you found the killer yet? No, you haven't. And now you come in here and accuse me of some kind of chicanery. What arrogance!"

Mac moved closer to him. "You're right, Darcy. You hired me. You are slick, I'll give you that. You hired me to act as your sweeper, to find out what the police knew, what evidence was out there that might implicate you or threaten your plans. And yet, because of our agreement of confidentiality, no one would know who I'm working for or reporting to."

Mac pushed Darcy deeper into the chair. "For your information, I did figure out who murdered your pal Silky. He's quite a dirtbag. He's killed a lot of people all over the globe. His big mistake, though, was trying to kill my wife and child. Thanks to several slip ups, I was able to connect him to you."

Darcy fidgeted in the chair. "I have no idea what you're talking about. Why didn't you just go to the location we agreed on and give that information to the man I sent to meet with you?"

Mac laughed. "Oh, I did go to that location, and I met with your man, Mr. Conroy."

"Who?"

"Come on, don't play stupid with me. I met with Conroy, the muscle you're using to execute your plan."

"My plan?"

"Funny how you skipped right over my mentioning of the name Conroy. Don't deny knowing him, or hiring him. You sent him to meet me. To kill me. And now that I've IDed him as the one who tried to murder my wife and baby, his days are numbered. I will track him down and reign terror upon his head. You, I could kill right here. But I need information right now. If you're truthful, you live. I won't hesitate to cut your throat, though, if I think you're lying to me. So, let's start with Conroy. What do you know about him?"

A bead of sweat broke across Darcy's temple. "I don't know much about him. He's an independent. Ortez hired him and told him to work with me. I never told him to kill anyone. I didn't think he'd kill Silky. Or Ortez. Why Ortez? He hired him. I certainly didn't send him to kill you or your wife or child."

"Is that why you dropped the name al-Satir?"

"He must have been the one giving the orders and money to Conroy."

Darcy continued. "What do you want from me? Are you going to kill me? You can't do that. You're a cop. Well, you used to be one. Now your PI license hangs on obeying the law. Why don't we make a deal. How much money to make this go away? I can make you a very rich man."

"Shut up!" Mac said as he moved behind Darcy. With his left

hand he took a knife out of his pants pocket. Darcy attempted to get up. Mac pulled him back into the chair with his right hand. Placing the blade of the knife against Darcy's neck, Mac said, "Tell me the plan or I'll cut your throat right here."

Darcy's eyes widened. "Can't we do this another way? I have money, lots of it. And I have contacts who can help you and your family. Please, let's talk."

"Your contacts won't even be able to help you. You've got to know you're on Conroy's hit list. Now, you have three seconds before I cut your throat. One."

"Wait. Think what you're doing!"

"Two."

"Wait, wait. I'll tell you what you want to know. Please don't hurt me."

Mac eased the knife off his throat. "What's the plan?"

"What plan?"

"I don't have the patience for this. I'll ask you one more time. Tell me about the plan. Does it have a name?"

"Well, yes and no."

"What the hell does that mean?"

"There are two prongs to the plan; the logistical end run by 'The Shield' and the operational end run by 'The Sword.' I don't know when the attack is scheduled to go off, but it should be relatively soon."

"Who's the Shield?"

"I don't know."

"Who's running this operation?"

"The man I told you about Satir, the Architect."

"Then who's the Sword?"

"Satir put the plan together but another higher-level commander is responsible for the operation."

"And who is that?"

"Again, I don't know. All the intermediates have been killed, most notably Ortez. The Sword is the one who probably gave the order to have Devin killed. Satir and Conroy are the only ones alive right now who would be able to answer that question."

"You know the code names, so you must be privy to inside info on this operation."

"No, no. Ortez was the inside man who knew Satir and Conroy personally. He was the one who told me all about the operation."

"Don't bullshit me, Darcy! You know more than what you're telling me. I want to know who's running this operation from the top. I want the name of The Sword, now! I know you know who he is!"

"Some Saudi sheik, okay? That's all I know. There are thousands of them, hundreds who would like to see the U.S. toppled by the Jihadists. I wasn't in that loop. As I said, Satir and Conroy would know who he is."

"What about the operation?" Mac asked.

Darcy squirmed in the chair and swallowed hard. "It's a surgical strike with suicide teams using small arms and chlorine bombs set to go off in several locations. That's it."

"Chlorine bombs?"

"Yes, very easy to make using undetected everyday chemicals like pool bleach and rubbing alcohol. Very volatile for the handlers, but effective in controlling and killing targets."

Mac pushed the knife closer to Darcy's jugular. "Where are these bombs to be exploded and what are we talking about in number of deaths?"

As a drop of sweat edged down the side of Darcy's face, he said, "Please, just ease up on the knife. I'll tell you everything."

Mac let the point of the blade drop from Darcy's neck. "Don't screw with me."

"Terrorist teams have already left Venezuela on a tanker. The tanker is loaded with enough chlorine and alcohol to create a chemical explosive that will kill thousands of people. The teams and chemicals were unloaded at a port on the west coast of Mexico.

There they were supplied with weapons by Mexican drug lords and transported in trucks to the Texas–Juarez border. From there, the teams and chemicals entered the U.S. through tunnels used by drug smugglers. At this point they're being transported to five designated locations by trucks purchased over the last few years with, I've been told, Saudi and some European money. I don't know where they are now, but they should be heading to their designated targets."

Mac griped the knife more tightly. "And where are those locations?"

"California, Texas, Missouri, New Jersey, and Florida."

"I need more specific locations," said Mac."

"Easy, easy. Rodeo Drive, the Alamo, the Gateway Arch, Newark Bay, and Walt Disney World."

"Is that it?"

"There's one more group entering through Canada. Don't ask me from where, 'cause I don't know."

"What's their target?" asked Mac.

"Minnesota's Mall of the Americas."

"Why that one and the other targets?"

"To attack everything American: its opulence, history, markets, entertainment."

"How are they to get close to these targets to set them off?"

"Each team will have sufficient fire power. Plus, once the chlorine bombs are set off, victims will scatter or die. A chlorine cloud will float with the wind and kill or incapacitate anyone in its path."

"Killing hundreds, maybe thousands in its path I suppose, depending on how many or how big the bombs that are set off," said Mac.

"One more thing, Darcy. "Who's paying *you*? I guess that would be the Shield?"

"I can't. Don't ask that, please. He'll have me killed."

"Yeah, if Conroy and al-Satir don't beat him to the punch."

Mac put the point of the knife by Darcy's right eye. He leaned close to Darcy's left ear and whispered, "I want a name. Don't try to squirm out of this. You know who the Shield is. Tell me, now!'"

"If I give you that, I'd be signing my own death warrant!"

"If you don't tell me, I'll kill you right here! A name. I want a name!"

"Aaron Ruger. Okay?!!"

"Who and where is this Aaron Ruger guy now?"

A bead of sweat fell from Darcy's cheek. "Bern, Switzerland."

"Switzerland? What's his stake?"

Mac moved the knife to Darcy's neck.

"He's the head of GNI."

"Why would the CEO at your parent company be behind all of this?"

"Ruger, like me, is an arbitrageur at heart. He deals privately, as well as publicly in currency exchanges. That's how I got drawn into this mess."

"And the benefit?"

"After the attacks, he plans to make billions off the fall of the U.S. dollar."

"He thinks he can get away with this?"

"Looks like he's been covering his tracks with Conroy," Darcy said. "And, with seed money from the Saudis, transportation from the Venezuelans, and weapons from the Mexican drug lords, the Americans will surely focus on them. Plus, of course, all eyes will be on Iran. That's not a hard sell. He'd be just a savvy investor who got lucky on a tragedy. With a trail of dead bodies, who's to find out?"

"And you thought you were going to survive with what you know of the operation?"

"He threatened to have me killed if I didn't cooperate. I had no choice. I'm just biding time, documenting everything and placing the records in a secured location, to be sent to the feds should I be murdered."

"You know he'd have you tortured until you gave up the location of the documents. Then he'd have you killed. Look what you gave up to me, and I didn't even have to beat it out of you."

"Yeah, but no matter what, he could never be sure I'd told him of every secured location, even if no more existed. . . . Hey, I know it's not the best plan, but it's been the only one available. My only other choice would have been to go to the police. Had I done that, I'd be dead already. You were my out. Al-Satir thought I contacted you to gather information on what the police knew of the operation to protect the operation. Actually, I hired you because I needed information on what the police knew of the operation to protect *me.* "

"Darcy, here's the deal: I'm taking you to the feds now," Mac said. "You'd better cooperate with them. Tell them everything you told me. There's no time to waste on this." He drew the knife lightly across Darcy's throat to demonstrate what would be in store for Darcy if he wasn't. "They'll work with you. Oh, and remember, when you talk with them, 'No threats, pressure, or coercion on my part was used to gather the information.' Understand?"

"Of course not, Private Investigator Taylor," Darcy replied in a quavering voice.

On the way to FBI headquarters, Darcy and Mac talked further about Conroy, Ruger, and the operation.

III

"And this is what ye have shipped for, men! To chase the white whale on both sides of land, and over all sides of earth, til he spouts black blood and rolls fin out."

Herman Melville
Moby Dick

Chapter Twenty-Four

February 9, 2004—PM

Agent Dillon was rubbing hand cream between her fingers, getting ready to turn off the light on her end table and go to sleep when the phone rang. It was Mac, cryptically advising her that something big was about to happen, and soon. He wanted to meet her at FBI headquarters. Agent Dillon contacted SAC Lindstrum and Agent Klein before dressing and heading out to the office.

Klein was the first to arrive. As he pulled into the lot behind the office building, he was greeted by Mac and Darcy standing alongside Mac's red pickup truck. The three quickly entered through the rear office building door.

As they entered the building, Mac said, "Agent Brad Klein, this is Lamar Darcy."

"Good to meet you," Klein replied. He would have liked to say, "Good to *finally* have met you," but he didn't want to give away the fact that he was intimately familiar with Darcy through surveillances and through studying the department's dossier on him.

"I didn't know you'd be here," Mac said to Klein.

"Apparently what you have to tell us is of extreme importance. At least that's what Sara said when she called me. And just so you are aware, Special Agent Lindstrum will also be coming. If any decisions have to be made, he wants to be present, instead of getting the information secondhand. He's a hands-on kind of guy."

The three walked down the carpeted hallway and took the nearest elevator to the second floor. Mac and Darcy stood behind Klein as he unlocked the door directly across from the elevator.

"Have a seat," Klein said, pointing to the upholstered chairs by the receptionist's counter. "I'll put on some coffee. I've a feeling we're going to be here for quite a while." He then disappeared through door on the far side of the counter.

In the next few minutes, Agent Dillon and SAC Lindstrum entered the reception area.

"Mr. Darcy. So glad to meet you," said Lindstrum. "And Investigator Taylor. I've heard so much about you."

I'm sure you have, Mac thought as he shook Lindstrum's hand. "Pleased to meet you," he said as he tightened his grip.

"Let's go inside," Lindstrum said.

The four of them walked through the door by the reception counter. Lindstrum turned on a switch that lit up an entire area, down both sides of a long carpeted hallway. Each side of the hallway had high glass walls. Looking through the glass, Mac noticed petitioned-off rooms consisting of metal desks, visitors chairs and sparsely adorned interior walls, mostly holding the FBI emblem and award plaques. At the end of the hallway, Lindstrum opened the door to a darkened room. He flipped on the light switch revealing a large conference room. Within it was a long gunmetal-blue table surrounded by upholstered gunmetal-blue chairs. This room did not have any windows. Mac observed a video camera at ceiling level in the far corner of the room, a white pull-down screen below it along the far wall, and several types of video equipment on the near wall.

Klein walked into the room behind the four. "Coffee's ready next door," he said.

"Agent Klein, why don't you bring Mr. Darcy into Interview Room One and see how he takes his coffee." Lindstrum turned toward Darcy. "And you, sir, please tell Agent Klein what you had told Investigator Taylor. And I mean everything. If your information is good and you're willing to work with us, we can protect you through our Witness Protection Program. I'm sure you've heard of it. Everyone has. It's as famous as Mr. Miranda's warnings."

"Who?" asked Darcy.

"Miranda," said Lindstrum. "You have the right to remain silent. The right to an attorney, and so on."

"And I do, don't I?"

"But, of course, and Agent Klein will give you a paper to sign listing all your rights, and that you were not coerced in any way to give the statement that will follow."

Darcy glanced over at Mac, who gave a blank stare back. Klein and Darcy then left the conference room.

"Let's get some coffee," Lindstrum said to Taylor and Dillon. The three walked across the hall and into a small kitchen area. They each took a cup. Lindstrum poured the first round of the dark-blended coffee. "Milk's in the refrigerator, sugar right here on the countertop. Help yourself."

Mac reached into the refrigerator and grabbed the already opened quart of milk. He poured only a small amount into his coffee and returned the carton to the refrigerator. "I've got some info you should know about before we get into what Darcy told me." Mac slowly stirred his coffee.

"Should I be afraid to ask?" said Lindstrum.

"Well, let's just say you might have to clear up this matter."

Lindstrum took a deep breath. "Let me have it."

Mac took a sip of the hot coffee. "Tonight I was to meet our ol' pal Dirk Conroy down in the Meadowlands."

"I don't like where this is going."

"I wasn't sure he'd be Darcy's courier, but I had my suspicions, so I set up the meet. I knew if he came, his plan would be to get whatever information I promised and then kill me. Either that, or kill me first and search my body afterwards for the information."

"Why the hell didn't you tell us? We could have caught the bastard!"

"I know, that's why I didn't call. I want him dead. He's not stupid. He could see a takedown coming a mile away. I know you guys are good, but he sees one car, one van in the vicinity, other than mine, and he'd be out of there faster than you can say, 'Adios motherfucker.'"

"I could have you brought up on charges for withholding information."

"I figured that would be your game. But as I said, I didn't know who the courier would be and I was, after all, working *for* my client. I'm here right now *with* him and with some very valuable information. That should account for my cooperation and override any concerns you might have on what I'm about to tell you."

Lindstrum crossed his arms and leaned forward. "Investigator Taylor, let's start over. Tell me what needs to be cleared up."

"As I said, I met Conroy tonight. He thought I had information to give him."

"What information?"

"I told Darcy I found out why Devin Barrow was murdered and I had a lead on some of the players involved in his murder."

"I hope you at least had local backup, in case something went bad, which I suspect did."

"No backup. I didn't want anyone else being put at risk."

"No, of course not. You just wanted to kill Conroy yourself, for revenge. And you didn't want any witnesses. You know killing him won't get us any closer to the overall plan. We want to take him alive. . . . He *is* still alive, isn't he?"

"Yes, he got away with two bullets in him. Unfortunately, two of his boys are lying dead in the meadows. They both opened fire on me. I had no choice. I killed both of them. It was self-defense."

"What?! You just killed two men in the Meadowlands!" Lindstrum turned and walked out of the room. "Follow me!" The three reentered the conference room across the hall. "Have a seat," he said. All three sat at the near end of the table.

"You're lucky this is a matter of national security, Mr. Taylor. Otherwise, I'd have you in handcuffs until this investigation is sorted out."

Lindstrum's demeanor suddenly changed. "Now, I know a lot about you, Mac, your style of doing business. I know you won't stop until you find Conroy and kill him. But this matter is bigger than your quest for revenge, as understandable as that might be. Nevertheless, I don't want Conroy killed. He can be our best state witness. We can bring down the whole enterprise with what he knows. And he has every reason to turn state's evidence. We have serial homicides hanging over his head. Look what Nunzi 'The Wolf' Sambogna gave us. Franco Antanucci and his crime family. The only ones who can bring down the big fish are those closest to them."

Mac put both his hands on the table. He'd heard the Sambogna story many times over. He leaned toward Lindstrum. "Well, I don't believe in letting one dirtbag walk to catch another one. I saw your act play out in Newark. A friend of mine, a retired patrol sergeant, became a local bank guard. Some gangbanger holding up the bank shot and killed him. You guys worked a deal giving him an early release because he gave you inside information on other gang members. My buddy's existence obviously wasn't worth a hell of a lot to you guys. As for Conroy, he tried to kill my wife and baby. If I get to him before you, he won't have a prayer to become state's evidence. I'll do this much for you, though. I'll squeeze out as much info I can before I kill him."

Lindstrum shook his head looking at Agent Dillon. "This is why I was hesitant to work with him. I see police interference written all over his face."

"Well, what now? It seems Mr. Taylor here doesn't want to play ball," Dillon said.

"We'll make this work." Lindstrum glanced over at Taylor. "Right, Mac?" Looking back at Dillon, he said, "Call our Bergen County liaison, Peter Marin. Tell him what we have so far and have him contact the local authorities down in the Meadowlands. They can work up the initial homicide case on those two bodies, but tell them this is a Homeland Security matter and our office will be handling the follow-up. Peter will know how to deal with the hoopla to follow. Tell him he can call me for the background on this case."

"I should call him now, shouldn't I, while the scene is still fresh."

"In a few minutes, Sara. Those bodies aren't going anywhere. And it's not like we'll be seeking a conviction here. Besides, you need to hear what we're about to be dealing with."

Lindstrum looked at Mac. "Now, you might not like our methods, but they will protect you when the smoke clears on these homicides. Our legal team with make this go away."

"Whatever you say. I don't think you'd want this case to go to trial anyway. It'd be hard for the prosecution to keep all these Homeland Security secrets under wraps."

Lindstrum took a sip of his coffee. He placed his cup on the table. "Then tell me, what have you learned from your investigation?"

"I need a pen and pad," Mac said.

Lindstrum pulled out a spiral notebook from a file cabinet behind him. Taking a pen from a drawer beneath the conference room table, he slid both across the table toward Mac. "Here ya go," he said. "Draw away."

Mac pulled the notebook toward him and opened it to a blank page. He picked up the pen and began to draw an outline of the United States. He looked up at SAC Lindstrum and said, "There are four parts to their plan. First, the money. Second, the weapons. Third, transports. Fourth, manpower. The money is reportedly coming from a guy named Aaron Ruger of GNI and an unknown Saudi. The weapons are Iranian. Venezuela is providing a ship to transport foreign terrorists here. "

"You said, 'Their plan.' Who are 'they'?"

"I have two names: al-Satir and a guy named Aaron Ruger. There's a third guy, an Arab sheik. Unfortunately, I don't have an ID on him. Give me time, though, I'll find out who he is."

"Good, we'll run checks on those two names, al-Satir and Ruger. Plus, we'll do what we can to indentify this third party. In the meantime, as the old saying goes, 'Time is of the essence.' So, how and when is this to take place?"

"Thanks to our Patriot Act transparency, those financing this operation know we are monitoring money transfers. So, instead of wiring money from one bank to another, they're dealing strictly with courier transfers. It's more cumbersome, but less risky. Several couriers will move the money to Iran for the purchase of weapons and to Venezuela for transportation costs—"

"That sounds risky, too," Lindstrum broke in.

"Not if the money is picked up by diplomats from Iran and Venezuela. Diplo immunity, plus a sympathetic host country won't prevent any exchange from taking place. Nor will any exchange be reported."

"What did Darcy tell you about the weapons to be bought?"

"Smalls arms for their attack teams."

"Like what?"

"Stinger missiles, AKs, 50 cals., grenades, mortars, Claymores, explosives, your usual assault team hardware."

"So what we're looking at here is a small-scale raid," Lindstrum noted.

"Not at all," said Mac. "This brings us to the third and fourth prongs of this operation, transportation and manpower. Over this last eight-month period, 50 Jihadists from various countries found their way to Venezuela. The money that was sent earlier was used to house, feed, and train them as leaders for the mission. These Jihadists will command the assault. In addition to them, approximately 100 Jihadists will penetrate our border with Canada, and another 100 more will cross from Mexico. Add to that 50 more from cells already in the U.S. All of them will remain in the dark as to the operation until notified by a coordinator. We're talking a total of 300 fighters."

"How do they plan on getting the weapons and 50 Jihadists from Venezuela into our country?"

"The weapons will be smuggled in over our southern border with many of the 100 fighters coming across the unprotected areas. The 50 Jihadists coming from Venezuela will be smuggled in on an oil tanker. It will arrive at Port Newark. If questioned, the fighters' cover will be as crew members. I don't have the particulars on the entry from Canada. That's something you can work on with our friends to the north if Darcy can't be more helpful."

Lindstrum nodded.

"So, what you're telling us," said Dillon, "is that 300 Jihadists will form up at separate locations throughout our country to destroy what, cities?"

"Not just cities," said Mac.

"Then what?"

"Our heritage."

"Our what?" replied Lindstrum.

"Heritage. Our oil refineries in Newark. Trade and Energy. Hollywood and Walt Disney World. Entertainment. Mall of the Americas. Capitalism. The Alamo. History. The Gateway Arch. Our Heartland. Oh, and, by the way, they want to kill a whole bunch of people in the process."

"All suicide runs?"

"Absolutely. Each Jihadist knows that there is a good chance he will die in the assault. He just needs enough weapons and ammunition to keep him going until he finds an opportunity to escape or is killed. The attacker also knows that victory is simple. Just inflict as much death and destruction as possible before meeting Allah. Oh, and one more small detail."

"What's that?"

"After the initial attacks, the Jihadists will set off chlorine bombs that, depending on the density of the populations and the wind conditions, will result in a death toll in the thousands. It will be catastrophic."

Chapter Twenty-Five

February 10, 2004—AM

"Sara, I have to call the Director. There has to be a Security Council meeting on this, as soon as possible," Lindstrum said. "I want you and Brad to stick with Darcy. Put him in a safe location and milk him for all he knows. I want daily, if not hourly, notifications on what he tells you. Let Peter deal with the Meadowland homicides. Hopefully, he can get some info off those bodies."

Lindstrum turned to Mac. "I'm sure you want to check on your wife. Hopefully, the locals are providing you with enough coverage. As you know, we've got money, lots of it, and technical support, but what we don't have is manpower. We just can't help you with that. So I suggest you spend the next few days with her. With any luck, we can hone in on Conroy and take him out of the picture. Especially now that you've slowed him down a bit. We'll be checking hospitals, clinics, doctors' offices, etcetera"

"Don't worry 'bout me," said Mac. "I'll take care of my wife. And I'll take care of the loose ends."

"Loose ends?"

"Yeah. I was hired by Darcy to find the killer of Barrow. I found him. He slipped by me once. It won't happen again."

"If you find Conroy before we do, I want him alive."

Mac let out a snort. "Can't guarantee his safety, Special Agent

Lindstrum."

"I'm serious, Mac."

"So am I." He turned to leave. "If you need me, Agent Dillon has my number."

Lindstrum shook his head as Mac left the room. "He's a good cop, Sara, but the man is uncontrollable. He's definitely not one to take direction from anyone, regardless of rank or office. Keep in touch with him. I don't want any surprises. This is going to be a circus case as it is. We don't need another ringmaster running his own show."

"10-4, boss. He's bullish, but generally a nice guy. After all, he did give us Darcy and the plan."

"I can just imagine how that interview went. No coercion, my ass. Taylor's middle name is Coercion."

Dillon smiled. "I'll check on those two names and let Peter and Brad know the plan." She left the room as Lindstrum picked up the phone in the corner and called the Director of the Bureau.

"I told you not to call me. I've given you other contacts," al-Satir said.

"I had no choice. I need your help, *now*," Conroy said as he pressed gauze pads onto his wounds. "I need someone to come get me, I need immediate medical help, and I need cover for the next couple of days."

"Where are the others? Can't they help?"

"I don't know if any made it out in one piece. I had to leave the job in a hurry."

"This is the third one you have botched."

"If this job is so easy, you should try your hand at it."

Satir realized Conroy was his best hope for cleaning house once the operation was over. Besides, he knew an awful lot about the missions and the people involved. "I'll make the arrangements," al-Satir said, "but you'd better take care of your personal business."

"Will do."

Chapter Twenty-Six

February 10, 2004—Late PM

NSA's spy in the sky locked in on the *Orgullo*. Three Coast Guard cutters out of Charleston, South Carolina were dispatched to intercept the oil tanker. The 408-foot USCGC *Liberty* with its 3-inch cannon, 20mm Phalanx CIWS closed weapons system, and heliport pulled out of its Newport, Virginia berth and charted a course due south. Once out of port it met up with two USCGC 110-foot, Island Class patrol boats, each equipped with 25mm chain guns and a pair of .50 caliber machine guns.

Off-duty Edgewood Police Officer Jason Strunella lowered the volume of the TV the moment Mac walked into the room. Cheryl sat back in her favorite living room chair. "Now that you're home can my brother leave? He's working midnights. He's going to need some sleep before going into work."

"Certainly," said Mac. "Thanks Jason. You've been a great brother in more than one way."

"Any time. I only wish I'd been here when that mutt attacked Cheryl. I would have put a couple of hollow points into that sucker. It's still hard to believe sis and the baby got through that ordeal unscathed. I am so proud of her."

"Thanks, bro," she said imitating his deeper voice.

Jason and Mac smiled.

"I'll be back in the morning. Mac, if you have to go anywhere tonight to find this cretin, just drop Cheryl off at my house. Ann is there. She knows how to use my off-duty gun. She hears any noise, she'll count heads, then take cover. Besides, the desk is aware of the situation. Patrol units will circle the house regularly and get out on foot to check the area."

"Thanks again, Jason. You take care," Mac said as he escorted his brother-in-law out his front door.

"He's a sweetheart," Cheryl said.

"He sure is."

"Now, I've got something to show you."

"I hope it's good news," Mac said. "I sure can use some."

"I believe it is," Cheryl said with a grin. She lifted her blouse, exposing her rather large midsection. "I thought you'd be interested in seeing this."

Mac looked down and saw the outline of a tiny foot print on her stomach.

"Wow! I guess the baby's getting ready to bail."

"It sure is, so don't go too far in the next few weeks. My due date is just over a month away, but this is my first, and the chances of an early delivery are high."

Mac kissed the footprint on her stomach. "Don't worry, I won't be going anywhere far. I learned my lesson with my first marriage. I should have spent more time with family. My daughter Rachel sure could have used a more attentive dad. Things would have been different with her if I'd been around more."

"Don't blame yourself for what happened to your daughter, or your ex-wife for that matter. People make choices. You can't control that. Just don't repeat your mistakes. Remember to spend more time with me and the baby."

"Message received," Mac said. "Unfortunately, as a cop you always think you can control a situation. That's why it's so hard to accept the fact that my first marriage and my obligation to protect my daughter were such failures."

"Well, in your case, Providence has given you a second chance." Putting Mac's hand between hers, she added, "I have faith in you. I've seen the gentler Mac Taylor."

He grinned and said, "Now don't let that get out. I've got a reputation to maintain."

Lindstrum entered the conference room and walked to the head of the table. "Listen up," he said to the group of agents before him. "The Coast Guard has been notified to board the Venezuelan ship, *Orgullo*, with force if necessary. NSA has been tracking its location along the east coast. Homeland Security, ICE, and the Texas and New Mexico National Guards have been informed of the southern entry of thirty terrorists and four trucks carrying granular chlorine to be used as an airborne chemical agent. The RCMP is on the alert for any suspicious border crossings from Canada into the U.S. The attorneys general and state police in every state have been alerted to the entry of other terrorists attempting to cross, or who might have already crossed, our northern border. California, New York, New Jersey, Florida, Missouri, Texas, and Minnesota are particularly vulnerable. County police, local police, and public and private security agents at various locations have been given high alert for a potential terrorist attack. They are being supplied with chemical protective gear and a constant stream of information. Our job now is to identify all parties involved in the impending attacks, locate all parties, disrupt their operation, and bring all involved parties to justice using all means necessary; that includes deadly force."

Lindstrum sat down. "Sara, will you please update everyone on the parties we feel are involved in this operation."

Agent Dillon stood up and pushed the hair from her eyes. "Subject One: Aaron Ruger, a currency exchange investor. Both he and his company, GNI, are based in Bern, Switzerland. He stands to make billions if this attack is successful and the U.S. dollar plunges. Subject Two: Mohammed al-Satir, a Saudi ex-patriot who to the best of our knowledge is the domestic organizer. Subject Three: Dirk Conroy, an enforcer who has killed quite a few people the last few months, is at the center of this operation."

"Question?" asked one of the agents. "I take it our CIA or Interpol will be taking care of this guy Ruger."

Lindstrum chimed in. "Not our concern right now; outside our purview. But be assured, he will be dealt with."

"I assume we got this information from a CI," said another agent. "Did he give us any leads on where we might locate these other targets?"

"Dirk Conroy is an ex-con," said Agent Dillon. "He's out of Newark originally, but he's been operating out of Bergen as well as Essex County; Fort Lee, Carlstadt, and Bloomfield, New Jersey to be specific. We have reason to believe he is responsible for the Senator Tremore shooting, the death of Devin Barrow at the GW lookout, the death and mutilation of a man named Eduardo Ortez dumped in a park in Bayonne, the death of a woman named Martha Thomlin, and the attempted murder of a woman in Bloomfield. Conroy is also the main target in two murders abroad; one in Edinburgh, Scotland, and one in Pisa, Italy. It is believed that those murders and the ones here in the U.S. are all related to this terrorist operation. Conroy has been shot in the left shoulder and left leg by one of our confidential informants. Based on that, we have notified all the nearby hospitals to be on the alert in case he shows up for treatment."

"Bravo to your CI. Too bad he didn't finish the job," whispered the agent closest to Dillon. He added under his breath, "I guess we all know who your CI is now. I hope his wife is resting comfortably."

Lindstrum broke in. "This will be Agent Dillon's case. Nevertheless, I want to be informed of everything that goes on. In other words, every interview, every scintilla of information relayed, every door checked, every canvass, every police action to be taken. You get the point."

At this time, Lindstrum began to hand out assignments.

The blue paneled van pulled into the driveway along the river side of the two-story house in Edgewater. Two men got out of the van and scanned the area before walking to and knocking on the rear door. The door opened and Dirk Conroy stood there brandishing an automatic handgun. "Come on in," he said, his left arm hanging limp from the gunshot injury. Bouncing on one leg, Conroy backed up and leaned against the living room wall.

"Did you clean the place out?" the taller of the two men from the van asked.

"As best I could," said Conroy.

"What about the car?"

"I dumped it last night into the Hudson. It'll be a long time before they find it and pull it out of the water."

"Then we should get out of here now."

"What about my injuries? I'm in pain, man. I need to get these wounds taken care of."

"That's why I'm here," said the shorter of the two men from the van. "I have what we . . . you . . . need in the van."

"Are you a doctor?" asked Conroy.

"I guess you can say so. We should hurry. The sooner we get in the van and get out of here, the sooner I'll take care of your wounds."

"First, grab the duffle bag on the floor over there. All my clothes and bathroom crap are in it. Put it in the van. Meanwhile, I'll shred the papers on the desk."

"Anything else?" asked one of the men.

"Yeah, get a plastic garbage bag from under the kitchen sink and throw all the bloody rags in it. I'll put the shredded papers in it. We can drop the bag off at some Dumpster along the way.

When their cleanup was complete, the three left the house, locked the rear door, and entered the van. The man behind the wheel, under the direction of Conroy, drove the vehicle south along the Palisades until he came to Hudson County Park. He pulled the van behind a row of vehicles by a soccer field. The driver of the van got out holding the bag of garbage. He dropped it in a nearby Dumpster. The other man had Conroy lie down in the rear of the van. He administered a local anesthetic to Conroy's shoulder and leg. All the time, Conroy held onto his pistol. The man methodically cleaned around the entry and exit wounds of Conroy's shoulder, disinfected both the shoulder and thigh areas, and applied dressings.

"All right, let's go," said the man to his partner.

The trio then headed toward al-Satir's house in the country.

Chapter Twenty-Seven

February 11, 2004—AM

The U.S. Coast Guard Helicopter Interdiction Tactical Squadron (HITRON) is based at Cecil Field in Jacksonville, Florida. The squadron specializes in Airborne Use of Force, primarily drug interdiction. In the early morning hours, 18 well-trained HITRON guardsmen headed north along the Atlantic coastline in three Augusta A109E Power helicopters—military designation MH-68A Stingray. Each helicopter was equipped with a semiautomatic Barrett M107 .50-caliber rifle semiautomatic sniper rifle and a 7.62mm machine gun.* Each HITRON onboard Guardsman was carrying an M14 Tactical rifle. Target: the *Orgullo*.

At the same time the HITRON crews were heading north, the USCGC *Liberty* was en route to intercept the *Orgullo*.

The *Liberty* first made visual contact with the *Orgullo* at 8:17 AM. The HITRON helicopters were twenty miles south of the tanker when the *Liberty* ordered the *Orgullo* to shut down its engines and prepare to be boarded. The *Orgullo* did not respond to the order.

"I must stop the ship," Captain Ramos said to Qutaybah.

"No, we head to shore. My men will fight the infidels. We must get to shore first." Qutaybah turned to the pilot. "Change your course. Do not stop the engines."

* http:www.uscg.mil

"I am still the captain here," said Ramos. "I give the orders to my men. Besides, we are too far out at sea. We can't make it through these Coast Guard ships. Even if we could, these tankers have too much draft. We'll bottom out way before we reach shore."

"Then we fight here . . . now!"

"Are you crazy? We'll all be killed. Nothing good can come of this."

"I knew you were a coward, el capitan. Now steer this ship toward the shore!"

Just then, another order came from the *Liberty* for the *Orgullo* to shut its engines and prepare to be boarded.

"I'm cutting the engines now. No sense—" was all the captain was able to get out before Qutaybah fired a shot from his Kalashnikov rifle into Ramos's head. Qutaybah turned to the pilot. "Head to shore now or I will kill you too!"

The pilot quickly adjusted the course.

"I must go below. If I suspect you have changed course, I will come back here and shoot you. Do you understand?"

With his eyes looking at the body of his captain lying on the floor, the pilot rapidly nodded his head.

Satisfied that his direction would be carried out to the letter, Qutaybah went below deck. Once he left the wheelhouse, the pilot made his way to the ship's rail and jumped into the water.

As the Coast Guard cutter made a wide turn to circle behind and run parallel to the large tanker, the three helicopters passed overhead. One of the aerial gunners fired warning shots across the bow of the ship.

After ordering his men to arm and prepare to do battle, Qutaybah hoisted a Stinger missile onto his shoulder.

The oil tanker had changed course from north to west, but because of its size it would take quite some time for it to make the 90-degree change in course. And time was one major factor not on the side of the terrorists aboard the *Orgullo*.

Suddenly shots were fired at the helicopters as they made a

second pass. The helicopters peeled off just as Qutaybah appeared on the deck of the tanker shouldering the Stinger missile.

Sirens sounded, then a voice boomed from the *Liberty*'s P.A. system, "This is your third and final warning. Drop your weapons, stop your engines, and prepare to be boarded!"

Armed terrorists ran out onto the deck of the ship. As Qutaybah ran toward the ship's rail and aimed his missile at the *Liberty*, the lead MH-68A Stingray came in low and took him out with several blasts from its 7.62 machine gun. The second and third helicopters proceeded to strafe the deck of the ship.

Shots continued to ring out toward the cutter.

The *Liberty*'s cannon turned on its turret. In the next instance, a loud burst, flames, and smoke exited the cannon. A second later, the control tower of the *Orgullo* exploded.

The pilot house was immediately engulfed in flames. One man crawled out from beneath the wreckage, flames burning his skin and clothing. He quickly jumped into the water.

The engines of the ship continued to move it forward.

The three helicopters immediately formed a triangle, hovering over the massive deck of the ship. The three six-man teams repelled from the copters and took up a circular position on the deck. The Guardsmen, moving in leap-frog fashion in four directions, exchanged fire with the retreating terrorists, some of whom managed to slip below deck. Several minutes later, all but three terrorists were killed.

Manpower from the *Liberty* began boarding the tanker. Firefighters quickly doused the flames in the wheelhouse. Engineers were then able to disengage the engines. In short order, the *Orgullo* was secured from the terrorists and ready to be searched for explosives, chemical weapons, and other forms of ordnance, after which the craft would be towed.

The HITRON Guardsmen returned to the helicopters and the three terrorists were transferred to the *Liberty* for interrogation and prosecution. The two men, who were pulled from the water, were treated for their injuries before joining the others in the detention hold of the *Liberty*. The cargo was secured and tugs were notified to pull the vehicle into port where the FBI would take the lead in the investigation.

"I don't like this," al-Satir said to Conroy as the man limped into the house.

"You think I do?" Conroy bellowed back.

"Well, you can't stay here. There are too many people looking for you and this is not a good place for you to be."

"You mean it's not good for you." Conroy moved closer to al-Satir and slammed his right hand down on the nearby coffee table. "You listen to me, you pompous ass," he snorted. "I've done your dirty work for the last few months. All the time your hands were clean. Well, not any more. It's your turn to look out for *my* interests."

"You were paid very well for your services. Besides, Ahmed, the work you have done will be rewarded by Allah."

"You're kidding, right? I did your bidding for the cash. That's it. I'm not one of your stooges who's going to fall on the sword for you or Allah."

Satir looked at his bodyguard standing by the living room doorway. Then turning back toward Conroy, said, "What do you want from me?"

"I want money and a car. And I want them now."

"You can take the van. Now how much money do you want? Two, three hundred dollars?"

Conroy laughed before saying, "Try five grand."

"Now it's my turn to laugh," al-Satir said. "Do you really think I have that kind of money lying around?"

"Absolutely! Don't try to bullshit me. What do you pay these goons you hire with, oil stocks? I know you've got cash lying around here somewhere. Listen, I need to get over the border. That ain't going to happen on three hundred bucks."

"That should be plenty to get you over the border."

"What do you think I'm going to do, hide out in some backwater town? I need cash to get back to Europe."

"We do have many protected areas in France and Syria. You can go to either of those places. I can get you some contacts and money once you're in Canada. They can help get you out of there."

"Don't mess with me. I don't need cash tomorrow. In Canada. I need it *now*!"

Satir scratched his head. "I know where you can get money. Minneapolis."

"Minneapolis. Why Minneapolis?" Conroy asked.

"Because that is where the Mall of the Americas is located. And that's where a truckload of men, weapons . . . and money are headed. All the money you will need to get you back to your boat in Paris or for you to get lost in Syria. Don't think small Ahmed. There will be plenty of chaos once the shooting starts there. With your resources I'm sure you'll find a way to get much of the, how would you say, 'escape money.' If our warriors do escape, fine. If they get killed, though, they will be with Allah and won't need the money. Then it will all be yours."

Conroy hesitated for a moment. Rubbing his chin with his right hand, he asked, "When is this attack supposed to go down?"

"In three days."

"That should give me plenty of time to get there," Conroy said. "I need a contact, though. Someone to coordinate with."

"When you're in the area call this number." Satir took a pad and pen off a nearby end table and wrote down the telephone number for a man living in Windsor, Ontario. "Here," he said, handing a page from the notepad to Conroy. "Tell the man who answers who you are and that I told you to call. Remember to say the Architect."

Conroy suddenly turned and struck al-Satir's bodyguard in the neck. The man dropped to his knees grabbing at his throat. Conroy walked behind him and punched him in the back of his head. The bodyguard fell, face first onto the floor. Blood spurted from his nose. Conroy pulled out a handgun from his coat pocket. With his free hand, he rolled the bodyguard onto his back.

"Is he dead?! Why did you kill him?" asked al-Satir.

Conroy ignored the questions and trained his gun on al-Satir. "Get me whatever cash you have stashed around here, or you'll be joining him."

"Please, don't shoot! I'll give you all I have," Satir said, his hands extended in front of him. "I have money in my office. Please, please follow me into my office. I will help you. Whatever you need. Okay?"

"Let's do it. I don't want to be here any longer than I have to. Just don't try anything stupid."

Satir led Conroy into a large office surrounded by tall wooden bookcases. Toward the far side of the room was a plush mahogany desk. On the desk were a blotter, several photographs, and a gilded copy of the Koran. In front of the desk were two dark leather chairs. Along the exterior wall behind the desk was a series of ceiling-to-floor glass panels. The view outside the glass panels was that of a long, downward sloping lawn ending at a stream. Satir walked toward the bookcase located just to the right of his desk and reached to remove a large, hard-covered volume from the bottom shelf.

"Hold it right there," Conroy said as he shoved al-Satir away from the bookcase.

Conroy removed the volume and handed it to al-Satir. He aimed his handgun at al-Satir's head. "I don't trust you one bit, so if there's a gun or any other weapon in there, I will blow your head off," he said. "Now open it slowly."

Satir opened the book. Inside was $1,200 in hundred-dollar bills. "That's all I have."

Conroy grabbed the book from Satir's hand, took the money, and threw the book on the floor. He stuffed the money in his pocket.

Then, without warning: *Bang!* Satir dropped straight to the floor; a small bullet hole in his forehead and a gaping exit hole in the rear of his skull. The Architect had not accounted for the potential threat a serial killer could bring to his grand plan. It was an oversight that cost him his life.

A second bodyguard and the two individuals from the blue van heard the shot. They came running into the house. Conroy, hiding behind a window curtain by the front door, shot all three, two in the back, the third as he turned to fire back. He searched their pockets and came up with the van key in addition to several hundred more dollars. Conroy left the house and headed west.

Chapter Twenty-Eight

February 12, 2004—PM

Dirk Conroy pulled into the parking lot in the rear of the three-story brick building. The structure, which was located on 5th Street in the downtown Dayton area, housed Ted's Bar and Grill on the first floor and four apartments, two each on the second and third floors. It was in an area known as the Oregon District, an historic section of the city. Conroy entered Ted's Bar from the rear door and sat at a table in the back. A waitress approached.

"Would you like something to drink?" she asked.

"A shot of whiskey and a beer."

"What brand of shot and beer would you like?"

"Surprise me," said Conroy.

As the waitress was about to walk away, Conroy grabbed her by the arm. "Ask 'Slash,' he knows what I like to drink."

She pulled her arm back. "We call him Evan here. He doesn't like to be called 'Slash' anymore."

"Don't care. Tell him I'm here."

"And who shall I say 'is here'?"

"Ahmed."

The waitress left. In less than a minute, Evan Herrick arrived at the table with a shot of Seagram's and a draft beer.

"I don't know what you're involved in now," said Herrick, "but here's the key to my apartment upstairs. I'm asking you not to cause any problems."

"Why would I do that?"

"I suspect you're on the run for some such reason. I cleaned up my act since getting the bartending job here three years ago. My boss gave me a chance. I don't want to blow it. The people here know my past. And now that they know you're here, they've got to be wondering if I did actually clean up my act."

"Now Slash—"

"Don't call me that. That was another time and place."

"You killed a guy with a box cutter. Don't play the saint role with me."

Conroy snapped his head back, gulping down the whiskey. He leaned forward and drained the draft beer from the 7- ounce glass. "Oh, I needed that," he said.

Conroy put the key in his pocket and got up from the table. "I also need some sleep. And when I wake up, I'm going to need a car and some cash. The van I just left in the back lot will have to be dumped or chopped up. See what you can do about that."

"Ahmed, I told you I don't want any trouble. I don't want to be involved in any illegal activity. I'm only putting you up as a favor."

Conroy laughed. "It's not a favor ol' bunkmate. Just do what I'm telling you to do and you'll never see me again. And calling the police would not be a good thing for you to do. I have a long memory. And I have friends. Do you understand what I'm saying?"

Herrick let out a sigh. "I'll see what I can do about the cars."

Conroy left through the rear of the bar. He walked along the side of the building toward the front. He entered the wooden door located next to the entrance to the bar. Once in the foyer, he opened the interior door and climbed the stairs. When he reached the second floor, he unlocked the rear apartment door. Conroy walked into the bedroom and fell onto the bed. He was asleep as soon as his head touched the pillow.

It was near midnight. Mac rushed out of the shower as the telephone rang for the fifth time. "Hello," he said, holding the receiver in one hand and the towel around his waist with the other.

"Hey, Mac, it's Marty."

"Marty, this must be important if you're calling me at this hour."

"Yeah, it is."

"Well, how can I help you bud?"

"Actually, I'm calling to help you. I heard about what happened to your wife, and that Dirk Conroy is the main target. So I had my crew hit the streets and put some pressure on the locals. One of my guys had Conroy as a confidential informant several years ago. He told me the gangbangers Conroy hung with still hear from him from time to time even though he moved out of the area. Conroy apparently has a crash pad in Edgewater on River Road."

"That's interesting," said Mac. "That's a few miles south of where Silky was killed. Do you have an address?"

Detective Lieutenant Presler then gave Mac the street address. "Just so you know," he said, "he's not renting the place under the name Conroy. According to the street urchins, he's been using different aliases. I don't know what name he's rented the apartment under but the address is solid. My guy's current CI has been there on several occasions. It's reportedly a two-story, white building right on the Hudson River. Apparently it has a great view of the Upper West Side of New York."

"Marty, I really appreciate the info. I'm curious, though. Why tell me? Why not call the Bergen County detectives?"

"Mac, come on. This guy tried to kill your wife. We had been brother officers for many, many years. My loyalties are still with you. I know you'll do what needs to be done. Besides, I'll call them tomorrow afternoon with the information. You know me. I'm a team player. Besides, I don't know how you got the info on the house. I just called to see how your wife was making out and if I can help in any way."

"Gotcha, my friend. Thanks for sticking your neck out for me and giving me a head start."

"Hey, what are friends for? If we don't look out for each other, who will?"

Chapter Twenty-Nine

February 13, 2004—AM

Mac slipped on a pair of latex gloves before shimming his knife between the door trim and jamb. The back door to Conroy's apartment popped open. He quietly closed the door and removed his Glock from his waistband holster. Mac scanned the area before moving slowly from room to room. Once he realized the apartment was empty, he went back and angled a kitchen chair under the rear door knob. He moved to the living room and slid a sofa behind the front door to prevent any surprise entries as he prepared to search the premises. A cursory search did not reveal anything. The living room desk, bedroom dresser, and kitchen cabinets were all empty except for a desk calendar, several pairs of socks, and a few eating utensils. Mac wasn't sure if this was simply a safe house for Conroy or if he had been spooked by their last go 'round and had left the apartment for good. *He's injured and on the run.*

Mac went into the bathroom and opened the medicine chest. Nothing. No drugs, no first-aid items, no toiletries, not even a bottle of aspirin. He got down on his knees, hoping to find some traces of blood. *I know I nailed him twice.* Nothing. The bathroom was clean. *Where would he go?* kept running through his mind. *Who would know?* Mac then noticed a shredder by the desk. He lifted the head off and looked into the plastic basket below it. Nothing. He looked at the bottom of the shredder head. It was a strip-cut shredder with metal rotating blades.

"Yes!" Mac let slip between his tight lips.

He took out his knife and began to pry out small strips of paper from between the shredder blades. He scanned several pieces before finding two when put together formed word fragments: "vin Barr". *Devin Barrow?* While attempting to find other strips of paper to match up, Mac saw a small piece of plastic, aqua colored with gold trim, lodged in the rotating blades of the shredder. *Business card?* It was then he realized his next move: *Time to talk with Darcy again.* He threw the shreds of paper back in the basket, replaced the top section, and quietly left the apartment.

"Where is he, Sara?"

"Mac, you know he's in protective custody now."

"Of course I know that. I brought him to you for just that purpose. I'm on his side. I'm on your side. I need to talk with him."

"I'll have to talk with SAC Lindstrum. You know your client is ours now, not yours."

"Do what you have to do, but I have some questions which I suspect he has the answers to. I think you might want to hear those answers."

Sara went out of the room and met with Lindstrum to relay Mac's request.

"Yeah, but we all know Taylor can be lawless. He's not big on Constitutional Rights. He thinks Miranda and Escobedo are a dance team. We go by the book here 'cause we have a lot of legal options available to us. No one is going to lose their job by going above and beyond what the legislature and courts allow. Don't get swayed by his Dirty Harry approach, Sara. Taylor can talk with him if I know what the questions are before he meets with Darcy and I want you present during the interview, that's if I agree to have one arranged."

Sara returned to the lobby where Mac was sitting. "Come with me." The two then went into a conference room. "Before any meeting can be arranged, I have to know what questions you want answers to."

"Take a guess," said Mac somewhat impatiently.

"Let's see. It must have something to do with Conroy. You still want to finish the job."

"Bingo. And I think Darcy knows where he might be headed."

"Why is that?"

"He worked for Darcy. Darcy was his contact. He might clam up when you guys pressure him, Constitutional Rights and all that, but we have an agreement, him and me."

"What's your agreement?"

"If he'll be honest with me, I'll act in his best interest, and make sure he's not seriously hurt."

"Am I to construe that as a threat to him?"

"Not at all. As I said, 'I'll act in his best interest.' Listen, if you want to get a lead on Conroy, I can help here. Darcy will play Pontius Pilot with you; wash his hands, don't know nothin'. I don't waterboard—not that I wouldn't, if need be—but I know how to extract information. Now, if you and *your boss* want to play nice and see a major terrorist attack occur throughout the country, I'll leave now. But if you want to be heroes, I'm here to help. Oh, and don't think I won't track Conroy down by any means necessary. Do you and your boss really want that headache too?"

"Is it all arranged?" Conroy asked Herrick.

"I have no connections with a chop shop, but we can dump your van down at the river. You'll just have to follow me there. I'll bring you back here and we can see what to do about getting you a car."

"Let's do it."

"Now?"

"I don't have time to screw around. I got too many assholes

looking to cut my throat or throw me in prison for life. So, yeah, let's go. Now!"

"It's daytime," Herrick said. "Too many people out and about. I want to dump the van behind one of the industrial buildings, but tonight when it's dark and no one's around."

"I don't have time to wait. I'll take your car now. And you'd better dump the van tonight. I really hate to have to come back here, or have one of my people come back here and take care of this matter."

Herrick knew his only chance of staying alive in the company of Conroy was to make sure Conroy needed him. He'd dump the van and hope never to see his old cellmate again.

"What are you driving?" Conroy asked.

"A white Mazda. It's in the back parking lot."

"I'll need some cash, too. How much do you have?"

"Only about $75," Herrick said.

"Credit card?"

"Just one but I seldom use it."

Holding his right hand out, Conroy said, "Well?"

Herrick reached into his front right pocket and pulled out the cash. "Here," he said. He then reached for his wallet, pulled out his credit card, and handed it over to Conroy.

"Will I ever see my car again? "he asked.

"You've always been a good bunkmate. Tell you what I'm going to do. I'll call you when I'm ready to dump it. I'll let you know where it is."

Herrick knew he'd never get that call. "I'd appreciate that," he said.

Conroy took the car keys from Herrick and left the apartment. He got into the 2002 white Mazda 3 with Ohio license plates, pulled out of the parking lot, and headed for I75 North.

Chapter Thirty

February 13, 2004—PM

The house was set back at the end of a long driveway. The countryside surrounding it was made up of rolling hills and single-lane roadways. The northwestern New Jersey house was a three-story, center hall colonial owned by the government; the proceeds of a drug arrest seizure under a RICO* statute.

"How have they been treating my client?" Mac asked as he sat in the leather chair across from Darcy and Special Agent Dillon in the first floor living room.

Darcy squirmed in the corner of the matching leather couch to Mac's left. "I'm still alive. People want to kill me or put me in jail. I can't go anywhere, and my future looks pretty shitty. Other than that, I guess I'm doing pretty damn good. Now, what brings you here? I thought the last time I saw you would have been the last time I would ever have to see you again."

"Well, there's been a new development."

"What now? I can see where this nightmare isn't going to end any time soon."

Mac slid from his chair and his knees touched Darcy's. "I want to know where your friend Conroy might be."

"That psychopath. Don't know and don't want to know."

* Racketeer Influenced and Corruption Organizations Act of 1970

"Here's the thing, though," Mac said as he put his hand on Darcy's knee. "*I* wanna know. And if you think he's a psychopath, you really don't want to deal with me. The feds will treat you nice until this case is finally settled, but you don't ever want to turn your back on me."

"That's enough, Taylor!" said Agent Dillon. "Remember, no threats, coercion, you know the rest."

Mac looked right at Darcy. "Yeah, you know the rest," he said.

Darcy bent his head and rubbed the back of his neck. "I don't know where he stayed. Somewhere in Bergen County, I think. But he was always on the move. He could be in Europe at this very moment."

"No, I don't think so," said Mac. "I put two bullets in him. He ain't going far."

"What? How? When?"

"Not your problem. What is your problem is hiding what you know about his whereabouts from me."

"I'm telling you, I don't know where he is. How would I? I've been stuck here for days."

"Let me try another approach. He's injured and on the run. Where would he go for help?"

"Well, unless he was dying, he wouldn't go to a hospital. He'd make a call for a backup team to help him out."

"What if his backup team is dead? Who would he call?"

"Investigator Taylor, you are amazing. And I trust you will kill everyone you can on this operation. Unless, of course, Agent Dillon and company keep you on a short leash."

Mac pointed his finger at Darcy. "There hasn't been a leash yet that I couldn't snap."

"Okay, that's it," said Agent Dillon. "Interview over."

"No it isn't," said Mac leaning closer to Darcy. "If you value your life, tell me where he would go."

Agent Dillon tried to place herself between Mac and Darcy, but

Mac's right arm prevented her from doing so.

"Where is he, Darcy?" Mac asked again.

Darcy swallowed hard. "Maybe with al-Satir," he said.

"Satir? Where the hell does he live?"

Agent Dillon backed off.

"He's got a place in Bayonne and another place in Pennsylvania. If Conroy needed medical attention and he had no backup to turn to, he'd probably call al-Satir; especially since I've disappeared from the scene."

Mac pulled out a pad and pen from his back pocket. "What're the addresses?"

Conroy pulled the Mazda 3 off the highway and into a service station. He proceeded to gas up the vehicle using Herrick's credit card. He hit "No" when asked if he wanted a receipt. Conroy then pulled up the car to the far side of the adjacent convenience store.

He got out of the car and approached the outside pay phone. Conroy pulled the piece of paper and some change from his pocket, put several coins in the telephone slot, and dialed the number al-Satir had given him. The telephone rang twice.

"Hello." Conroy detected a heavy Mideast accent.

"This is Ahmed Sal Mohammed. I got your number from al-Satir. I'm heading to Minnesota. I want to hook up with your guys, so I need to know exactly where and when."

"I don't know who you are or what you are talking about," the man on the other end of the line said.

"The Architect told me to call you. I need to know who I'll be meeting with, where and when. Don't bother calling al-Satir, he's dead and the cops are after me. I don't know what they know, but we have to stay one step ahead of them if we want to complete this jihad."

"I will have to call you back. Give me a telephone number where you can be reached. I will get back to you."

"Let's just say I'll call *you* back within the next few hours. Check with whoever you have to." He then hung up the phone.

Conroy entered the store. He picked up some snacks, a pack of chewing gum, and poured himself a hot cup of coffee. He liked his java black with three scoops of sugar. *The snacks and coffee sugar should satisfy my sweet tooth for a while*, he thought.

After paying the clerk with cash, he walked outside. Sipping his coffee, Conroy suddenly noticed a man standing by the trash can to his immediate right.

"Where ya headed?"

"What?"

"Just asked, 'Where ya headed?'" the man said. "I'm running a load of pianos to Toledo. I was just wondering if you're hauling anything that way."

Conroy looked beyond the man and saw several large rigs in the lot. It was a cold night. All the truck engines had been running with their parking lights on.

"None of those are mine," Conroy said, pointing at the trucks lined up in the lot. "And where I'm going is my business."

Without waiting for a response from the trucker, Conroy quickly stepped off the short step outside the store and walked to the Mazda 3. Once inside the vehicle, he backed out of the spot on the far side of the lot, threw the shift in drive and tore across the front of the store and out onto the highway.

What a prick, the trucker thought.

The office telephone rang. Cheryl picked up the receiver.

"Hi, this is Lieutenant Marty Presler of the Newark Police Department. I'm looking for Mac Taylor."

"This is Mac's wife Cheryl. Mac's not here right now. How can I help you?"

"Mrs. Taylor. I was sorry to hear of your ordeal. Thank God you're okay. I do have some good news that will interest Mac. Does he have a cell phone I can reach him at?"

Cheryl proceeded to give Presler Mac's number. She then asked, "Is there anything I can do, Lieutenant?"

"If you reach him before I do, tell him to contact me. I might know where the guy who attacked you is headed."

No one was at the Bayonne address. After posting several local police officers at that location and calling out the FBI's BCI unit, Agents Dillon and Klein left the scene in their Caprice and headed west. Mac followed, insisting on taking his truck. The two vehicles turned onto Route 80 West, heading for the Delaware Water Gap and on into the Pocono Valley of Pennsylvania. SAC Lindstrum had called ahead and notified the nearest Pennsylvania FBI office to have a Swat team set up outside al-Satir's chalet. He was told it would take approximately one half hour to put together the team and have them in position. The trip for Mac, Dillon, and Johnson was estimated to take about 2 hours.

The four cars carrying federal agents from Pennsylvania set up a perimeter around the house and waited for the Agents and Mac to arrive.

Mac's cell phone activated. While stepping down on the accelerator, he pulled the phone from his left pocket. "Hello."

"Mac, it's me, Marty. I spoke with my CI, the one who gave me the info on where Conroy was staying in Edgewater. Well, he's come through again. He heard on the street that Conroy is looking for money and a place to lay low before heading out of the country. . . . Can you talk?"

"Yeah, go on. I'm alone in my car."

"I'm told there's a good chance a guy who shared a jail cell with Conroy in Ohio would put him up at his apartment in downtown Dayton. The name is Evan Herrick, aka 'Slash.' Are you ready to take down the address?"

"Shoot." Mac wrote it down.

"Marty, you are The Man. Thanks for the information. I'm on the way to another location as we speak. I'm traveling with a bunch of feds. Our boy might be at the place where we're going. If not, I'll be heading to Dayton. I owe you a steak dinner. And I will reimburse you for anything you laid out for your CI. So far the info this guy has been giving you is gold. I hope he's right on with this one. If the information pans out, I owe him a steak dinner, too."

"Mac, we go way back together. After what this guy tried to do to you and your wife, well, my only regret is that I'm not there with you. Good luck hunting. Call me if you need anything and if I hear anything else I'll call you."

"Thanks, brother."

It was just before midnight when Sara, Brad, and Mac rolled up to the Pennsylvania location. Mac got out of his truck and walked to the Caprice.

"I hear PA is a Commonwealth State," Mac said. "A judge isn't going to let us execute a search warrant during evening hours or execute an arrest warrant at this house once the sun sets. Unless—"

Sara smiled. "Unless it's a federal agency. We supersede state law. A federal arrest warrant for al-Satir and a search warrant on his house have already been drafted and signed while we were heading over here. The information Darcy gave us was ample evidence for the arrest and search warrants. We don't quibble over how much or how little evidence is necessary for warrants when a national security issue, such as this, is at stake. We're short on manpower, but not on money, political clout, methods of detection, and powers of enforcement. If we want you, you're done."

"So, let's do this. Are we good to go?" asked Mac.

"We've got the green light. I just have to touch base with our PA agents."

After a brief conference, the federal agents and Mac rushed the house from all sides. The first agent who rushed in the front door nearly tripped over one of the bodies lying in the hallway. Mac, Dillon and Klein cleared the main floor and the basement. The Pennsylvania agents cleared the second and third floors.

"I counted five dead," Mac said to Agent Dillon.

"We should have them all IDed within several hours."

"Too bad my boy Conroy wasn't one of them."

"Mac, please. You know we want him alive. There's a wealth of knowledge in that guy's head."

"You mean like Nunzi The Wolf, who killed 19 men and you guys let him walk."

"Again with that. Didn't you have this conversation before with Agent Lindstrum?" Sara asked rhetorically. "Let it go. Sambogna brought down an entire crime family. A lot of lives saved in that one."

"I know at least 19 people who would have disagreed with you on that."

"Let's just focus on the case at hand. Can we, Mac?"

"It's your show."

The team of officers all gathered in the first floor living room. Agent Dillon took out her cell phone and called her office. After one ring, SAC Lindstrum answered.

"Sir, we executed the warrant. Five dead bodies, none of them Conroy. One of them might be Satir. The others are unknown, possibly bodyguards, drivers, house help. We won't know until we do some background."

"How are our people, Sara? "

"All safe, no injuries on our side."

"Good, good. I've been in touch with the Philly office. They have their identification unit waiting for the signal to enter. Stay there and go through any documents that are found. I know they have to photograph and dust first, but we're on a tight schedule, so slap on some gloves and check for any documents that pertain to the planned attack."

"I'll get right on it," said Dillon.

"Is Taylor there? I want to speak with him. I don't want him interfering with the evidence or the ID guys. You know how he can get."

Agent Dillon looked around the room, then hollered, "Mac, Mac Taylor!"

No response.

She called out his name again.

And again, no response.

"I don't know where he is," she said into the cell phone.

"Well, find him. I don't want any game running on this case."

"10-4. I'll call you back once I find him."

Dillon went outside and saw Mac approaching his truck.

"Where are you going?" she asked.

"I'm heading out. Not much I can do here. I'll only be in the way. I know how your tech guys get antsy having people traipse through their crime scene."

"What if we come up with some good leads?"

"Call me. You have my number."

"Are you holding out on me?"

"Why would I do that?"

"Answering a question with a question. Evasion 101. What's going on, Mac?"

"Ya know, there's a Bergen County Homicide detective who thinks I'm holding out on him in the Barrow case. It must be my face. I really am a trusting individual."

Sara crossed her arms and tilted her head to the right. "Mac, what's going on here?"

"Here's the deal. You know and I know that Conroy killed these people. He might have actually done us a favor in that regard. Nonetheless, those bodies look to be fresh kills. He can't be too far ahead of us. He's not going to head back east. That's where all his troubles lie. He'd go either south, west, or north. That'd be my guess. I'm banking he'd head west. I've got a one in three chance of being right."

"You're telling me you're going to drive aimlessly west, hoping to run into him. That's a pipe dream and you know it. You know something you're not telling me."

"Look, Sara. Conroy will probably stay on the Interstate highways. He'd want to put distance between here and where he intends to hide out. He knows if he hides in one of the local towns it won't be long before he's found out. Safely distancing oneself from the crime scene is what every smart fugitive looks for. And Conroy's no dope. He also knows we'll soon find out what vehicle he's driving. Along the way he'll figure he'll have to dump it. I want to be in or near that area when that happens. I don't want to be sitting on my ass in Bloomfield, New Jersey.

"Here's some advice for you: check out the stolen vehicle reports the next two days; north, south, and west of here. Send out a nationwide AP* with a description and recent photograph of Conroy. Note in the AP that there's a federal arrest warrant out on him for the attempted murder of a U.S. senator. Consider armed and dangerous. And have the Pennsylvania State Police and the locals check the gas stations, convenience stores, rest areas, etcetera, located within the next several hundred miles from here. That's coming from an old street cop. That's how we'd do it. But I'm not telling you anything new. I know your department has means of discovery that I'm not even aware of. That 'need to know,' mentality.

"Now, I'm wasting precious pursuit time discussing with you my reasons for heading out and what needs to be done to catch up with this psycho. So, Agent Dillon, if you find out any information in that house or through the efforts of your department as to where Conroy might be going, or what type of vehicle he's driving, I'd appreciate a phone call. As I said, 'You have my number.' I'll call you if I learn anything." Mac jumped behind the wheel of his truck and slammed the door shut.

---

* AP or APB: All Points Bulletin. Shortened to AP: common police vernacular.

"I'm not buying it!" Agent Dillon yelled as Mac slapped the vehicle into gear. With the rear tires of his truck screeching off the smooth, gray pavers, Sara jumped back. "You know something you're not telling me!"

As Mac disappeared down the long driveway, Agent Dillon took out her cell phone and punched in her office number.

"Paul, it's me, Sara. Taylor took off heading west in his truck. He won't be a problem around here. But knowing him, he's going to a problem somewhere else. I think he knows something he's not willing to tell us."

"Well, we don't have the manpower to follow him all over creation right now. We're not his babysitter. He knows if he wants to maintain his license to conduct business, he can't withhold information from us. Let's just hope his hatred for Conroy doesn't overshadow his need to earn a living to support his family. Stay in touch with him by phone. If we have to, we can triangulate his location when you call him."

"I'd better get back inside and see what I can find out." Agent Dillon went to her car and took out a pair of latex gloves. As she snapped them on, her thoughts were about Mac. *What does he know that he's not telling me?*

Conroy pulled his vehicle into the rear of an all-night diner, went in, and had dinner. He then went into the bathroom and washed his face. *Refreshing*, he thought. After dinner, he got in the back seat of Herrick's car and slid down to get some sleep. He knew he had a long couple of days ahead. He needed all the energy he could muster. Right now he had enough money to last him for a while. The $1,200 he took from al-Satir, plus the cash from the dead bodyguards and Herrick, provided him with more than enough money for food, a motel room if needed, and transportation costs. *I could get by with Herrick's credit card for a day or two*, he thought. *Slash won't report it stolen and by the time the police get to trace it I'll be long gone.*

Chapter Thirty-One

February 14, 2004—AM

The four trucks entered the United States and headed to the safe house to pick up the terrorists who were going to wreak havoc on the cities of San Antonio, Texas; Orlando, Florida; Saint Louis, Missouri; and Anaheim, California. An NSA satellite surveillance team was able to pick up all four vehicles in transit. The DEA happened to have a Texas border house under surveillance for its drug-running operations the past few months, the same house where the trucks were headed. A little luck (Providence?) was always welcomed in an investigation. The NSA and DEA teams relayed the information to their FBI liaison officers. Within less than an hour, various law enforcement agencies scrambled assault teams to respond to the safe house location. When the first truck arrived, federal and state police Swat teams, backed by the Texas National Guard air and ground support, the DEA, and local agencies, quickly arrested the vehicle's occupants, secured the truck, and simultaneously stormed the house. A firefight ensued. Twenty-two terrorist and drug traffickers were killed in the melee. The rest, who attempted to make it back to Mexico through the tunnel, were either captured or surrendered. The three other trucks, while en route to the safe house, were intercepted without incident by the Texas State Police and National Guard. Canines, HAZMAT units, and Explosive Ordnance teams were dispatched to the various crime scenes where all the weapons and potentially dangerous materials were uncovered, tagged, bagged, and removed to a secured location.

"One location left to worry about," Lindstrum told his group of agents. "The Mall of the Americas. This last bunch of Jihadists we're waiting on will more than likely enter from Windsor, Ontario. Just a guess, but with its large Mideastern population, there's less likely a chance they will be noticed forming up and crossing the border. Or so they might think."

SAC Lindstrum turned to Agent Klein. "Anything from our brothers to the North?"

"The Mounties have been shaking the bushes. They've got some leads. And yes, fingers are pointing at Windsor. Possibly a run across the Detroit River. We should know more soon. They're still pumping their informants."

"Well, the second you learn anything, let me know."

"Yes, sir."

Mac took a slow ride down 5th Street. It was early morning. Ted's Bar and Grill hadn't opened yet. Two quick turns and he entered the parking lot in the rear of the bar. The three-story building had an outcropped structure in the back. *Probably a keg room*, Mac surmised. The upstairs apartments were stepped back about 10 feet. A fire escape stretched across the second and third floors. The drop ladder was only three feet above the first-floor roof. There were seven cars in the rear lot. Mac noticed that one of the vehicles, a blue van, had Pennsylvania license plates on it.

After parking his truck on the far side of the lot, he got out and walked along the side of Ted's Bar to the front of the building. He entered the front foyer leading to the upstairs apartments. The right side mailbox read: Apt. #1 Herrick. Mac pulled out his .45 caliber Glock and silently climbed the stairs. Upon reaching the landing, he approached the first door across from the top of the stairs. On the door was a gold metal number 1. *A rear apartment.*

Mac exited the building and mounted the outcropped structure in the back of Ted's Bar. Once on top, he pulled down the fire escape ladder and climbed it slowly. Reaching the second-floor window, he peered inside. Seeing no activity, Mac slid his knife between the double-hung window sashes and unhooked the lock. He raised the lower sash and, with gun now in hand, slipped into the kitchen. He heard music playing in another room, presumably the bedroom.

Mac crept around the kitchen table and moved into the living room. The music got louder. It seemed to be coming from down the hallway to a room on the right. Mac hugged the wall, his gun pointed at a 45-degree angle from the floor. As he entered the bedroom, he quickly raised his weapon to a point-shoulder position.

When he noticed the person lying on the bed, who appeared to have been in heavy REM sleep, was not Conroy, he eased out of the room. In checking all other areas within the apartment, he realized Conroy was not there. Mac went back to the bedroom of the sleeping man. He moved to the side of the bed and shook its occupant with his right hand, holding his gun in his left. After a few moments of heavy shaking, the occupant, Evan Herrick, opened his eyes.

"Whoa!" Herrick said, his hands now outstretched above his head. "Please, put your gun down. I'm not armed."

"Quiet," Mac said as he moved to the corner of the room. "Where is he? Is there a place in the apartment where he could hide? Is he sleeping in the back of his van? Where is he?"

"Who?"

"You know who. Where's Conroy?"

"Sir, are you the police? You didn't say that when you pointed your gun at me."

"Never mind who I am. Is Conroy here? Tell me now or you'll be dead in five seconds. I'm starting now—"

"Hold it, hold it! I'll tell you what you want to know. No, he's not here. He left yesterday morning with my car and money."

"And you're still alive? How odd."

Mac scanned the hallway again, then asked, "Where'd he go?"

"I don't know." Herrick got up from the bed and edged toward the bedroom window. "Who the hell are you?" he asked again.

Mac ignored the question.

"Come over here, now!"

As Herrick approached, Mac hit him in the stomach with a right hand. Herrick doubled over. Mac pushed him onto the bed.

"Right now, I'm your worst enemy. You're going to answer *my* questions or you won't live long enough to say, 'Who are you?' Got that? Now come with me."

Mac grabbed him with his right hand, his left hand still holding his .45.

They left the bedroom and headed down the hall to the kitchen.

"Sit!" Mac ordered, placing a chair in the corner of the room. Mac took another chair and hooked it under the front door knob. He sat down next to Herrick.

"I'll ask again, where'd he go?"

"He didn't tell me, I swear."

"If he just needed your car and money, why are you still alive?"

Herrick sat back in the chair. "Why would you care? I know Conroy always had run ins with the law. You must be a cop."

Mac put the barrel of his gun on Herrick's forehead and started to pull the trigger. "I warned you!" he said.

"No, no! Stop! I'm sorry. I won't ask again. I promise."

Mac eased his finger off the trigger and brought the gun back to his side. "For the last time, don't worry who I am." Mac brought his face to within inches of Herrick's face."What you need to focus on is that I'm going to kill you if you don't give me the answers I'm looking for. "

Herrick put both of his hands up and back. "Whoa, whoa, I gotcha. I guess Conroy didn't kill me because he needs me to dump a car for him. I couldn't do that if I was dead. Right?"

"What car?" Mac knew full well it wasn't a car, but a van. *Use the guy's own words. Test him. See if he's telling the truth.*

"A blue van. I told him I'd have to wait 'til dark to dump it. I was buying time. I knew he wanted to leave immediately. I know this guy. He'd kill me in a heartbeat, but if he had something for me to do first, he'd hold off on that. It worked . . . so far."

"What car is he in now?"

"He took mine, a 2002 white Mazda 3." He gave Mac the license plate number.

"Money?"

"Seventy-five dollars and my credit card."

"How much gas was in the car?"

"About a quarter of a tank."

"Did he ask for any directions?"

"Nope."

Do you have a GPS in your car?"

"No."

"Did you give him anything else?"

"No."

"Okay, here's how it goes. Don't leave your house for the next hour. Don't go near the blue van. Don't call anyone. Don't do anything. Cops will be swarming this area. The feds will be here to talk with you. You can tell them what you told me. We talked, but I never threatened you. Remember that or I will find you and kill you. Understand?"

"Understood. As a matter of fact, I don't even know who you are. I'd like to keep it that way."

Chapter Thirty-Two

February 14, 2004—PM

Mac's telephone call to Agent Dillon brought out the local feds. Sara and her posse were en route to the Dayton location. She was not happy with Mac's freelance style of handling an investigation. Agent Dillon went by the book: keep the lines of communication between coworkers open; know your legal limitations and stay within them; when executing arrests or warrants, wait for backup; make sure all evidence is properly obtained and secured; get clearance from supervisors for continued actions; and document in writing everything you do. In her mind, Mac held fast to none of these procedures. In dealing with him, Sara felt, at times, that she was chasing a ghost. He held back on information vital to the case; he ran solo, leaving a trail of unsecured evidence behind him; he made no effort to clear his actions with anyone in authority, and his interviewing techniques were extremely suspect by any normal police standard. Nonetheless, Mac was effective. He'd produced some very valuable information over the course of the investigation. Locating this so-called safe house for Conroy in Dayton, Ohio, was just another example of Mac's ability to keep the chase alive.

"Wait for me, Mac. We need to talk," Agent Dillon shouted into the telephone as a large semi truck streaked past her on the left. "I'll be at the location in a few hours. I notified our Dayton and

Columbus offices. They should be there shortly."

"I'd love to wait for you, Sara," Mac said rather abruptly, "but I don't want that Mazda getting too far ahead of me."

Dillon held out little hope that Mac would agree to wait for her. *He runs his own game; does what he wants, with little, if any regard for the chain of command.* There wasn't much she could do to get him to play by the rules. Still, she had to try.

"The State Police from Ohio, Kentucky, Indiana, and West Virginia have all been notified to be on the lookout for that vehicle. Plus the locals have been notified. Let them do their job. Instead of driving around aimlessly, hoping to run into Conroy, why don't you wait until I get by you and we can go over what we've got and what's to be the next move?"

"Sorry, no can do," Mac said in a somewhat nonchalant matter. "He can't be too far ahead. I've got to believe he'll still be heading west, either getting gas directly off the highway within the next few hours, or changing cars soon. Probably the later. He's not stupid. He knows it won't take long before we're on him. Remember the plan to attack the Mall of the Americas? I think he'll be heading out there. That's the direction I'd be heading if I needed to meet up with some contacts that could get me the hell out of the country. I don't think he'd head directly to Canada. I could be wrong on that, but sometimes you just have to rely on instinct. Mine tells me he's heading to Minneapolis. I'll keep you updated on my activities. I'd appreciate it if you would do the same."

Sara doubted Mac would, in fact, keep her updated 'on his activities.' She did, however, have one ace-in-the-hole that she was going to play before he'd disconnect the call.

In a weird configuration of geographical boundaries, Windsor, Ontario is directly south of Detroit, Michigan. In the early morning hours, the *Malaga*, a 50-foot party boat pulled out from a local marina. Aboard the fishing vessel were the captain, three crew members, and twenty multinational terrorists disguised as fishermen. They were on the first leg of their journey to the Mall of the Americas where they were to kill shoppers until they ran out of ammunition. Over the course of their trek in the U.S., the terrorist were to meet up with eighty additional Jihadists.

The *Malaga* started to take its normal route to the fishing grounds, but at the last minute changed course and headed toward a small docking area by the outskirts of Detroit. Waiting at the dock for the fishing boat was a large truck. In the vehicle was an assortment of weapons that included fully-automatic rifles, flack vests, boxes of ammunition, explosive devices, and cash, lots of it. These terrorists were more mercenary than religious. Escape plans had been hatched for each one of them, but such plans did not come cheap. Some would be caught. That could not be avoided, but the terrorists weighed the odds—a lot of money and a trip home, or capture and jail time in the U.S. No surprise, they decided to play the odds. Nobody in the U.S. gets the death penalty anymore unless they get charged in Texas, Florida, or Oklahoma. Those who are given the death penalty in the other states usually spend years on appeal before dying of old age or as the victim of a fellow inmate attack. Moreover, since U.S. prisons, compared to those in the Mideast, were like country clubs, the decision to kill as many Americans as they can and get paid handsomely for it seemed to be a no-brainer for the Jihadists.

"Mac, are you a team player?" Agent Dillon asked.

"I'd like to think I am."

"Well, you see, I *am* a team player. So, I'll give you some information you might not be aware of. Why? Because we are *a* team. You wait for me and I'll share some information that will save you a trip to Minnesota. That is, of course, if you'll agree to play by the rules of the Federal Bureau of Investigation. What do you say?"

Mac thought for a moment. "That depends on the information."

"Fine. Here it is. I have reason to believe that Conroy will be heading to Detroit. If he's looking for some ready cash, weapons, and a way to slip out of the country, I think he'd head directly north, not northwest as you suspect."

"You sound pretty confident. Reliable information?"

"The best. Only Conroy is going to miss his boat by a few hours."

"His boat?"

"Here's the scoop. Based on information provided by the Royal Canadian Mounted Police, a charter boat carrying a host of terrorists is preparing to dock in Detroit. The group is coming from Windsor, Ontario which, by the way, has one of the largest Muslim populations in Canada. Agents from my Bureau, along with Homeland Security Agents, Border Agents, and local undercover Detroit Police Officers are currently awaiting the arrival of that boat. A large truck is by the receiving platform where it's set to dock. We suspect the truck is loaded with weapons and other items that would assist in the assault on the Mall of the Americas. The boat, the truck, and all parties will be taken down within the next few minutes."

"And you're only telling me this now," Mac said with a bit of irritation in his voice. Then sarcastically, "I thought we were a team?"

"First off, you know how we operate—need to know basis. You didn't need to know. There were to be no communications regarding this raid. You remember WW Two, the Big One, 'Loose Lips Sink Ships'?"

"I missed that one," Mac responded gruffly.

"Secondly, you've been holding out on me. There's no way you just happened to stumble upon Conroy's safe house in Dayton. I was born at night, but not last night."

"Okay," he said. "Let's cut to the chase. Literally. Where do you want to meet? I will be very disappointed in you if I find out you're playing me and you actually do know exactly where Conroy is at the moment. I know you feds have various ways of knowing things, whether it's tracking through bugs, GPS, electronic transactions, eyes in the sky, informants, you name it."

"Yes, we do . . . and you have yours. I like ours better," Agent Dillon replied.

"I'll take street justice, Old Testament style, eye for an eye. It's more honest, fairer. You can keep your courtroom justice."

"Are we done, Mac?"

He laughed into the phone. "Sure. Tell you what. Why don't we meet somewhere near Toledo? I'll head north, in case Conroy ditches the car. We can keep in touch and decide on a meeting place as we get close to each other. I'd hate to see Conroy make it all the way to the border. So, if we can cut out some traveling time, I think we both can benefit. What say you?"

"All right, but make sure you stay in touch and let me know where you are."

"You mean you didn't put a bug on my truck?" Mac laughed again.

"Its signal has been weak." Mac couldn't see the smile on Sara's face.

"Mac."

"Sara, go ahead."

"The bust went down without a hitch. All parties were arrested and none of our guys or gals were killed or injured. The truck was impounded. Multiple weapons and blocks of cash were recovered from the vehicle."

"What about Conroy? Was he picked up in the sweep?"

"No, which is odd."

"Why odd?" Mac asked.

"Because we had him using Herrick's credit card for gas at a station near Bowling Green. He had to be heading in that direction."

"Maybe, maybe not."

"Well, where else would he be heading? We don't have any inside info on whatever *he* might be planning, unless you're holding out on me."

"Look," Mac said, "if he used Herrick's credit card once, he'll use it again. So keep an open line on that. If he continued north, he might have wanted to slip into Canada and disappear. With all those Muslims in Windsor, it seems to be a good place for him to hide."

"Any other possibilities?"

"I'm still thinking Minneapolis. The Mall of the Americas. If he hadn't got wind of the arrests, he could still be thinking the crossover from Canada was a success. He might have headed north on I75 to throw us off. The logical route to Minneapolis would be Route 70. Still, there isn't much difference between north then west as opposed to west then north." Mac was quiet for a moment. "Sara, any way of keeping these arrests quiet for a day or two?"

"No way. I wish we could, but there were too many agencies involved in the coordination, takedown, and processing of people and evidence. It can't be done."

"Well, hopefully Conroy won't be watching TV or listening to the radio for the next 24 hours or so. . . . Wishful thinking, I know."

"Yeah, well, meet me at our Detroit office and we'll decide on the next move. Maybe we'll get some actionable intelligence by that time."

Agent Dillon gave Mac the FBI Detroit office address before placing the red revolving light on the dashboard and pushing her government vehicle well above the speed limit.

Chapter Thirty-Three

February 14, 2004—PM

The takedown at the Detroit dock went as planned. Law enforcement personnel, helicopters, search and evidence dogs, bomb sniffers, and patrol boats swarmed in on the *Malaga* and the white truck by the Detroit dock. All cell phones were collected, tagged and brought to the FBI's Detroit office. Special Agent Anwar Malachi, along with two other agents who spoke Arabic and Farsi, were assigned to log all missed and sent calls on each phone. They were also to respond to all incoming calls and maintain conversations in hopes of gathering additional information on other terrorists within the circle. By prolonging conversations with these callers, agents were provided an opportunity to triangulate the calls and zero-in on general locations from where these calls were being made.

Conroy woke up. He had been sleeping rather soundly all night in Herrick's car. He grabbed a bagel and coffee at the diner before gassing up and heading for the Mall of the Americas. His first stop after Bowling Green was along I90 between South Bend and Gary, Indiana. After a jaunt on 294, the second stop was again on I90 in the town of Portage located just north of Madison, Wisconsin. He was at a service station in Portage when he placed another call to the contact al-Satir had given him.

The phone rang three times. "Hello," said a man with a Mideast accent. It was not the same person Conroy had spoken with on the last call.

"Who is this?" Conroy asked.

"A friend," replied the man on the other end of the call.

"Well, were you or your other bud able to arrange something?"

"We are trying to do that now," said the voice on the other end.

"You had plenty of time to arrange a meet place and the person I'm to meet with."

"Where are you now?"

"Never mind where I am. Answer my questions!"

"Okay, okay," said the voice on the other end of the line. "Meet the driver of a large white truck in the south parking lot of the Mall of the Americas."

"Tomorrow, right?"

"Tonight."

"I thought this wasn't going down until tomorrow."

There was a hesitation on the other end of the line.

"We need to look over the area first. How do you say, 'a dry run.'

"What time then?" asked Conroy.

"Be there at 8 PM."

"From where you're coming, how could you get to the location by 8 PM?"

Again a pause.

"How many teams we have and where they will be coming from is not your concern. Be assured the truck will be there."

Conroy's gut was telling him something wasn't completely right about all this. Still, the thought of missing out on the cash and making a quick getaway gnawed at him.

"All right," Conroy said. "I'll be there. Make sure your guys are, too."

"Good," said Special Agent Anwar Malachi before hanging up.

Sara and Mac entered the large conference room on the third floor of the federal building. They approached the agents sitting at the long table along the wall opposite where they entered. "Any luck so far?" she asked.

"And you must be who?" one of the agents at the table asked.

Pulling out her ID, Sara said, "I'm Agent Dillon from the Newark Office. This here is Investigator Mac Taylor. He's assigned to our office to assist on this case."

"Sorry 'bout that," said the agent who asked. "But you know how it is, 'need to know'."

"I understand, believe me, I understand," Sara said, shooting a quick stare at Mac. Then looking at the three agents at the desk, she again asked, "So, anything so far?"

Agent Malachi smiled. "Yes. We've had six calls and were able to hit pay dirt on two of them. We have our people and the Canadian Mounties at those locations. So far, they've made quite a few arrests at those locations. We're setting up surveillances at two other spots right now."

"Any of those perps go by the name Dirk Conroy or Ahmed Sal Mohammed?" asked Mac.

"Ummm, no . . . but I haven't got all the names yet of those pulled in."

"You said there were six calls. What's the story with the last two?" It was Sara asking the question this time.

"One of the calls was to a weather channel. Nothing there to report. "

"And the other."

"It was some guy who wanted to meet up with this group we just arrested on their way to the Mall of the Americas."

"Whoa! Yes! That's got to be our guy." Mac shot a fist into the air. "Were you able to get a location on the caller?"

"Yeah. A pay phone at a service station in a place called Portage in Wisconsin."

Sara crossed her arms and tipped her head forward. "How'd your conversation go with him?"

"Good. I have our agents and Homeland prepared to set up tonight in the south parking lot at the Mall of the Americas. The caller expects to meet with the driver of a white truck at that location at 8 PM tonight."

Sara patted him on the shoulder. "Great job! Hopefully, we'll catch this serial killer tonight. Make sure the guys out there know that the target, Dirk Conroy, aka Ahmed Sal Mohammed, is armed and dangerous. Proceed with extreme caution."

"What do—," Sara turned and her shoulders slumped. She shook her head and let out a breath of air. Mac was gone.

He's going to be the death of me.

Sara pushed her way through a half dozen or so law enforcement agents and local police personnel before spotting Mac by a table in the far corner of the room. He was holding a slice of pizza in one hand and a can of soda in the other.

"So there you are," Agent Dillon said. "I thought you skipped out on me again."

"And why would I do that. We're a team. Aren't we?"

"Very funny. I still haven't figured you out yet."

"Well don't kill yourself trying. I haven't figured myself out yet, either."

Agent Dillon laughed. Then in a serious tone said, "So tell me, Investigator Taylor, what are you thinking now about the investigation and how we operate?"

"I'll give you guys an A for the work you've done so far. Unfortunately, the politicians and lawyers will screw this whole thing up in the end. Thanks to the ACLU and bleeding heart politicians, these terrorists will eventually be released on good behavior to go out and try again to kill more Americans. And once the pols run to the media to report the takedown of this group of radicals, our boy Dirk Conroy will be heading for parts unknown."

"You don't think our people will get him tonight in Minnesota?"

"Nope," Mac said, taking a big bite into his slice of pizza.

"Why not?"

"Because he's not stupid. Once he hears about the arrests on the news—I'm sure he's listening to a radio or he might stop somewhere and see the report on the TV—he'll realize the meet is either off or it's a setup. When it sinks in that the person he spoke with was not someone he had had contact with in the past, his suspicions will be confirmed."

Sara grabbed a slice of pizza from one of the many opened boxes on the table. "You seemed pretty happy when you learned that the caller heading to Minnesota was probably Conroy. Why the about-face?"

"Don't get me wrong. There's still a chance that he might be caught. And at least we have an idea where he is and that he's using a credit card we can trace for locations. There are two downsides, though. One, if he does show up at the agreed location, I won't be able to get there in time to meet and exact a little street justice on him."

"And two?"

"Two, if he gets word that he's being played, he'll be in the wind. Then he'll go on your Most Wanted List and we won't see him again. Well, *you* won't see him again, but I will. I will track him down no matter how long it takes or how far he runs. That cretin tried to kill my wife and child. I won't rest until he's . . ." Mac saw the look of concern in Agent Dillon's eyes . . . caught."

"You mean killed. By you. Don't you?"

"Are you still trying to figure me out?"

"Ah, a question for a question. Don't try to dodge the bullet. You know I can't condone your style of vigilante justice," Sara said.

Mac took a long swig of his soda, then threw the empty can in the garbage bin alongside the table. "Let me educate you, Agent Dillon, on life and what you call vigilante justice. In World War Two the German SS were given orders not to take Allied prisoners.

They were told to kill all captured. The Japanese burned to death or hacked the heads off of American prisoners. The Viet Cong and North Vietnam Army tortured and killed our American soldiers. And these animals that were just arrested were hell bent to indiscriminately shoot, poison, and kill innocent Americans. Unfortunately, the only justice these enemies know is street justice, vigilante justice."

"That's not how we operate," said Sara. "We have to set the example of a civilized society. That's just how it is. We are the last bastion of sanity in this world."

"I have a priest friend who agrees with you. But then again, why wouldn't he, he's a priest. He keeps thinking about the next world. Unfortunately, we're stuck in this one, and it's a dangerous one."

"Mac, you know I can have you taken off this case. Especially since you have a personal vendetta against Conroy and it might compromise the investigation. We want him alive, if that's doable. You only want him in one condition, dead."

"Look, Sara, I'll go by the book with you. I don't know what, if any, valuable information Conroy could supply, other than a list of victims, but if catching him for interviewing and interrogation purposes is your goal, as long as we're working together, I'll not go immediately to my kill response."

"Is that a promise?"

"Cross my heart and hope to die."

First Polsani, now her. What's with this compassion for a serial killer?

"Breaking News, the Governor of Michigan, the FBI, and the head of Homeland Security will be holding a press conference within the next hour. Apparently, it's in reference to the arrest of a large group of alleged terrorists entering the U.S. from Canada. The arrests reportedly occurred in Detroit and Windsor, Ontario. We will break to the press conference once it starts. Now back to our regularly scheduled program."

Conroy, switched channels on the car radio.

". . . confiscated was a Canadian boat and a truck registered in the U.S. It is unknown at this time the nature of the planned attack. . . ."

He switched the channel again.

". . . arrests appear to be connected with other arrests made earlier off the Eastern Coast and in Texas."

"Damn it!" He slammed his hand down on the wheel of the car. "Time to unload this bag of bolts and get far away from here!" he yelled as if there was someone listening.

Conroy now knew the meet in the parking lot at the mall was a set up. Moreover—though he couldn't be sure—he figured the feds knew the vehicle he was driving. *The credit card has to go. Only use cash from now on. Stay away from Minneapolis.* Conroy was not one to suffer from paranoia, but he was sharp enough to realize when it was time to leave a very small footprint. He knew the feds had a lot of tracking capabilities, many of which he wasn't even aware of.

Best course of action is to disappear for a while, Conroy thought. *New car, new identity, time to find a place to lie low, somewhere out of sight.* He started looking for the next service area.

Conroy sat in his car by the air pump at the service station. He waited, checking out the cars and trucks that pulled in to get gas or diesel. He watched a family in an RV come and go, a guy and his wife or girlfriend in a blue pickup truck gas up and leave, and a group of teenagers stop for some snacks. Then the target he was waiting for appeared. He was a middle-aged black male, alone in a newer model silver Chevrolet. The man gassed up the car and pulled it to the front of the convenience store.

Conroy pulled the Mazda 3 toward the rear of store. He walked around to the front and waited for the black man to exit.

"Where ya headed?" Conroy said as the man let the glass door shut behind him.

"Excuse me?" the man said.

"Oh, I was just wondering where you were headed. I'm heading north, hauling pianos. My rig is over there," Conroy said pointing behind the man.

The man turned to look in that direction. "I don't see any truck over there," he said. Then turning back and peering down at the handgun Conroy was holding by his hip, he whispered, "Oh, man. What do you want?" He attempted to pull out his wallet. "Here's all the money I have."

"Stop right there. Keep your hands where I can see them. Now follow me around the corner."

"Hey, I'm not crazy. I go 'round that corner, I ain't coming back."

"Well, here's how it goes. Your choice. I shoot you right here or you come with me. I'll take your money when we 'round the corner, I'll put you in the trunk of my car so you can't call the police, and I'm off. By the time you break out of the trunk or someone hears you, I'll be long gone and I'll ditch your car. You'll get it back and we'll all be happy. Okay?"

"I don't have much of a choice, do I?" the man said looking around, hoping the store clerk might see what's going on or someone might pull up to the pumps and scare off this would-be robber.

The two men walked to the rear of the store. The area was dimly light, but the victim could still plainly see the large, black gun in Conroy's hand.

Conroy took the car key out of his pocket and popped the trunk.

"Get in," he said.

The man got into the trunk.

"Give me your wallet and keys."

The man handed over both.

"No!" the man yelled, just as Conroy raised the gun and shot him in the forehead.

The victim's body went limp. Conroy put the gun in his pocket and closed the trunk. He knew when the Mazda 3 was found—which it will be in the next day or so— he'll have to ditch the Chevy. Still, he thought, *it should buy me enough time to get far away from here.*

Conroy came around the front of the building and approached the victim's car. The store clerk was standing outside.

"Did you hear that loud bang?" the clerk asked.

"Yeah, it was a large semi passing through. It backfired. Must be some bad gas or diesel. Don't know what causes those big rigs to backfire."

"Hmm," said the clerk. Then shaking his head, he walked back into the store.

Conroy got behind the wheel of the silver Chevrolet. He took out the wallet the victim had given him and opened it.

"James Stark," he said. "Good name. I can look like a James Stark," he said aloud to himself. Conroy then quickly pulled out from in front of the store and got back on the highway, only this time he headed due north . . . toward Canada.

IV

"I won't be reconstructed, and I don't give a damn."

Innes Randolph
A Good Old Rebel

Chapter Thirty-Four

March 15, 2004

"I am not happy about this!" Aaron Ruger hollered as he stood, bent over his mahogany desk. "There was a lot of money to be made, a lot of money, and now we're back to square one."

The Saudi prince sat back in the plush French Louis XV chair. "We both lost. My people would have scored their victories. Now, no victories, only victims. Our victims."

"Wrong, Amel, your victims, not mine. My losses come with dollar signs." Ruger shook his head in disgust. "So, what are we to do now?"

Prince Amel folded his hands and placed them on his lap. "We must be patient," he said.

"I'm not a patient man, and I don't take financial losses lightly."

"Nevertheless, we must face reality. We need to eliminate anyone and anything left connecting us to this operation."

"And how are we to do that? We've lost everything! Men, weapons, money . . . everything!"

"Not everything," said the prince. "I have been able to bring back to my country a man who has been a part of our plan from the start. His name is Ahmed Sal Mohammed. He is an American."

"You mean Arab, er Muslim. Unless he's changed it like Cassius Clay."

"Yes, his American name was Dirk Conroy. He's had other aliases. He was able to hide out in a city called Windsor in Canada, after that crossing from Canada into Detroit failed. We have our people there. He was able to blend with a new identity until we were able to bring him to my country in a private plane."

"Why all the fuss for this Dirk Mohammed, whatever the hell his name is?"

The prince leaned forward, "Because Ahmed Sal Mohammed knows, how do the Americans say, 'where all the bodies are buried.' Actually, he has killed most of them. If he were to be captured, we both might be in trouble."

"Then why not have him killed?"

"Not so easy. He is a deadly killer himself. If we do not succeed in killing *him*, we are as good as dead. He will hunt us down. At best, even in his death, he could attach my family name to international terrorism. Who knows what files, names, or documents he might have hidden away, or given to a friend or attorney to send to various governments if he dies a mysterious death. He is not a stupid man. It is better to keep him alive until we learn if there is more to fear from him. At least for a time."

"And when will that time come? I don't like anyone, I mean anyone, knowing our business and who we are. It should be easy to lock him up somewhere and squeeze out any information he has hidden. If he has anything that can hurt us, kill him."

"Oh, if it were only that simple. Who knows what might be the signal to release any information to the government that he might have, worse yet, to the press. The information could be on some computer requiring the mere touch of a button to go out to whomever. The days of tapes, CDs, and hard copy documents are long gone."

"So, what shall we do if we can't kill him?"

"As I said before, we must be patient. We wait."

"Wait for what?!"

The prince held up his hand in an attempt to calm Ruger down. "Please, please, listen to me. Once Ahmed arrived in my country, he said he had business to attend to in Genève."

"What's in Genève?"

"He said he was going to Genève, but he is not there. He is in Paris. He is staying with a Syrian girl who we will find out more about. We can threaten to kill her entire family if she doesn't tell what, if anything, Ahmed might have on us. If she betrays us, we will have to kill her, her family, and, of course, Ahmed. But we must be patient, methodical in our planning, if that's to happen. Ahmed will be a very formidable enemy if he slips by us."

Ruger turned and looked out the stained-glass window behind his desk. "When is he expected back?" he asked.

"Soon, I suspect. He left several days ago. I got the impression he wouldn't be there long. He said something about seeing an old friend."

"And you know who this friend is?"

"It's the girl."

"Are you sure?"

"Yes. We have people who live in his building. He hasn't moved from the apartment since he arrived there."

"Maybe you should call him back, then have someone work over the girl."

"He'll be back, don't worry, Aaron. Patience, my friend, patience."

"Patience my ass, Amel. I don't like unfinished business. And this guy Mohammed *is* unfinished business."

Ruger paced back and forth before slamming his hand on the desk. "He doesn't have anything on us! Besides, if he did, we could deny it! You know he has to be eliminated! You have people loyal to you and your cause. All it takes is a bullet, one bullet. Why did you let him leave your country? You and I have developed a good relationship with Washington. We can't afford to have some lowlife killer ruining all that for us."

The prince stood up. "I told you the timing is not right for killing this man. You say all it takes is a bullet. What do you know about killing anyone? You know how to make money. That's it. Money is your goal and your god."

"Please, don't make me laugh. Spare me the righteous indignation. You're telling me money is my god as you sit there in your fine robes with a private helicopter and plane waiting for you, with a family wealth that's greater than the GNP of some countries. Don't give me that crap about money being important to *me*. You want not only wealth, but power. Why else would you risk your precious family name for a few extra gold bars in your stockpile? Why, because of your dream of a caliphate where you will be a big part of the ruling class beyond Saudi Arabia."

"I don't deny that jihad is in my blood as it is in the blood of all true believers of Islam. We will succeed in our jihad. It will take time but it will eventually happen. Meanwhile, I do not want to prematurely draw attention to me or my family. And I will not risk my family's safety. Had I not offered to bring Mohammed, or as you'd prefer to call him Conroy, back to my country where he has a home, he would return eventually, and his return would be problematic for me and my family. He is a ruthless killer who expects people to do what he asks. Had I not brought him back when he asked, I know he would make it a point to get his revenge. And that I am sure of even if he never learns that I have reached out to have someone kill him. Again, there is yet another possibility. The one where I find a loyal subject or subjects to kill him, and the attempt fails. In that event, my death and that of my family would be certain."

Prince Amel clasped his hands together and bowed his head.

"If you wish to arrange for his death," he said in a calm voice, "go right ahead. Just leave me out of your plans. But be prepared for what may follow. As they say in American, 'the unintended consequences.'"

Ruger let out a breath of air slowly, "You enjoy quoting the

Americans, even though you want to blow them to hell. Well, I see where your point is well taken. Kill him when you're ready. I'll leave the matter to you."

"I thought you would see it my way," said the prince. "Now, I think it is time for me to leave. Should anything new develop regarding Ahmed, I will meet again with you. No intermediaries. Agreed?"

"Agreed."

The Saudi prince left Ruger's mansion and walked to his private helicopter. The bird whisked him to the airport where he boarded his Leer jet and headed back to his palace in Saudi Arabia.

March 16, 2004

The phone rang.

"Mac."

"Martin, how have you been?"

Detective Lieutenant Presler stood at the phone booth watching a truck blocking traffic in the middle of the busy intersection. "Same old, same old," he said. "Listen, I've got some information on Conroy."

"What do you have?" asked Mac.

"One of my guys has a snitch on University Heights, if you can believe that."

"Sure, why not. Even the well-to-do need a confessor once in a while."

"Well, as you know, they're not all well-to-do in that area. Nevertheless, my guy's snitch told him your boy Conroy phoned him about a month ago looking for a contact."

"Did he say where he was, or where he wanted to go?"

Drivers were laying on their car horns for the truck to move.

"What did you say, Mac? I didn't hear you with this racket."

"Did your guy say where Conroy was, or where he was going?"

"He said he was in Canada but wouldn't give the confidential informant any specific location. Conroy asked the CI what the word was on the street, were the cops talking to anyone about his whereabouts? —ironic twist, heh Mac? Conroy's confidential is the guy snitching on him."

Mac chuckled. "We should be thankful there's no honor among thieves."

Presler had to raise his voice over the traffic noise. "How true, how true."

"Is that it, Marty?"

"No, no, here's some actionable intelligence you and your team might want to jump on. Conroy reportedly told the informant he was planning to leave Canada soon, that he would be heading to Europe. He said he had a passport."

The light changed and the truck cleared the intersection.

"A passport? He wouldn't have gotten ten feet past a terminal gate if he presented a passport in the name of Dirk Conroy or Ahmed Sal Mohammed. He must have another identity."

"Well, Mac that's for you, your buddies at the Bureau, and the RCMP to figure out. I know checking flights records from Canada to Europe for the past month could be a monumental task, but with computers now, it should be a lot easier."

"Easier yet, if he took a chartered flight," said Mac. "This informant, I'd be curious to know why he's so close to Conroy that Conroy would call *him* for help."

"He knew Conroy from the old neighborhood. He helped initiate him into the Muslin brotherhood, particularly into a group called Jalil ul-Anmar. We picked him up on various street crimes. None related to terrorism; otherwise, we'd have lost him to the feds. He agreed to work with one of our detectives if a deal was made to give him credit for time served. He's low level, but he had, and still has, a wealth of street information. So, the deal was struck. He was released from jail. He's on parole, though, so we still have our thumb on his neck."

"Could we use him as bait, to lure Conroy to a particular location?"

"Sorry, Mac, that ship left the dock. Apparently Conroy made it to Europe. Unfortunately, our guy hasn't heard from him again and he doesn't know where in Europe he is."

"I guess I'm forced to bring the feds back into play."

"Just cut out the middle man. I'd be in a very bad place if they knew I was feeding critical terrorist information to a PI instead of to them. I'm paranoid enough to think they might even be monitoring every conversation."

"Martin, I know from listening to all that traffic noise in the background you're not calling me from the PD. When they start wiretapping public phones just for the hell of it, we'll all be in more trouble than you think."

"Mac, you know better. Right now I'm taking a chance that they aren't tapping your phone. Nonetheless, I trust you to keep me out of any conversation you have with your buds at the Bureau."

"I will. I'll say the information was received from an anonymous source, a conscientious citizen, who heard of me from the street and knew I was looking for Conroy. I have no further information or means of contacting that person. But have no fear, my good friend, I'm working *with* the feds, so, if your identity is revealed—which it won't be—you come under *my* umbrella. Now that's a switch.... Listen Martin, I owe you a lot for all you've done for me. I'll not forget that. If you need anything, and I mean anything, don't ever hesitate to call. Thanks again."

Mac slowly put the phone down onto its cradle and began to consider all his options.

"You can relax, honey," Mac said as he entered the living room.

Cheryl was sitting in an upholstered chair, her feet up on an ottoman. "Relax? What? Why?" she asked.

"Apparently Conroy is somewhere in Europe at the moment."

"Well, that's comforting, for the time being."

"Still, in case the information is wrong, I want Jason to stay with you when I'm not here."

"What? Where do you intend to go?"

"I'm working with the feds, so I can be shooting off anywhere, any time, any day. I just want you to be safe and sound. Jason can adjust his shift so he can be with you."

"Don't worry. I don't think that guy Conroy will be coming back. Besides, I now bring your gun with me wherever I go. And yes, even when I do the laundry. Plus, I keep the phone nearby. You did say the local police will continue to watch the house, didn't you?"

"Well, I'm glad to hear you're taking precautions. Nevertheless, I don't feel comfortable with you being home all alone, especially at night."

"I don't want to put Jason out. He's got a life of his own to live."

Mac grinned. "No, he doesn't. You know him. He's always looking for something to do. This security detail will do him just fine."

"But—"

"No buts. Honey, I love you. It's my fault you're dragged into this whole mess. I'd never forgive myself if something happened to you."

"Fine, fine," she said. "I'm not going to fight with you over this."

"Good, because you might want to fight with me after I tell you what I'm going to do next."

"Oh God, what now?"

"I'm going to get in touch with the FBI and see what, if anything, they have on Conroy's location right now. They have tracing abilities beyond what most people imagine. If they don't have hard evidence on his location, maybe they will after I tell them what continent he's now on."

"And this research is supposed to upset me into fighting with you why?" Cheryl said, a stern look on her face.

"Because, if I get an actionable location on this dirtbag, I'll be out of town for a few days."

"You mean 'out of country.' Don't you?!"

"Well, yeah."

"And what if I go into labor while you're gone? What then?"

"You still have a few weeks before your due date."

"You're not that stupid, Mac. You've heard of premature deliveries. I suspect you delivered a few preemies of your own when you were a cop in Newark."

"Honey, you'll be fine. Jason and Annie are here if you go into an early labor. The police and ambulance are a phone call away. They'll be here within five minutes."

"I'm not going to the hospital in a police car or ambulance! I'm not sick. I'm having a baby, *your* baby!"

"That's why I have to finish this with Conroy. I don't want you or the baby becoming one of his future victims. I know how this guy thinks. He won't rest until he gets his vengeance."

"Sound familiar?"

"Listen, I don't want to be looking over my shoulder the rest of my life. And I surely don't want to worry about your safety and the safety of my child every day this man walks free. You can add to that that I am not going to let the safety of my family rest with the authorities. The same authorities who will set this guy free for providing information on the arrest and conviction of higher level criminals, all for his information and testimony. They'll let him go for the so-called greater good served. Then I will definitely kill him unless he kills me first. But, even if I get to him first, it might be too late, too late for the ones I love." Mac dropped to one knee next to Cheryl, picked up her hand and kissed it. "I'm going to kill Conroy. Not for vengeance. Not for justice. But for the survival and defense of my family. Nothing can deter me from that goal."

"I don't want you to go."

Mac went to kiss Cheryl on the lips. She turned away from him. "I have to," he said in a deliberate voice as he rose from his kneeling position.

Cheryl turned back facing him. "If you won't listen to me," she said, "please speak with your old war buddy Father Polsani. Maybe he could talk some sense into you."

"We've talked many times before about matters like this. He's not going to change my mind." Mac then walked into his office and sat at the desk. For the next several minutes he looked around the office—at the filing cabinet, the office machines, the plaques—until his eyes rested on the telephone in the corner of his desk.

Chapter Thirty-Five

March 16, 2004

"Sara, it's Mac, we have to talk."

"Yes, we do. I've been meaning to call you about some new information we just received. Meet me at my office."

Ten minutes later, Mac was at the Federal building in Newark. Agent Dillon met him by the reception desk and escorted him to her office area. The room contained eight desks, each with a two-drawer filing cabinet. Four agents were seated. The other work areas were empty.

"When you called it sounded like you had something you wanted to tell me," Agent Dillon said as she walked behind her desk and sat down.

"Maybe I do, maybe I don't," said Mac with a grin on his face. "You mentioned that you had some info *I* might be interested in. Do you want to go first?"

"Not really. What do you have?"

Mac leaned on the corner of her desk. "A little bird told me that Conroy is in Europe right now."

"Who told you?"

"An anonymous caller."

"Would that be one of your snitches from your old department?"

"Not important right now. What *is* important is that he is out of the country. More specifically, he's in Europe."

"That's a pretty big place, Europe," Agent Dillon said sarcastically. "Do you know where in Europe?"

"Not yet."

"Well, I do."

Mac pushed away from the desk. "What?! Were you planning on telling me, or is this another one of these 'need to know' jobs?"

Agent Dillon got up from her chair. "I'm telling you now! More than I can say about you. You've been holding back information from me since the first day we met. Right up to that time in Pennsylvania when you left me in the dust, then held out on me in Ohio. I'm not new here, Mac. And I'm not stupid. We've been playing this hide-and-seek game for too long. No more games. If we want to put this case to bed, we have to be totally honest with each other. So, I'll be up front with you with the information I can share. Will you do the same?"

Mac thought for a moment and said, "Agreed. I'll give you all the information that I, too, can share. The operative word being 'can.'

"So you can still hold out on me?"

"Sara, I understand there are things *you* can't tell me. CIs need to be protected, undercovers need to be protected, witnesses need to be protected, and certain information that can jeopardize a case or a life needs to be closely guarded. I've got those issues to deal with, too. But I'll never hold back on anything that can hurt you or your agency in any way. I will do all I can to honor our agreement. Remember, I did give you Darcy."

Agent Dillon sat back down. "Fair enough," she replied before gesturing for Mac to take a chair from the empty desk to her right.

He pulled the chair over, turned it around, and sat with his arms crossed over the back of it. "Shoot," he said.

Agent Dillon pulled out a case jacket from a drawer on her desk. She opened it and removed a photograph of a French-styled apartment complex. "Here's the scoop," she said. "Interpol has been surveilling this apartment on Finlay Street in Paris for some time."

"That's funny," Mac said.

"What's funny?"

"Finlay Street. Finlay's an Irish name. It's Gaelic. It means 'Fair Hero.' Something our guy Conroy is not."

"And you know Gaelic how?

"I'm Scottish. My former name was MacPherson."

"Former name?"

"A story for another time. It's just a funny name for a street where that mutt Conroy would live. Finlay is not Parisian, and our target is anything but a hero."

"Forget Finlay, Mac—Pherson. I'm sure there's a Parisian-named street somewhere in Dublin," Agent Dillon said. She then added, "Let's stay on point, okay?"

"Gotcha."

"Here's where we come in. We believe Interpol has made a connection with our target, Conroy, and an apartment on this Finlay Street. Their computer checks of bank accounts in France owned by Arab nationals disclosed several accounts in the name of Zeala Romandi and Malcolm Terrell. Ms. Romandi is a Syrian national with no reported employment. We don't know yet who this Malcolm Terrell is. We think we know. I'll explain in a minute. Meanwhile, Romandi made, and continues to make, various cash bank deposits into various accounts. Each deposit appears to correspond with a terrorist act, two of which were made within days of the murders in Scotland and Italy. Interpol had set up surveillance on her apartment, but until recently there has been little activity to report."

Mac perked up. "Until recently?"

"Yeah. Our boy Conroy pulled up to the apartment yesterday and entered the building. He hasn't been out since. Interpol made a positive I-dent on our guy. They had him entering the apartment back in November of last year, but were unable to make any connection with our guy's rampage here in the States or with the killings in Scotland and Italy until they tied bank deposits to the times of the murders. Now that they know he's been involved in various activities in the U.S., they're checking with us before deciding whether or not to move in on him and Romandi. The French National police have identified a 1996, 40-foot Mainship yacht docked along the Seine River at Port Grenelle, not far from the apartment in question. The yacht is reportedly owned by one Malcolm Terrell."

"So you're thinking Conroy is definitely using the alias Malcolm Terrell, and he's using this Syrian woman to hide his blood money and this boat to get around Europe?"

"We still haven't confirmed that yet. We're checking with several other outlets of information, but we are pretty sure that Malcom Terrell is another one of his covers. And, if that's proven the case, which we believe it will be, everything else falls into place—the girl, the money, the boat."

"Why not just grab the both of them? Interpol has two homicides they can solve, and a whole lot of money to confiscate."

"You know how this works, Mac. Get the bigger fish. Our European counterparts want to know who's supplying the money. If they take down Terrell, who we believe to be Conroy, and this woman Romandi, and confiscate the money, they might lose the bigger fish. They might be able to roll one or both of them, but odds are not good that they can get to the supplier in time. Once he hears of their arrests, he'll be in the wind or under the protection of an enemy country."

"Enemy country? We sure have our share, don't we? Anyway, what is Interpol or the Paris police planning to do at this point?"

"They want to follow both parties, see who their contacts are. Once they can put a fix on the money trail, they will take everyone down."

"Come on Sara. You say you're not new. You should know this game better than me. International politics. International intrigue.

International bullshit. That's what it is. Where else could the money be coming from? Who has that kind of cash and vested interest in terrorism against Europe, the U.S., and Western interests? The Iranians, oil-rich Arabs, the Russians, the Chinese? Interpol might find the culprits, but there ain't a hellava lot they're going to do about it."

"That's a lot of maybes."

"Well, here's one definite for you. What about that guy that Darcy fingered? Rudder."

"His name's Ruger, Aaron Ruger."

"Well, that's a solid lead."

"We only have Darcy's word. The powers to be want some corroboration before they give the signal to act on him."

"And who in particular makes that decision?" Mac asked.

"This decision will be made by a higher up. I can't give you a name. I don't have the name. Whoever makes the call will conveniently remove himself or herself from the trail. Think about it. When was the last time you ever saw a top politician or administrator take a fall for an operation gone bad? Their hands are always clean. We're the ones who need the lawyers to keep us out of jail. They're the ones who make the calls, then claim ignorance and moral outrage."

Mac laughed. "I never heard a Fed talk like that. It's refreshing. So, what's our plan?"

"For you and me . . . we wait."

"Wait for what? We know where Conroy is. We suspect this Aaron Ruger is supplying much, if not all, of the cash. We know where the cash is. I don't understand this 'wait and see' attitude."

"There might just be things here we aren't privy to, that only certain higher ups are aware of. Think what you will, but we're only pieces in this puzzle. There is surely a bigger picture here."

"That's the problem."

"What is?"

"The so-called 'higher ups.' They try to project an air of competence, of justice with their well-scripted speeches, their nuanced decisions regarding 'the bigger picture', but they don't have a clue. They know little about the viciousness of the enemy. How quickly these pariahs could strike. And why are the 'higher ups' so clueless about the intentions and actions of these animals? Because they're insulated behind all the protections we afford them. They live in their fantasy world believing they hold all the cards with their power. Meanwhile, the bad guys are blowing up the world and killing innocent people at will. This is a war we're in. Either they just don't get it or they don't give damn. Bigger picture, my ass!"

Agent Dillon leaned forward and put both her hands palms down on her desk. "So what would be *your* answer to this?"

Mac got up from his chair. "Simple. I'd act now! I'd take down those two in Paris, freeze the bank accounts, and arrest anyone who tries to get at the money. Then I'd drain those two of any information they have on who supplied the cash for deposit. If they corroborate the information from Darcy that the money came from Ruger, I'd have him killed. Or maybe just arrested and interrogated. He might be just another middleman. If the money originates with the Iranians, I'd let those Persians know, in no uncertain terms, that I know what they did. Payback's a bitch. I'd then take out one of their military or nuclear facilities with some smart bombs. If it's an Arab—surprise, surprise—I'd tell the country he came from to have him killed, or all foreign aid to them would be cut. If the perp was a Russian or a Chinese, I'd tell *that* country's leaders—those old Soviet and Maoist relics—unless they take action against that citizen, I have no choice but to fund factions seeking their overthrow. That's just starters."

Sara shook her head. "You make me laugh."

"You asked what I would do."

"What dream world are you living in? That would never happen."

"Bingo! That's what I'm telling you. What difference does it make who the supplier is? Nothing's going to be done. That is, of course, unless the supplier is some kind of lone wolf. Then, and only then, might the higher ups act outraged and send a cruise missile up his ass. But they'd first have to check to make sure they don't offend any country, group, or religion. We have to always be concerned about the political fallout. Take Iran or Syria, for example. Those maniacs have been supplying money to every Tom, Dick, and Harry terrorist group that wants to kill our people. So, how's that Ayatollah doing today? Or Syria's Assad? Last I looked, they were still living the lap of luxury. It's all bullshit!"

"Is that it?"

"No. You need someone with balls to take these big guns out. Think Kaddafi? Reagan bombed his palace, nearly killing the idiot. Haven't heard much from him lately, have we? Without someone having the balls to hit the big targets, though, the money supply can still be cut off, and it can be done without stepping on too many toes of world terrorist leaders. How? Destroy the organization from the ground up. Kill every terrorist you get your hands on, except, of course, the ones who want to give up information on manpower, strategies, tactics, and, yes, where the money supply is coming from. Shoot 'em or blow 'em up, makes no difference to me. The money people will run and hide once they know they're next on the list to be destroyed. And they *will* be next if one of your respected 'higher ups' has the balls to finish the job."

"Done yet?"

"One more thing. With all this talk about higher ups, puzzles, pictures, and money suppliers, I forgot to add a very important step in my plan."

"And what might that be?" Agent Dillon said matter-of-factly.

A hard look crossed Mac's face. "I'd put my money where my mouth is, starting with the interrogation of Conroy."

"How's that?" asked Agent Dillon.

"I'm a simple man, Sara. I'm not really cut out for your style of justice, rolling and releasing perps. Or the slick style of your brothers at The Firm, turning enemy spies into 'friendlies' for cash. I never cared for chumming up with liars, cheats, thieves, rapists, or murderers. So, as for Conroy, once I got through squeezing him for all he's worth, I'd kill him."

Agent Dillon got up from her desk and walked to the center of the room. Several agents watched her as she turned and faced Mac. In a loud voice she said, "Well, that's not going to happen under our watch. I've heard enough to know that it's time we go our separate ways, Mac. Several times my bosses wanted me to take you off this investigation. They didn't feel you could be trusted to comply with our authority. I defended you each time. I felt obligated to you for the work you've done so far, for turning in Darcy and for all the information you've provided us. A lot of lives were saved. My bosses reluctantly agreed to give you additional chances to prove your value to the Bureau. Sadly though, I now have to agree with them. We're done working together. Your style of doing business doesn't comport with the way we do business here. I'm afraid you've become a liability, and, since that's now the case, we'll have to part ways. I'm sorry, Mac. Thanks for all your help." She motioned for him to follow her to the office door. Before reaching out to shake his hand goodbye, Agent Dillon said, "I wish I could say 'It's been a pleasure.' I really do."

"Me too," Mac said with a smile as he shook her outstretched hand. "Hopefully, we will meet again under more agreeable circumstances." He turned and walked out the door.

Sometimes I hate this job, Agent Dillon mused.

Chapter Thirty-Six

March 16, 2004

It wasn't difficult for Mac to get a plane ticket on such short notice. There were always overbookings and last-minute cancelations. The downside was paying full price for the ticket. He knew he couldn't bring any weapons aboard the plane in his carry-on case, so it simply included his toiletries, a change of clothing, a map of Paris, and a mini-compact pair of 8x21mm binoculars. The bag he checked in at the gate contained additional clothing and a new set of kitchen steak knives, which he bought on the way home from the FBI office. He wrapped the boxed knives in gift paper, adding a red bow and a wedding card addressed to Zeala and Malcolm. He also placed in the check-in bag a box of clear plastic disposable hospital gloves, a small toolkit containing several plastic electrical zip straps, electrical tape, a wire cutter, box cutter, a flat-head screwdriver, Phillips screwdriver, pliers, and insulated gloves. He suspected the bag checkers were more interested in explosive devices being loading into the cargo bay of the plane, than they were about handheld tools that couldn't be accessed by the passengers. What a person did with a handheld weapon once the plane landed and all the passengers were off it was no concern to them. Besides, if he were to be questioned on why he was carrying a wedding gift and work tools, he could bluff his way through that. At least that was Mac's feelings.

Apparently the loading of the cargo went well. Mac did not get called to be present if or when baggage security opened his bag, and he wasn't quizzed on its contents. He thought to call Cheryl, but decided not to. She hadn't fully forgiven him for heading off to Paris to track down Conroy. Mac knew she wanted him to slow down a bit. He'd been there before, with his first wife, and that relationship did not end well. He wanted it to be different with Cheryl. He vowed that once this case was finished, he would settle down with her and the baby. No more wild and crazy adventures. He'd only take the easy cases—small thefts, cheating husbands, runaway kids; cases that don't deal with serial killers and international terrorists. That's what he was thinking when his cell phone rang.

"Hello."

"It's me, your wife."

"Hi, honey. I was just about to call you," Mac lied.

"No you weren't. I know you."

"Well, I was thinking about it and decided not to, because I knew you were still upset with me."

"That I am, but I still love you and worry about you. Please be careful, whatever you're planning on doing. Remember you have me and the baby to take care of now."

"I know. I'll be back as soon as I can. And when I do, I'll be spending all my time with you two. I won't take any high-profile cases anymore; just nice easy ones. I promise."

"Yeah, you say that now, but I know you. You won't change. This craziness is in your blood. Just do me a favor—be safe, and come back in one piece."

"Will do, honey. I love you."

"Love you, too."

Just as Mac disconnected the call with Cheryl, a voice came over the loudspeaker. "Flight 704 to Paris is now ready for boarding."

It took approximately 30 minutes for all passengers to be seated and all overhead compartments to be filled. Not long after,

Continental Flight 704 taxied down the Newark Liberty Airport runway. Within minutes, the sound of its turbo-jet engines filled the aircraft's interior with a high-pitch whirl. Racing down the runway, the airbus quickly reached for the sky. Once airborne, the large plane banked left. It crossed over lower Manhattan and headed out over the Atlantic Ocean. The plane, en route to the Charles de Gaulle Airport in Paris, France, was scheduled to land at 7:30 on the morning of March 17. Mac closed his eyes and tried to get as much rest as he could, knowing only too well the overnight flight and the time changes would take their toll on him. He planned to accomplish much once the plane landed, and, for that to happen, he would need all his wits about him.

The two Saudis had followed Conroy ever since he landed in Paris. The men were to keep a loose tail on him and wait for further orders. Currently they were standing under a street lamp a block away from the apartment complex on La Rue du Docteur Finlay where Conroy and his girlfriend were staying.

"We should get something to eat," Tamir, the taller Saudi said, as he stretched his arms above his head. "We've been here for too many hours and Ahmed has not moved from the apartment."

"The Royal Family will have us beheaded if we lose him," said Obaid, the shorter of the two. "You go and get something. I will move closer to the apartment. If anything happens when you are gone I will call you. If nothing happens while you are gone, I will get something to eat when you get back."

Tamir nodded, then walked in the direction opposite the apartment complex. Obaid remained under the street lamp. After a few minutes, he moved closer to Conroy's abode.

Before he reached the complex, his phone rang.

"Obaid," the caller said.

"Yes, this is me."

"Is Timar with you?" asked an intermediary.

"Yes, but he is at a different location at the moment."

"The plans have changed. Remember what we talked about before you left?"

"Yes, I remember."

"Let it be done."

"I understand," Obaid said.

He disconnected the call and dialed Tamir's number.

The phone rang three times before Tamir picked up. "Yes?' he asked in a muffled voice.

"Tamir?"

"Yes, it is me." His voice was much clearer this time. "I was just swallowing a bite of my sandwich." Then he asked, somewhat annoyed, "Why are you calling me? Are they leaving?"

"No, no one has left. We have some important things to talk about when you get back."

"Couldn't you have waited to tell me when I got back?"

Obaid bit his lip, "No, I could not," he said. "Our plans have changed. I thought you would want to know as soon as possible. It is what we have trained for."

Jason and Ann Strunella showed up at Cheryl's door. "We're here," they said in unison.

"Why?" asked Cheryl.

"Because Mac called before he left for the airport. He wanted us to stay with you in case you go into an early labor."

"I don't get it. If I start getting labor pains I could always call you and you could pick me up and take me to the hospital."

"Well, it would be quicker if we stay here. Plus, Mac is concerned about your mental state. He doesn't want you to be alone."

"Okay, come on in." Cheryl looked at Jason. "Mac and I talked about you coming over," then she turned to Ann, "but he didn't say anything about you. Don't you have your own kids to worry about?"

"They're with my mom. They'll be fine. They love it there. My mother spoils them rotten."

"All right," Cheryl said, "if you're going to stay, I'll put on some coffee."

The three of them went into the kitchen where they sat and talked for about an hour. As Ann got up to pour another cup of coffee, the doorbell rang. They looked at each other.

"Who could that be?" asked Jason.

"I don't know," said Cheryl.

Jason got up, pulled his .380 ACP Walther from his hip holster, and walked to the front door. Cheryl grabbed the telephone and held it in both her hands.

"Who is it?" asked Jason as he stood by the hinged side of the front door, pistol at the ready.

"Nick Polsani," came the response.

"Father?"

"Yes, I'm here to see Cheryl and Mac Taylor."

Jason quickly moved to open the door. Once Father Polsani stepped inside, Jason looked out into the front yard. Satisfied that no one had been following the priest, he reentered the house and double locked the door.

"For what do we owe the pleasure, Father?"

Cheryl and Ann entered the room.

"Father," said Cheryl with a concerned look on her face. "Is there a problem?"

"No, no. I stopped by to see how you and Mac have been, particularly you. I know you've had that incident. I want to make sure Jesus' flock is doing well. Where's your husband?"

"Mac left a little while ago. He's headed for Europe, Paris actually, on a case."

"I suspect I know what that's about. He's a driven man. But you do know that you are the most important thing to him."

"I wonder sometimes, Father."

"No, Mac is a good man who cares deeply about you, and about others. He just has a funny way of showing it."

Ann stepped closer to the priest, "Father, would you like some coffee? I just made a fresh pot."

"Yes, I'd like that."

For the next few hours, they sat and talked in the kitchen. Though the hour was not late, Father Polsani thought it best to say his goodnights. When Jason got up to escort him to the door, the priest noticed the butt end of the gun protruding from Jason's waistband. The two walked to the door while the ladies tidied up around the kitchen.

"I hear you're a police officer, Jason."

"That's right."

"Do you live far from here?"

"A bit, Father, but Annie and I will be staying with Cheryl until Mac returns, in case she goes into labor."

"And?"

"And what?"

"To protect her from another incident."

"Well, yeah," Jason said as he opened the front door. "We don't expect anything like that to happen again, but she doesn't need any more stress and worry, especially with Mac gone. She should be spending her time thinking about the baby."

Father Polsani stood for a moment by the opened door. "How can I help?" he asked.

"We should be fine, Father? I'm here, Annie's here. Cheryl will be okay."

"Well, I don't know if Cheryl told you or not, but Mac saved my life once. How do you repay a man for that? You do what little you can. There might not *be* much I can do—other than provide comfort and care for his wife—but if that's all I can do, it is what I will do. Please let me know what is going on. If Mac is not home when Cheryl goes into labor, promise me you'll call. I want to be at the hospital when she delivers the baby."

"Yes, of course. If that's what you want."

"That's what I want."

Chapter Thirty-Seven

March 17, 2004

Continental Flight 704 landed at Charles de Gaulle Airport several minutes before its 7:30 AM scheduled arrival time. During the flight, Mac was able to get his fill of airline food and several hours of shut eye. Once off the plane, he passed through customs, gathered up his bags, and headed to the car rental area. He was not particular in his choice of cars. He agreed to take whatever small or medium-sized vehicle was available. Mac ended up leasing a four-cylinder, white Peugeot 307. When he got to the car, he removed the gift of knives and toolkit from the larger bag and placed the bag in the trunk. Mac dropped the knives and toolkit on the front passenger floor and tossed the smaller carryon bag onto the front passenger seat. He then hopped into the driver's seat and turned on the ignition. Before putting the vehicle in gear, he adjusted the driver's seat and familiarized himself with all the gauges on the dashboard. He then took out the map of Paris, unfolded it, spread it across the steering wheel, and began to chart his way to La Rue du Docteur Finlay.

Mac wound his way through the city of Paris until he arrived at Finlay Street. He traveled down the one-way thoroughfare at a normal speed so as not to draw any attention. About three quarters of the way along the roadway he spotted the apartment building he remembered seeing in Agent Dillon's office. He drove past it, looped back, and parked on Rue Emeriau across from the complex. Mac reached down and picked up the box of knives. He opened it, took out one knife, and slipped it into the left pocket of his coat. He got out of the car and walked up the avenue. Mac remained for a moment on far side of the street, beneath where he suspected the hidden surveillance camera was placed.

After scanning the area, Mac crossed the street and passed the apartment complex. He made a mental note of the two front entrances. Both were glass paneled with steel or aluminum frames. He also noted that each street-side apartment unit in the building had a large walk-on balcony. As he moved past the building, Mac sensed he was being watched. He glanced down the road and saw two men sitting in a red Citroen. They both had eyes on him as he walked down the street. *A surveillance team,* he guessed. *But whose? From where?* After a second glance in their direction, Mac concluded the two men were Arab nationals. *That was not good,* he thought. *Why are they in Paris, sitting outside Conroy's apartment? Are they with him, protection for him, or are they out to do him harm? Either way, getting to Conroy is going to be trickier than I thought.*

Mac took out a baseball cap from his right coat pocket. He put the cap on his head and turned up the collar of his coat. He slipped on a pair of the clear plastic disposable gloves as he walked back to the front entrance of the apartment complex. The outer glass-paneled door was unlocked. He entered the hallway and scanned the list of tenants on the mailboxes. *Bingo!* The name ROMANDI UNIT 303 jumped out at him. Mac checked the glass-paneled interior door to determine the security of the building. That door *was* locked. *It could be popped,* he thought, *or the glass can be broken if need be.*

Realizing the timing for a break and entry was not right, Mac tipped his head down and walked out of the building, across the street, to his car. Entering his vehicle, Mac removed the plastic gloves and took out the mini-compact set of binoculars. He trained the binoculars on the front doors of the complex.

The two Arabs looked at each other.

"I do not like the looks of that man," Tamir said as he watched Mac walk out from the front door of the apartment complex."

"Nor I, Tamir. Nor I."

"What should we do? Kill him?"

Obaid laughed. "Tamir, what do you want to do, kill everybody? We don't know who that person is. Our job is to focus on Ahmed and the girl. That stranger could be anybody. He might even be working for the police. If so, there will be others watching. We cannot take the chance of killing anyone here. Besides, our main plan is a much better one. Before we do anything else now, I think it best that we go and plant the bomb."

No sooner had Mac placed the Citroen in his sights than the driver put the car in gear and proceeded to pull out into traffic. Mac quickly slid down as the car passed him. He pulled his car into the intersection and watched the Citroen continue along Finlay. Mac turned and raced down Finlay to Quai de Grenelle where he had seen the Citroen make a left turn. For concealment, Mac maintained a loose tail, keeping three cars between his Peugeot and the Citroen. The driver of the Citroen turned into a parking lot at the Port de Grenelle.

Mac drove past the Port so as not to attract any undue attention. At the first opportunity, he made a U-turn and pulled into a park across the street from the port. He shut off the car's engine. Mac quickly slipped a second knife, several plastic electrical ties, and a roll of electrical tape into his coat pockets. As the two Arabs got out of their car and headed toward the pier, Mac sat back and placed the binoculars to his eyes.

"How'd you injure your shoulder and leg?" Zeala asked Conroy.

"It was a car accident."

"Was anyone else injured?

"No, just me."

"What happened?"

"It's a long story. One for another time," Conroy replied. He then handed her a slip of paper. "Here, take this," he said.

"What is it?" she asked.

"It's a list of banks in Egypt and their routing numbers. I want you to begin transferring money from our French accounts to these Egyptian banks. Only make one transfer a week. And each transfer has to be fewer than ten thousand American dollars, so do the euro to dollar conversion before you transfer any money. I think the governments track any money transfers over that amount. I'm not sure, but I don't want to take any chances."

"You have five banks listed here. Do you care which bank gets what amount?"

"No. Just keep the transfers going to different banks. Don't transfer money to the same bank twice in a row. Can you handle that?"

Zeala nodded and said, "But of course."

"I'm going to take two thousand of those euros in the other room. You can use the rest for food and expenses."

"Where will you be going?"

"I'll be taking the boat back to Yambu. It'll take me some time to get there, but you'll be busy the next few months, anyhow, transferring money."

"And when I'm finished?"

"When you make the last transfer, call me. I'll come get you and bring you back home with me."

"Promise?"

"I Promise."

"One more question, then I'll leave you alone, my love. When will you be leaving?"

"Tomorrow morning, early, before sunrise."

"Aah, we still have tonight," Zeala said as she put her arms around Conroy and kissed him on the cheek.

"All night," Conroy whispered back in her ear.

Tamir took a package from the trunk of the Citroen. It was approximately one-foot square and six inches deep. The package contained explosive material, a fuse, cell phone, and wire contacts. He placed the package under his right arm and walked to the Mainship lashed in its berth. Obaid, the lookout, got out of the car and leaned on the hood.

Mac sat low in his seat, maintaining an "eyeball" on the two men.

Tamir casually slipped onto the platform deck of the boat. He took out a screwdriver from his coat pocket and popped the lid of the tackle box on the aft deck. He placed the package inside the box and closed it. Tamir looked across the parking lot and nodded to Obaid.

When Tamir and Obaid got back in the car, Obaid asked, "Any problem with the box?"

"No. I broke the latch. It still stays closed though. If he looks closely at it, he will notice it's broken."

"Fortunately, he won't live long enough to notice," Obaid said with a smile.

"Now we just have to worry about the girl. If she does not go with him on his boat, we will have to kill her in the apartment or out on the street in a private place."

"That will not be easy after we blow up the boat. Too much attention and investigation."

"Can we kill her first, without Ahmed knowing?" Tamir asked.

"Only if she comes out of the apartment alone. He will have to wonder where she is. That might make him decide to leave here. Then, once he gets on the boat, 'Boom!'"

"Yes, I understand, but we have to make sure we are watching him when he gets on the boat. If we don't, and he finds the bomb first and throws it overboard, they will not be happy with us. Ahmed is not stupid. He will find out who did it. When he does, we are all in for trouble."

"You worry too much, Tamir. All will go well. If the girl leaves the apartment first, we kill her. If Ahmed leaves first and goes to the boat, we kill him. I am not worried about the girl if Ahmed dies first. She is not a big threat. We will kill her, eventually."

Chapter Thirty-Eight

March 17, 2004—PM

The sun had set, leaving a reddish glow in the western horizon. The two Arabs kept their vigilant watch on the apartment complex. Mac had just finished eating a sandwich he bought from a vendor down the block from the apartments. Inside apartment 303, Conroy sat at the kitchen table counting out the euros he was to take with him on his trip back to Saudi Arabia. Zeala took some of the euros from the table and placed them in her pocketbook. She then went to the closet and removed her coat from the hanger.

"I must go to the store," she said. "I have nothing for you for breakfast."

"Good thinking. I should have a big breakfast," Conroy replied. "I'll be on the water all day. And while you're at the store, pick up cold cuts and drinks. I'll make some sandwiches for lunch."

Zeal kissed Conroy, grabbed her pocketbook, and headed for the door of the apartment. "I won't be long," she said, closing the door behind her.

Outside, Tamir and Obaid took turns watching the entrances to the apartment complex.

"There she is!" Obaid said to Tamir who was resting in the passenger seat.

"Are you sure?" he asked, rubbing his eyes.

"Yes, yes. There she is walking down the street. Do you see her?"

"Now I do," said Tamir. "I wonder where she could be going."

"No matter. Just do what you have to do, what we came here for."

Tamir got out of the car and felt for the knife in his front right pocket. He crossed the street and walked at a fast pace, hoping to close the gap between himself and Zeala before he lost her around the corner.

When Zeala reached the specialty shop on the corner of Finlay and Nelaton, she turned right. Tamir was now only thirty yards away from her. Nelaton had apartments above various businesses on the left and apartments set back from the street on the right. In front of the apartments on the right was a long row of hedges, approximately three feet high. Once the street lights came on, all the businesses closed and the area emptied of pedestrians. The street was strangely quiet considering the location. Straight ahead was a picturesque view of the Eiffel Tower.

As Tamir got within ten feet from Zeala, he reached into his pocket and gripped the knife. He planned to stab her between her shoulder blades, piercing her heart, then quickly tossing her over the hedges. Seven, five, three feet behind Zeala, Tamir took out the knife and brought his arm back.

Suddenly he felt a grip on his wrist. As he turned, Mac struck him twice with the heel of his left hand, once on his temple directly below his right eye, and again on the back of his neck where his spinal cord connected to his skull. Zeala turned in time to see Tamir drop to the pavement, unconscious.

"Are you okay?" Mac asked.

Zeala couldn't talk at first. She held her hand to her mouth and nodded her head yes.

"Do you know him?"

"No, no," she said. "And I don't know you. What is going on? Are you the police? Is he a mugger?"

"No, Zeala. He was sent to kill you and your boyfriend."

"How do you know my name? You must be a policeman."

"That doesn't matter right now. Had I not stopped him, you would now be dead. That knife that's lying there had your name on it."

"But why would he want to kill me? If you're not the police, we should call them now, right now!" she said.

"I don't think Malcolm would like that."

"Who?"

"That's right, you like to call him Ahmed. And I know him as Dirk Conroy. Malcolm Terrell is just another alias. But you know that. Rather than discuss the history of your boyfriend, though, let's get away from here before this mutt comes to, or someone spots us here."

"I'm not going anywhere with you."

"Suit yourself. Without me you'll be dead before you ever step foot back in your apartment. There are others wanting you and Ahmed dead."

"And you don't?"

"Maybe I do, maybe I don't, but we're not going to find out here. Let's go." Mac pulled out a pair of clear latex gloves and placed them on his hands. He then bent down, picked up the knife, and went through Tamir's pockets. Like most assassins, Tamir didn't carry any ID on him. "Don't think about running, Zeala," Mac said as he felt around Tamir's ankles for any other weapons. "Others will find you, if not me. You're better off with me. I have no intention of hurting you."

Mac got up, grabbed Zeala by the elbow, and led her by the arm back toward the apartment complex.

Obaid drove down Finlay Street. He knew something was wrong when he saw Zeala walking with the man he and Tamir had seen earlier in the day. Obaid sped around the corner onto Nelaton Street. He slowed and looked down both sides of the roadway. It was then he spotted Tamir lying on the sidewalk. He stopped his car and got out. He ran to where Tamir was lying. Obaid noticed that although Tamir was unconscious, he was still breathing. Obaid propped him up and rubbed his head and face.

"Wake up, Tamir! Wake up!" he said between clenched teeth.

Tamir's eyelids began to flutter.

"Get up!" Obaid ordered. "You should be ashamed. How could you not have killed her? You're bigger, stronger. You have a knife. This other man, where could he have come from? And what is his purpose?"

Tamir sat up and looked around. "Where is my knife?"

"I see he not only knocked you out and protected the girl, but he also took your knife. This is not good."

"I will take joy in killing this man when we find him."

"I've just seen him with the girl walking back to the apartment building," Obaid said. "Soon you will get your chance to avenge what he has done to you."

Zeala and Mac arrived back at the apartment complex. Entering the outer door, Mac said, "Take out your key and open the inside door."

She did as she was told. "What are you going to do? Are you going to hurt me or Ahmed?"

"I'm going to get some information. I can get it the hard way or the easy way. Which way depends on you and your boyfriend."

The two turned down the hall and entered the elevator. Mac pressed the button for the third floor. "You do live on the third floor, don't you?" he asked.

"Yes, apartment 303."

The elevator door opened on the second floor. A woman was standing there about to get on. "We're going up," Mac said in English while holding the knife to Zeala's back.

The woman looked confused. She backed away as the door closed. Mac pressed the third-floor button a second time. When the elevator opened on the third floor, Zeala and Mac got out and stood in the hallway. Mac noticed the exit stairway was about twenty feet to his left, just past the trash chute door.

"This way," Zeala said pointing down the hall to the right.

When they arrived at 303, Mac pulled out the cap from his coat pocket, placed it on his head with the brim down, just above his eyes, and stood behind Zeala. "Open the door like you usually do. And don't go running into the room. I don't want any surprises. I don't want to hurt you, but if you give me any cause to, I will."

Zeala unlocked the door and pushed it open. The two moved into the dimly lit foyer. With his right hand, Mac closed the door to the apartment, but did not let it click shut.

Conroy was still sitting at the kitchen table, reading a sea chart map. "That didn't take you—" was all he could get out before looking up and realizing that Mac was behind Zeala, now with the knife held to her throat.

Conroy reached around his back and pulled out his 9mm Browning automatic handgun.

"Put the gun down or I slit her throat!" Mac said as he pushed farther into the room.

Conroy hesitated before placing the gun on the table well within reach.

"Push the gun away from you. Now!"

Conroy smiled. "That ain't going to happen. Who are you? Come on in, let's talk. Remember, I'm the one with the gun."

"And I'm the one with the knife to your girlfriend's throat. So I guess we're even."

"Not really. I'll humor you for a while, but—." He stopped in mid sentence. He wanted to finish by saying *if I have to kill the two of you I will.* Conroy knew he needed Zeala to transfer all the money into the bank accounts he set up in Egypt. After she completed that task, he was planning on killing her anyway. But for now, he needed her alive.

"But what?" Mac asked.

"But why don't you put down the knife so we can talk? I'll push away the gun. See." Conroy then pushed the handgun across the table . . . still within reach.

"No, let's talk like this," Mac said. "Let's talk why there's a pile of money on the table in front of you? Or why you go by three different names? How about why you've been traveling between the U.S. and France under one of your aliases? And the million-dollar question, why there are two men outside, one of whom just tried to kill your girlfriend?"

"Who are you? And what business is it of yours?" Conroy said.

"We've met before. You know who I am. I'm here for some information. Information you have."

"I know you? Your voice sounds familiar. Come closer, tip that hat back. Let me see who you are. And the information you want. If I give it to you, then what?"

"I get the information I want, I leave you and the girl alone." Mac lied.

"Really, now, you expect me to believe that?" Conroy said. "Regardless, I'll play your game. You don't want to come here into the kitchen, fine. What do you want to know?"

"For starters, where does all that money on the table come from? Who's supplying you with the cash?"

"And you need to know this, why?"

"Let's just say I don't want to see you hurt." Mac lied again. "Whoever is paying you might now want to kill you. There have been two Arabs outside your apartment for the last day or so planning on killing you and her." Mac made a head motion toward Zeala.

"So you're telling me you're here to help me." Conroy smiled. "That's rich."

"A name. I need a name."

"You want a name. Here's one. Ortez, Eduardo Melo Ortez."

"You mean the one you killed, cut up, and left in a Bayonne,

New Jersey park."

A stern look came over Conroy's face. "We're not going to play this game much longer. Either move closer and let me see your face or tell me who you are. And let go of Zeala. We can handle this like men. You're not much of a man threatening a woman."

"You know me Conroy. Those bullets you took in the swamp were mine."

Conroy realized he was now facing the man he was hired to kill in New Jersey. He reached across the table for his gun. Mac was quicker. He took the knife from Zeala's throat and threw it, hitting Conroy in his chest just as he picked up the handgun. A shot went off, but the bullet found a home in the ceiling. Mac reached into his pocket and pulled out the steak knife. A snap from his wrist and the knife found a home in Conroy's stomach.

Zeala fled into the living room on her left. Conroy, clutching the knife in his stomach tried to get out of his chair. The knife in his chest had punctured a lung. He began to wheeze. Mac picked up a kitchen chair and cracked it over Conroy's head. The serial killer hit the floor like a rock. Mac picked up the gun that fell from Conroy's hand.

"Don't go near that door!" Mac yelled as he saw Zeala moving toward it. He then walked to it and looked out into the hallway to see if the gunshot had attracted any attention. An elderly woman was standing down the hall looking at him. Mac quickly closed and locked the door.

"Hopefully, no one called the police," Mac said to Zeala who was now sitting on the floor in shock over what had just occurred. Seeing the condition she was in, he didn't wait for a response.

Conroy began to come around. The wheezing continued. "I need a doctor" was all he was able to get out.

Mac grabbed him by the collar of his shirt. "You say I'm not much of a man for threatening women. There's your woman right there. She's going to be fine. You made the big mistake of going after *my* woman, my pregnant wife. You're not much of a man, are you? You're paying now. I might be getting soft, but there is one way you can come out of this alive. The money," Mac said. "Where's the money coming from?"

Conroy looked at Mac, realizing his only chance of survival was to answer his question. "Two," he said between the heavy wheezing.

"What two?"

"Rue . . . garrrr."

"Ruger?"

Conroy nodded his head yes.

"Who else?"

"Per . . . ence Ahhhh mmml."

"Prince who?" Mac asked.

"A . . . mel."

"Prince Amel?"

Again Conroy nodded yes. Then, as his eyes closed and the wheezing slowed to a whisper, a sudden death rattle shook his body. Conroy exhaled his last breath.

At that moment the sound of sirens was heard in the distance.

Mac looked at Zeala seated on the floor, her arms locked around her knees. "The police should be here any moment," he said. "They'll help you." He then rushed toward the door, unlocked it, threw it open, and ran down the hall. He took the stairs two at a time until he came to the main lobby. Seeing the flashing lights of a patrol unit pull up in front of the building, Mac tore down the hall to the rear of the complex. He pushed open the emergency exit door and found himself looking into a large parking lot. Once outside the building, he decided to head west to Rue Saint-Charles, then south hoping to find a cut-through to where his Peugeot was parked on Rue Emeriau. At that moment, a 2-door, blue Renault pulled up alongside him.

The driver, a Ukrainian male in his 40s, said, "Get in, Investigator Taylor!"

Chapter Thirty-Nine

March 17, 2004—PM

Mac looked at the driver of the Renault "How do you know me?"

"Get in the car. We don't have a second to spare. The police will be here any moment."

As Mac slipped around the other side of the Renault and got in, he said, "If you're not the police, who are you?"

The driver quickly stepped on the gas pedal and drove the vehicle out of the parking lot. As he drove down the block, a police car, lights blazing, sirens blaring, zipped past him.

"Close, my friend. That was close. Getting out of there in time saves us a lot of explaining."

"What are you talking about?" Mac asked as he took off the plastic gloves and placed them in his pocket. "And why do you care what happens to me?"

"A friend of yours asked us to keep an eye on you. You are a tough guy to keep up with."

Mac leaned back on the head rest. "How about an explanation?" he said. "I don't know who you are, who you work for, or what friend wanted you to keep an eye on me."

"For starters my name is John. I work for your country. That's all you need to know about me right now. Your friend, Agent Sara

Dillon, reached out for you this morning. When she learned you flew out of Newark, she checked the flight manifests. She saw that you were flying into Paris and knew it could only be for one reason. That's when she called the agency who hired me and several others. We've been tailing you since you got off the plane."

"And the video coverage at the apartment?"

"No, that's not us. I'm sure your government will be good enough to have those tapes buried somewhere deep, not to see the light of day, except for a select few."

"You seem to know a lot. Who are you working for?"

The Ukrainian ignored the question.

"I liked that move on Nelaton Street."

"You saw that?" Mac said. "If I hadn't knocked him out, he would have killed the girl. You wouldn't have stopped that?"

"Investigator Taylor. The girl didn't fit into our assignment. We did not get involved with the incident on Nelaton Street for a very good reason We're covert. Mission oriented. We like to stay that way."

"I thought you boys at the CIA were more compassionate than that."

"We're not CIA. Our group takes contracts from many different countries and organizations. In this matter, you are our mission. We are concerned about your safety for two reasons. First, because Agent Dillon and your country apparently want you well and alive. And second, because you have information on your boy, Ahmed. Information he has probably given to you regarding others in his sphere of influence. Possibly, high-ranking officials. "

"Conroy."

"What?"

"He's Conroy to me."

"Conroy, Ahmed, Terrell; no matter. We need to know what you know."

Mac sat forward in the passenger seat and put his hand on the dash for balance as the Ukrainian driver made a sharp right onto the highway leading south.

Mac reached in and clutched a knife he kept in his other coat pocket. "And why should I trust you?" he said.

"Because I'm on your side."

"You're on whoever's side pays you. You've made that clear."

"And that happens to be your side in this case. They need to know who . . . Conroy . . . is dealing with. If you wish to speak with Agent Dillon, I could arrange that."

"Yes, I would like that. In the meantime, where are you taking me?"

"To a safe place, outside of Paris. If you would please, give me the keys to your Peugeot parked on Emeriau Street. One of my men will bring it to where we're staying."

Reluctantly, Mac took out the car key and handed it to the Ukrainian.

The Paris Police surrounded the apartment complex. The first responders entered the building and climbed the stairs to the third floor where there had been reports of gun fire. An old woman was standing by her door at apartment 305. She was pointing to 303. The officers entered apartment 303 and observed Conroy lying on the floor in the kitchen with two knives stuck in his body and blood covering his face where Mac struck him with the chair. Zeala was holding the hand of his lifeless body and mumbling words in a language the arriving officers did not understand. They searched the other rooms as a second team entered the apartment and started administering first aid to Conroy and Zeala.

Boom!

Just then the Mainship yacht exploded.

Within seconds, flames engulfed the entire deck of the boat. Once the heat and flames reached the fuel tanks, a large second explosion occurred. The flames curled and reached a hundred feet in the air.

It was then that a red Citroen with two Arabs pulled out of a parking space across the street in the park and headed south along Quai de Grenelle. The car and its occupants soon disappeared.

Everyone on Finlay Street heard the loud explosion several blocks away by the river. Because of their close proximity to the river, two police cars, originally assigned to the apartment complex scene, were redeployed to the explosion site. Fire department vehicles and a second ambulance were also dispatched to that location.

Police and paramedics at the apartment building on Finlay Street continued with their investigation and first aid. Zeala was able to give the police a cursory description of Mac as the paramedics worked, in vain, on Conroy. Both Zeala and Conroy were transported to the nearest hospital. Doctors at the hospital noted in the intake form that the patient known as Malcolm Terrell was dead on arrival. (The medical examiner's report completed days later listed the death of Malcolm Terrell, aka Ahmed Sal Mohammed and Dirk Conroy as the result of exsanguinations, specifically, massive hemorrhaging in the chest cavity and stomach.)

Zeala was taken to a quiet conference room in the hospital where she was told of Conroy's death and interviewed for several hours. She had little information to tell the police about Mac, other than how he saved her life several minutes before forcing her into the apartment, confronting her boyfriend, and killing him. When asked who tried to kill her on the street and why, Zeala had no answer. Nor did she have any answers as to why Mac wanted to kill her boyfriend.

"He called him a name I didn't recognize," she said.

"Your boyfriend, Malcolm Terrell?"

"Yes, Ahmed. He called him Connerly or Conroy. But that's not his name."

"Did Malcolm, er Ahmed, correct him?"

"No, he just got angry."

The detective moved closer to Zeala. "Did this fight have anything to do with all that money sitting on the table?"

"I don't think so. Otherwise, the man who stabbed Ahmed would have taken some or all of it."

"Well, maybe after that gun went off and we were called, the attacker decided to get out as soon as he could, deciding not to take the money."

Zeala shook her head. "No, I don't think so. He asked Ahmed where the money came from. This man, attacker as you say, wanted some information about suppliers."

"Drug dealers?"

"I don't know."

"Do you know how Ahmed made his money?"

"He told me he dealt in the exchange of money, mostly in dollars and euros. That's why there was so much cash lying around."

The detective sat back and folder his arms. "Miss Romandi, none of what you are telling me makes sense. A man you've never known, nor met, saves your life and then tries to take it. He seems to know Ahmed and Ahmed knows him, but he knows Ahmed by another name, a third name, one you've not heard him called before. And this attacker only wanted the names of Ahmed's suppliers. Suppliers of what? Money? Ahmed transacts money, but not his own? Suppliers give him money to transact? And this attacker wants to know who these people are? Enough to kill a man. It's not making sense to me. I'll tell you what's going to happen next. I have an investigator from the GAFI coming to speak with you. His organization is the Groupe d'action financiere. They are headquartered here in Paris. They investigate money laundering and other forms of criminal financial activity in our country and abroad. They have access to all bank accounts and other bank transactions in France, and they work with other countries regarding the transfer of funds. I have no doubt he will know what all the money found at the time of the assault is about. I suggest you cooperate fully with him."

Zeala was transported to Paris Police headquarters and placed in a small interview room. Agent Pierre Latoure of the GAFI entered the room.

"How are you, Miss Romandi?"

"Do you really have to ask after all I've been through?"

"I was just being courteous. Excuse me. I see I should be more direct with you."

"No, I'm sorry. I'm just upset over all that has happened. How may I help you?"

"Ahmed is dead. He was involved in major criminal activity. You lived with him. You deposited money for him. That makes you complicit in his activities."

"I had no idea he—"

Agent Latoure put his hand up to cut her off. "It does not matter whether or not you were aware of the nature of his activities. The fact that you helped to execute them is a criminal act. Tell me, how did you think he accumulated so much money?"

"He said he was a money exchange investor. There's a name for it. He told me the name but I can't remember it. I've never heard of it before."

"The form of investing you are talking about is arbitrage trading. He's an arbitrageur. At least that's what he portrayed himself to be with you. We have much evidence, though, to the contrary. So much so that all your joint accounts and any other property owned by you and Mr. Conroy—I'm sorry, I was told you call him Ahmed—will be frozen, and once those assets are determined to be the ill-gotten gains of criminal activity, which they will be, they will be confiscated by our government."

"Blessed be Allah, what was he involved in? I loved Ahmed. He provided for me. I was going to move to Saudi Arabia and live with him after all the money in our accounts were sent to banks down there."

"How were you to do that?"

"I would send small amounts to several different banks over a period of time.

"And that didn't make you think Ahmed might have been acting outside the law? That he was using you?"

"No, he loved me. I was going to live with him."

"The man was a serial killer. I doubt you would have lived long after making the last transfer of money."

"That's not true. He loved me."

"You can keep believing that, if it makes you feel better. I'm here to find out how much you know about his involvement with foreign agents, terrorist groups, and homicide victims."

"Believe me, I don't know anything about what you just said. This whole thing is a nightmare."

"And it's about to get worse. You will be charged with violation of our terrorism statutes, conspiracy as well as complicity. If convicted, you will be put away in one of our prisons for many, many years."

Zeala began to shake. Her eyes tearing up, she cried out, "I didn't do anything but deposit money!"

Agent Latoure remained stoic. "That's enough to get you a long prison term."

Before Zeala could react, Agent Latoure said, "But it doesn't have to be that way."

Zeala looked up. "What do you mean?"

"If you take a polygraph to prove to us that you do not have complicit knowledge of any of Ahmed's criminal activities, we might be able to offer you a plea deal."

"No prison time?"

"No prison time."

"That's it, just take a polygraph?"

"Well, it's not that simple," Latoure said. "Where are you from in Syria?"

"In the North, Aleppo. Is that important?"

"So you speak Aleppan Arabic."

"Yes, I do."

"Do you speak any other languages?"

"Some Turkish."

"Good."

"Is that it?"

Agent Latoure pursed his lips. "For the moment. We will need to talk extensively about Ahmed. After that, there might be a way for you to prove your loyalty to France."

Zeala looked perplexed. "How do I do that?"

"Miss Romandi, we have many mosques in Paris," Latoure said. "It would be awfully helpful if we knew what was being said in them. Should you agree to help us in that regard, I'm sure a judge would see that you are loyal to France, and, therefore, he'd be willing to waiver any time behind bars."

Chapter Forty

March 18, 2004

"Agent Dillon. May I help you?"

"Agent Dillon, how are you? Private Investigator Taylor on this end."

"Mac, it's good to hear from you. I hope you're still in one piece. Once I found out you left for Paris, I was furious. But then I decided to do what I could to see that you were safe."

"Really, Sara? I know what's going on here."

"Oh you do, do ya. Then, tell me, 'what's going on here."

"I should have seen it coming."

"Seen what coming?"

"When you showed me the photo where Conroy was staying, right down to the street name. You knew I could find that apartment building in Paris, and that I'd find Conroy. You feds don't give up much. Why would you have shown me that information?

"Because we were working together," Agent Dillon fired back.

"Come on. I know enough about how you guys—excuse me, in this case, gals—operate. Everything is on a 'need to know' basis. Your boss wouldn't let you clue me in on that information unless there was a reason. You knew I wanted Conroy dead. That after he tried killing my wife, I would stop at nothing to get him. You also knew that I was going to get the name or names of his money suppliers. Which, by the way, I had. And, you knew you could disavow any knowledge of your agency working with me. I'd just be a renegade, a vigilante. Maybe even a lone wolf. Yeah that's what your agency might call me. That's what all that talk was about in your office. If I remember correctly, you said to me something like, 'Now you've become a liability. We'll have to part ways. We're done working together.' You said that in front of several agents, agents who could corroborate your statement that I was no longer working with your agency. I was acting alone. Saves face for your gang should things go bad."

"Boy, you think you have us all figured out."

"Yeah, it didn't all make sense until this guy you people hired to watch me said one thing that got me to thinking."

"And what might that be?"

"When I asked him about the surveillance tapes on Conroy's building, he said, 'Your government will take care of those recordings.' Why should *my* government have anything to do with it, unless *we* were doing the surveillance? Or, at least had a hand in it. In that case, you were aware of Conroy's involvement from the beginning of this investigation, when you saw him entering the building several months ago. You knew through financial records that he was also going by the name Malcolm Terrell. I couldn't figure out, though, why he wasn't stopped from flying out of Canada, if he was using that alias."

"And there ends your guessing game," Sara said.

"No, not really. After I gave it some thought, I realized Conroy was—to draw an analogy once more—Nunzie the Wolf in the Antanucci organization you wanted to take down. You needed to be sure who the kingpins were, the money suppliers in this case. You didn't know whether to trust Darcy on his fingering of Ruger. Plus, you had your suspicions about a member of the Saudi Royal Family, but you couldn't confirm which one sent a plane for Conroy who was languishing in Canada. I just have one question that needs to be answered."

"What's that?"

"Why me? Why'd your agency come looking for me? I know your bosses don't like me."

"You're right about that, my bosses don't like you. It's because of your way of doing business. And that's the truth. But they, we, needed you. We needed Darcy. You had him as a client. We didn't want to spook him. We knew we could hold your license over your head and that you'd more than likely agree to cooperate."

"Did you see, or care about my wife, that she almost got killed?"

"Honestly, I don't think anyone in my agency saw that coming. And no one wanted it to happen. But since it did, the higher-ups thought it could be turned to our advantage. They overrode my immediate boss's objections and decided to keep you on. To some of them up top, it's all just a chess game. You were the knight. You could jump over people and get the information we needed.

"When you called and said you had some information on Conroy, it seemed like the right time to bring you in and take a look at where he was hiding. How he slipped out of Canada, we still don't know. We couldn't find any of his known aliases on scheduled flights out of Canada, or the U.S. for that matter. We suspect a Saudi corporate jet took him out of the country. Which family member commissioned the flight is still a mystery. We're holding off on contacting the Saudi government or Saudi officials to get that information. We don't want the Saudis to shut down our investigation into the charter, or possibly give the target a heads up, if we could find out through other, more secure, means, who in the Royal Family is the bad apple. That's why we wanted to find out who the supplier was through Conroy. Worst-case scenario, Conroy dies without giving us a name or names. Then, we go to the Saudis to help with the investigation. Best-case scenario, Conroy dies, but not before spilling the beans. So, I'm told through channels that you did get the names?"

"Yes, I did."

"And?"

"And I would have given it to the fine young gentleman acting as my bodyguard here in France, but I'm afraid if I gave it to him or to you right now over the phone, I might not make it back home. My usefulness will be over."

"Don't be so cynical Mac. I might have been part of a plan to deceive you—for the good of the country, I might add—but you are always safe with us and the people our sister agency abroad contracts out to. Trust me."

"There's little I trust these days. And contracts can work both ways, depending on the client and which one of them puts forth the highest bid. I will do one thing for you, though. I'll meet you halfway. Darcy was right. Conroy confirmed that Ruger is one of two suppliers. That should be enough to take him down. The only downside is that Conroy won't be around to testify against him. So, it might be best to take Ruger out."

"What do you mean Conroy won't be around to testify? I was told he was taken to a hospital."

"Well, last time I spoke with him, he had trouble breathing. I think he had respiratory problems. I'd be surprised if he pulled through."

"We'll deal with that issue when you get back. I won't discuss that now even over this secured line. Let's get back to the other supplier. Who is he?"

"The name of the Saudi royal will have to wait 'til I get back to the States. Nothing is going to be done with him anyway. That's my guess. And I need to know my PI license is still good. Besides, I'm going to need some money to cover all the expenses I've incurred for the protection of our country."

"You're just lucky you're still on this side of the grass," Agent Dillon said. "You'll get some money, but I need a name, Mac, and I need it now, not tomorrow or the next day."

"Fine. His name is Amel, Saudi Arabian Prince Amel."

"To be honest, I've never heard of him," Agent Dillon responded. "The Saudi royalty is quite large. I think there are over 1,000 relatives in the king's family."

"I'm happy having just one relative," Mac said. Then, after a moment's thought, he followed with, "soon to be two."

"If you want, I can call her and tell her you're all right?"

"Don't bother. You've done enough," Mac said sarcastically. Before hanging up on Agent Dillon, he added, "I'll handle it."

Cheryl sat in Mac's chair and spread her hands across his desk.

"Miss him?" Ann asked as she walked into the office.

"Yeah. I should have known I wouldn't've been able to slow him down."

Ann smiled. "Leopards don't change their spots, Cher. Mac loves you, you know that. But he's one of those guys who's not going to give up the game. I don't know what goes on inside the heads of guys like that. Jason's a bit like that, too. Not as bad as Mac, but still, he likes the game."

"What is it about this 'game' you're talking about?"

"It's the energy, the excitement, the danger. But it's also good things, like fairness, justice, protecting the innocent, the vulnerable."

"And don't forget vengeance," Cheryl said.

"Well, one man's vengeance, is another man's justice."

"How do you know the difference? Mac lost his daughter and the love of his first wife because of his obsession with the job. I don't want to lose him, but he's got to realize a man's responsibility is not only to God and Country. He has a responsibility to take care of his family."

Ann came around the desk and picked up Cheryl's hand. "He knows that. He'll be back soon. I'm sure of it."

Just then the telephone on the desk rang. Both Cheryl and Ann stared at it. A moment later, Cheryl picked it up.

"MC Investigations. Cheryl speaking. How may I help you?"

"Hi, honey, it's me."

Cheryl sat straight up. "Mac? You sound so distant."

"It must be the connection. I'm calling from France."

Cheryl put her hand over the phone and, with a smile on her face, said to Ann, "It's Mac. He's fine. I think."

She took her hand off the phone and said, "Are you okay?"

Mac chuckled. "Yeah, I'm fine. Hopefully, I'll be home in a few days. There are several things left to be tied up here, but the rough stuff is over. I'm looking forward to coming home and being with you and the baby. How are you feeling?"

"So so. I miss you. It would be nice if you could be here when I go into labor. My due date is a few weeks away, but I guess I can go anytime."

"I'll do my best, honey. Meanwhile, please make sure someone is there with you."

"I'll be fine. I'm not an invalid. I'm pregnant. That's a healthy condition. It's not like I have a disease. Besides, I have a telephone. Family, friends, and the police are just a phone call away."

"I know. I've heard all that before from you, but I'd feel better if someone was with you . . . for a lot of reasons."

"Don't worry. Ann and Jason are staying with me. And Father Polsani has been stopping by every day to see how I'm doing, or if I need anything."

"Why is he doing that?"

"He said you saved his life once and that, although he could never pay you back fully, he owed it to you to help us—you, me, and the baby—in whatever way he can."

"That guy is too much."

"*That* guy is in good with the Lord," Cheryl shot back. "Don't knock him,"

"I know, I know. Just rest, and I'll see you in a couple of days."

"When?"

"I don't know when, but it should be soon. I'll be out of here as soon as I can."

"I love you."

"Love you, too."

Mac hung up the phone. He looked at the Ukrainian seated across from him and asked, "Why do I have to wait several days before I get out of here?"

"Many reasons. Investigators will be checking airport security cameras to see who fits the description of the guy Zeala gave a composite of to the police. Two, you might have left prints on those knives stuck in your boy, other prints possibly on a chair, table, door knob, and any other place you might have touched in the apartment. The French will eventually get your prints from the U.S. government. I'm sure between your police records, PI records, and possibly criminal records—weren't you arrested in New York State recently? Too soon for an expungment. Anyway, I'm sure your fingerprints are all over AFIS.* Three, if you're IDed, we'll have to have Mac Taylor disappear and another person take his place."

"Say what?"

"We have to create a new set of records for you. A new name with a personal history. These things don't happen overnight. It takes a few days to create a whole new history of a person."

"First off, I don't think the girl got a good look at my face. It was dark on the street. Then I walked behind her most of the time. In the apartment, I was behind her with a knife to her throat. She went into a bit of shock when the shit hit the fan. She shouldn't remember a whole hell of a lot, maybe my voice or my height, color of skin. I'd be surprised if she recalled any physical details. Secondly, unless these tech guys in France are magicians, they're not going to find any prints. I wiped the steak knife clean and I put on gloves before I picked up the shit 'um's knife. I had the gloves on both times I was at that apartment complex. And your guys should have swept the

* Automated Fingerprint Identification System.

Peugeot clean of prints before it was returned."

"That's true, but we can always have a death certificate drawn up for you. No one will be told about it. Just a record of it will be placed in the county clerk's office should an inquiring mind want to know."

Mac leaned toward the Ukrainian. "Who are you shittin'? Don't try to bullshit me about filing a false death certificate with the county. It takes more than a death certificate to put this case to bed. Even if they don't have prints, the authorities will be looking for a body, DNA, dental work, tattoos, surgeries, or x-rays records. I would need to be convincingly dead if no body was found. That would be a tall order, even for you spooks."

Mac sat back in his chair and laid his chin on his interlaced fingers. He sat still for a moment. Then, smiling at the Ukrainian, he said, "You might want me dead, but I'll take my chances alive."

Chapter Forty-One

March 18, 2004

"If I wanted you dead, you'd be dead," said the Ukrainian.

"Maybe yes, maybe no. But leaving that aside, something's not making sense here," said Mac.

"Like what?"

"Your tail, for instance."

"What about it?"

"Simple. You said you had me followed from the moment I got off the plane at de Gaulle Airport. Correct?"

"Yes, go on."

"Well, remember the boat? It's got to belong to Conroy. When you had me followed, were you or your snoops there to see the man place a package in the storage box? The same man I took down on that street around the corner from the apartment complex? The package was probably an explosive device. Why would he want to blow up that particular boat? It had to have belonged to Conroy. That should've been easy enough for you to check out."

"That's been done already. The boat is his, under his alias. And, yes, we're aware of the man and the explosives."

"Why then didn't you take those two mutts down and squeeze them for information?"

"They were not our main concern at the time. You were. We did take note, however, that someone, other than you, wanted Conroy dead, that they were Arabs using a rental car to get around. We were tailing them, until you decided to create a scene at the apartment. We needed to get you and your vehicle out of there."

"Well, I suggest you find those two. They have the code to detonate the explosives. Unless you want to play around trying to create your own detonator? I wouldn't recommend that, though, if these two are still out and about. They could blow you sky high."

"I see where you're going with this. I like it. But it's a mute issue," said the Ukrainian.

"What the hell are you talking about? If you could grab those guys and keep the explosive device under control, I could take that boat up river."

"You want to take the boat? Do you even know how to operate a 40 footer?"

"No, but if I have to, I could, I guess. You could come with me."

"And you want us to do what with it?"

"Take it up river and out to the Channel, or out to sea," Mac said." I'll get a witness or two to see me getting in the boat, maybe getting gas. If the boat isn't full, I'll need to top off some diesel before heading to the Channel. The authorities will think I assaulted Conroy over something to do with the boat, or money owed me. That would work to our benefit. Once out at sea, we could have another boat meet us; at night—of course."

"Then what would you suggest we do?"

"Once out there, out of the shipping lanes, we can get on the other boat and blow Conroy's into a million pieces. The authorities can look for a body or bodies all they want. But they're not going to find anything. It'd be assumed, when no body parts are found, whatever the explosive didn't destroy, the fish ate."

"Not a bad idea," the Ukrainian said. "Too bad it's not going to happen."

"Why not?"

"Because the boat was blown up last night."

Mac clapped once and stood up. He then placed his hands in the small of his back and stretched. "I know, John. It's John, right?" Mac said forcing air from his lungs. "I'm not as dumb as you might think. I heard the explosion when we left in your car. It had to be the boat. You didn't mention anything to me about it, though. Nor about the Arabs who apparently blew it up. Something deeper is going on here. That had to be part of *your* plan. I don't have you in checkmate yet, but I do believe I have just placed you in check."

Chapter Forty-Two

March 18, 2004

"What are you talking about?" the Ukrainian asked.

"You want me to start at the beginning?" Mac replied.

"Sure, why not? It's as good a place as any."

"How's this then?" Mac said. "You're not a company that contracts out from the CIA, you *are* the CIA. You hired those two Arabs to kill Conroy, just as your agency conspired with the FBI to have *me* kill him."

"Why would I want to do that, run two operations at the same time on the same target? It doesn't make any sense."

"Sure it does. You just told me you had me covered ever since I left de Gaulle Airport. And then when I told you about the boat, you said you knew all about it. But when I asked you about those two Arabs, you said you didn't know them and you made no effort to find out who they were, or any effort to get hold of them and their detonator. That's what you led me to believe. Then when I hit that one guy who was trying to kill the girl, you didn't do anything to intercede, nor did you seem interested in finding out who he was. The thing that really convinced me, though, that you knew who they were and didn't want to do anything to stop them, was the explosion last night. Letting those two blow up the boat under your watch, without your authority to do so—knowing there were explosives aboard—is not something I'd expect you, as a professional, would let happen."

"And that's why you believe I know these Arabs? That's a bit of flimsy speculation, even for a PI," said the Ukrainian.

Mac shook his head in disgust. "Not at all. It's as Agent Dillon said to me, 'It's a chess game.' Politicians and their minions, like you, see this whole terrorism thing as a game. The puppeteers pull the strings and people die, the good along with the bad. It's just part of the game. Right? You wanted me to believe I was operating alone, and you were going to play that for all it's worth. Maybe I'd get the information on the suppliers. Maybe I wouldn't. But it's a good chance I'd kill Conroy. And if I didn't kill him, you had those Arabs doing your bidding. But they, too, didn't know they were working for your agency. You had them believing they were hired by someone else. They didn't know who, but you probably had them thinking they were working for a fellow countryman, some sheik with a whole lot of pull. You've been their contact all along, walking them through every step. Though they never met you, they believed you were working on behalf of a friendly Arab nation.

"It took me a while to figure out how Conroy was able to get out of Canada without being caught. You guys wanted him out of the country in order to follow him, learn of all his contacts, all his suppliers, maybe be able to flip one or two of them so they could work for you. You guys love double agents. The game. Remember, it's the game. Am I right? Do I still have you in check?"

"Tell me why I'd want those two Arabs to kill Conroy if I needed information on his suppliers."

"Because you wanted him dead, period. You already knew who two of his suppliers were. You knew that my man Darcy had fingered Ruger, and you knew that Prince Amel commissioned that plane to pick up Conroy and bring him to Saudi Arabia. You were hoping to learn of any other contacts Conroy had. If that failed, you planned to have me kill him, with the Arabs as insurance. Neither of us connected with your organization in any way known or provable."

"Well my friend. Believe what you wish. All's well that ends well. We know who his main suppliers are, Conroy's dead, and you're alive."

"One big problem, though."

"What's that?"

"The girl."

"Aah, but that's your problem," the Ukrainian said. "You could have killed her. You should have. After all, she *was* working with Conroy. Her fingerprints are all over the blood money. He tried killing your wife. That would have been a just revenge, killing Conroy's girlfriend."

"A man of God once condemned me for thinking there is such a thing. I believe, like you, there is a just vengeance, only I see it when the target is the one trying to kill me, a family member, or a friend. Unlike you, though, killing someone merely to seek vengeance upon another isn't in my DNA. Plus, I don't believe in killing women, unless they try to kill me or someone else in my presence. This wasn't one of those cases. "

"Well, Conroy's girlfriend saw your face. She can identify you in photographs, videos, surveillance cameras. Maybe you said something to her that rings a bell with the police. She could be a problem."

The Ukrainian stood up and looked out the safe house window. He continued, "You were careful enough not to leave fingerprints at the apartment when you put Conroy out of commission for good. But the problem is the girl can describe you to the police."

"I don't kill innocent people. For all I know, this girl could be a dupe. Conroy has been known to play people. I'll take my chances by not hurting her."

"Very well," the Ukrainian said as he stared out the window. "I see you are an honorable man. And because I can appreciate that, I've decided the girl can live."

"You decided! Who—" was all Mac could get out before the

Ukrainian turned and looked directly at him.

"Yes," he said, "and your plan could have worked. I like what you proposed. Too bad it's only academic at this point. I could have had several witnesses see you with Conroy's boat. That could've, in some way, been construed as a reason for you to whack him. Since the boat was going to be blown anyway, we could have killed two birds with one stone. No pun intended. With the boat taken out to sea and blown up, the police could close out their case. Conroy dead, suspect killer dead, boat containing any damaging information, gone. Then again, I could just have the girl killed."

Mac rubbed his eyes and ran his hands over his head. "Something's missing here—aside from the fact that you're nuts. Something you're holding back from telling me. You seem to have gone through a lot of trouble setting this whole thing up when a simple bullet to Conroy's head would have done the trick. You had all the information you needed from him: the suppliers, the money in the bank, the boat, the girl. Why the game? All this intrigue?" Mac approached the Ukrainian and grabbed him on the right arm. Looking him squarely in the eyes he said, "Unless . . . ."

"Don't think about it," Mac said as the Ukrainian tried to break free and pull the gun that was on his right hip. "I'm not buying any of what you're telling me; your name, who you work for, your grandiose plans. Understand? If we're on the same side, I need to know all of what's going on here. If we're not, I need to know that, too. I've had enough of this guessing game. So, tell me what you know about Conroy, all of it, or one of us is not going to get out of this room alive. Now, I'm sure you've killed your share of people. So have I. And, believe me, if you want to have a go at it, I'm game. But we can avoid all this if you tell me everything you know about Conroy. I mean everything."

The Ukrainian smiled, then relaxed. "My turn now? Where would you like me to start?"

"You tell me," Mac said.

"Very well," he replied. "How do you think Conroy got an early release?"

"Go on."

"We offered him a deal. In prison, he was approached by a terrorist group known as Jalil ul-Anmar."

"So he offered *you* a deal?"

"Actually, it was the Bureau who got him out early and put him on their payroll. He joined the group and provided a lot of information on that organization. He took on a cover name: Ahmed Sal Mohammed. When he moved out of the country to Saudi Arabia, the feds turned him over, in part, to my agency. He started working for us. We'd keep the Bureau informed of his activities. We basically had to out of obligation. After all, he was originally their CI. Now, the girl has been with him a while. They set up in the apartment in Paris where he then purchased the yacht and learned how to operate it. He said it was his way of relaxing. I guess you need some place to get away to, when you're a serial-killing, double agent."

"You should have known you couldn't trust that dirtbag," Mac said.

"The majority of people we deal with can't be trusted . . . and I'm including those on *our* side."

"You, yourself, proved that to me."

"Anyway, when our counter-terror guys finally got around to checking out the girl, they found she was depositing large sums of money into several bank accounts. Banking records showed that she had joint accounts with a guy named Malcolm Terrell. Same with the apartment. We then realized Conroy was double dipping. It wasn't our money he was having her put in the accounts. And Malcolm Terrell wasn't an alias we had given him. When our boys checked the dates of the deposits, they matched up with recent terror-related killings."

"I heard. The killings in Scotland and Italy. The feds told me at least that much. But you know how the misinformation game is played. They laid the information gathering on French intelligence," Mac said.

"Well, there is some truth in that. We have liaisons with their financial counter-terrorism bureau. Ever since 9-11, the French have been very helpful to us. Only God knows how long that will last. If this mission turns bad, all that could change."

"Meaning?"

"If they find out that Conroy has been working with us and we hadn't let them know about it, that he's been operating in and out of their country with our knowledge and not theirs, it could create a problem, one of trust between our two intelligence agencies, which means there will be a shutting down of information. As you probably know, information gathering is our lifeblood."

"Aah, the 'ol trust issue. I don't know how you guys don't cut your own throats when you shave in the morning. Can you even trust yourselves?"

"Make jokes if you will, but we do it for one main reason: we love our country. Most of our guys, those who aren't specialists in the sciences or undercover, are former military: Seals, Special Ops, Delta Force, Marines, etcetera. We put our lives on the line every day without any recognition. You, of all people, a former serviceman, should know that, should appreciate that."

"Loyalty, yes. I appreciate that, if that's what we're talking about. Honorable men, honorable causes. But there are lines here not to be crossed. My friend of the cloth keeps telling me that . . . in so many words. I suspect you've been over those lines many times."

"I do what needs to be done for our country."

"Like considering to kill an innocent girl."

"We don't know if she's innocent. She was living with a known terrorist."

"Then find out first if she's innocent, before you sign her death warrant."

"In this business, by the time we find out if she should be killed or not, it could be too late. She may just be another fanatic to strap a bomb to her chest and take out fifty of our people."

"I just think you should make the effort of finding out, for your conscience, if nothing else. That is, of course, if you have one." Mac held his stare with the Ukrainian. "An interesting conversation to have at another time. Right now I want to know the rest of the story about Conroy."

"And so you'll get it. Once we were able to connect him to the killings, we knew we had to eliminate him. His usefulness to us was over. He was working with our enemies, taking money to kill Americans. Beyond that, he was a renegade who could hurt our relationship with France, hurt our reputation at home, give those in Congress a reason to neuter our agency again through legislation and withholding of money, and we could risk losing our ability to find and develop human assets to fight terrorism from within these pariah organizations."

"You knew he was back in the States wreaking all kinds of havoc. Why didn't you have him killed then and there?"

"Not our jurisdiction. The feds pulled rank on us. They said they'd take care of it. That's when you came on the scene with your guy Darcy and your dead pal Barrow. The feds underestimated Conroy. They never thought he'd try to kill your wife. They knew your reputation from the Newark PD and that situation in New York when your daughter was killed by those lowlife bastards. It was then the Fed bosses thought it was a good idea to take the leash off you and let you go rouge. No accountability on their part. Once you arrived here, though, my group was to keep an eye on you. I was assigned that task. I was also given orders to get another hit team in place, one that couldn't be tied to *my* agency."

"I don't understand, though, why knowing all this about Conroy, you didn't take him down in Canada. You must have known he was flying out of that country in one of the Royals planes."

"For one, not enough time to do a clean job of it. Two, we wanted to confirm who the Saudi Royal was behind his escape. Three, we needed to know if he had anything relating to our arrangement: documents, tapes, videos, contact information, anything. Could you image if it ever got out that a U.S. senator was almost killed by a government CI? We checked and couldn't find any record of a safe deposit box in his name or the girl's. We have no record of him contacting attorneys. This boat was his sanctuary. If he had hid anything, it more than likely would be there. We couldn't be sure of that, but we also couldn't take any chances. The boat had to be searched. If there wasn't time, it had to be blown up. That's why the Arab hit team dropped the explosives in it. But, like war, on the first contact with the enemy, you can throw away your game plan."

"So the boat's blown and your Arab hit team are on their way home."

"Yes, and I had to convince them to forget trying to locate and kill you. The last time I spoke with Tamir, he was still fuming over your attack on him."

"Tamir? So that's the creep who likes to kill innocent women."

"The world is full of guys like him . . . and me," said the Ukrainian.

"Aren't you worried the French bomb experts will figure out where the explosives came from?"

"I hope they do. Our hero EOD* warriors dig up enough Iranian-made IEDs** to blow half the Middle East to hell. Let our French allies think it's a gift from the Ayatollah."

"Then what about the apartment? Conroy could have stashed anything that would implicate your agency in there."

"We took care of that. Before Conroy arrived in Paris, some of my people searched his apartment while the girl was out and about. They were very meticulous not to raise any suspicions. They came up dry, nothing there that could hurt us, which was good news for us."

* Explosive Ordnance Disposal

** Improvised Explosive Device

"Why didn't you shake down his boat when you did the apartment?"

"We thought about it, which was going to be the next move. Then Conroy arrived. The more I thought about it, I liked the idea of simply having our Arab friends lay the boat up with explosives. Best case, Conroy gets on the boat, we get rid of him and any possibility of a connection with my agency."

"Why, then, get me involved in all this? Your original plan seemed to be fine."

"My bosses liked the insurance of having a second hit man out there. The boat could always be blown—best done at night, fewer witnesses, and more time, after the explosion, for it to burn."

"So, it was never about finding who the money suppliers were. You knew they were Ruger and Amel. Did the Bureau know this all along, too?"

"No. You were going to tell them . . . which you did. Congratulations. They need 'beyond a reasonable doubt.' We just need doubt. A much lower bar to cross over."

"Why, then, go through all this cloak and dagger, unless you want me dead, too. Is that the reason?"

"That's what you think? It might be hard for you to believe, but we don't kill friendlies. And you are a friendly."

"So, where do we go from here?" Mac asked.

"You sit tight for a day or two. Your reason for being in Paris is to do business with an American company known as Security International Corporation—SIC. You were here to discuss a job opening you heard about on the Internet. Your contact here is a man named Mark Andrews. He was the one you scheduled an interview with."

"Will I meet this guy?"

"You're meeting with him now."

"You? I thought you said your name was John?"

"John, Mark. Does it really matter?" said the Ukrainian. "That will be your cover in case anyone asks."

"Do I get the job?"

"There are others to be interviewed. I'll call you if you get it."

"You guys are into everything, aren't you?"

"Security *is* our business. Now that's no lie."

Chapter Forty-Three

March 20, 2004

Continental Flight 1076 from Paris to Newark Liberty Airport was without incident. A strong tailwind and lack of air turbulence made for a smooth and comfortable ride. Though it was an early afternoon flight, Mac slept most of the way. It had been a rough couple of days for him, both mentally and physically.

"Please fasten your seat belts, we will be landing soon," said the flight attendant.

Mac looked out the window of the plane and saw the Statue of Liberty in the harbor. *Good to be home*, he thought.

The wheels of Flight 1076 hummed as they touched down on the tarmac. Then the engine roared in reverse. The plane soon taxied to a slot at Gate B. Mac gathered up his belongings from the overhead compartment, offered the attendant and captain standing by the exit door of the plane a well-deserved thank you, and headed to the baggage claim.

As he approached the carousel, he noticed an individual standing by the glass exit door. The man watched him pick up his bag as it popped off the conveyer belt and landed on the moving metal sleeves. Mac then walked past him and headed toward the row of cars along the curb where a Port Authority police officer was clearing out the traffic that was building up. The individual followed

Mac from a distance. Another individual waited for him in a blue Honda alongside the curb.

"Hey, Taylor, over here!" yelled Jason, his head sticking out the driver's side window.

"Glad to see you, brother," Mac said as he threw his bags into the back of the Ford Explorer, then got into the front seat. "How's Cheryl doing?" he asked.

"Fine, just fine. She misses you. But don't expect a friendly welcome. She's still mad you left her so you could track down that a-hole in France."

"Well, I'll just have to make it up to her. Can you stop at a florist on the way home?"

"Sure."

Jason pulled out from the line of cars and headed toward Route 78.

"I hope all went well for you over there in Gay Par-ree." Jason said.

"Yeah. I took care of business and helped in the game."

"What game?"

"Why our game, of course."

"I don't know what you're talking about."

"I'm talking about what we do. What the feds do. Finding the bad guys, arresting them, killing them, turning them. It's all a game, a deadly game, but a game no less."

Jason looked over at his brother-in-law and smiled. "Man, the way you look at things sometime is just plain weird."

Mac laughed and slapped Jason on the shoulder.

After a few moments, Mac turned serious. "You're a good cop, right, Jason?"

"Where are you going with that comment?"

"Look in your rearview mirror. Keep an eye on that blue Honda."

"What about it?"

"One of the guys in it—the passenger—was watching me at the

airport. Now that car just made the same three turns we've made. Plus, it's hanging back, using several cars as cover. You slow, the Honda slows. You pick up speed, they do the same. I don't know what it's all about, but I'm not liking it. I think we should find out one way or another. It might just be paranoia. But if it's not. . . ."

Jason reached down his right side and tapped his hip. "The fun never stops with you, does it?" he said.

Mac caught the maneuver. "Are you packing?"

"Always, brother, especially when I'm with you. You are high-octane trouble."

"Yeah, well, take the next exit. I'm not bringing any trouble home with me."

Jason sped up, then at the last second turned off on Exit 55. Before the blue Honda reached the exit, Jason made a sharp left onto Fabyan Place. The blue Honda, about 200 yards back, turned off at the exit. Before the Honda reached Fabyan Place, Jason made a quick three-point turn on Selvage Street. They watched as the Honda came to a jarring stop where the off ramp intersected with Fabyan.

"Did you pick up that plate number?" Jason asked Mac.

"Sure did. I'll call it in now and see who or what we're dealing with."

Just then the Honda made a left turn and brought the vehicle nose-to-nose with Jason's Explorer. Jason exited his car quickly, pulled his .380 Walther, and held it at his side. Mac dropped his cell phone on the center console, then stood by the opened passenger door.

Jason took the offensive. "Out of the car!" he yelled.

Suddenly the two men bolted out of the Honda and open fired. Several shots hit the windshield and opened doors of the Explorer. Mac ducked back into the car as Jason fired back. Mac reached over and pulled the gear shift into drive. He then grabbed the steering wheel with his extended left hand and turned the wheel to the left, putting the impenetrable engine block of the Explorer between his brother-in-law and the attackers.

Jason's bullets dropped the passenger of the Honda. Mac rushed from the Explorer and headed toward the driver of the vehicle, drawing fire away from Jason. The driver fired three shots at him, hitting Mac in the right shoulder, lower right chest area, and right leg. Jason had one bullet left in his gun. He steadied his Walther, then pulled the trigger. The bullet passed through the opened window of the Honda and hit the driver squarely in the chest. The attacker fell face down onto the pavement.

Jason ran to where Mac was lying. He felt for a pulse. It was weak. He listened for a heartbeat. It was faint. Nonetheless, Mac was still alive; barely, but alive. Jason quickly called 9-1-1 on his cell phone. Mac lost quite a bit of blood before the ambulance and paramedics arrived. He remained conscious until the ambulance pulled into the emergency entrance of the Newark hospital. As he faded to black, he was quickly rushed through emergency up to the operating room.

Jason was allowed to call his wife before being subjected to a barrage of questions from prosecutors and detectives concerning the shooting. Because of Cheryl's delicate condition, Jason asked prosecutors to let Ann break the news to her about Mac. It was granted.

Mac's friend, Martin Presler, was called to the hospital. His primary concern was to learn of Mac's medical status and if he could help his family and friends in any way. On his way to the hospital, Presler contacted other officials who had recently worked with Mac. He was fully aware of Mac's involvement with the feds and suspected the shooting had something to do with that relationship. He wanted their help in the investigation that was to follow.

The driver of the Honda was dead on arrival at the Newark hospital. The bullet from Jason's gun punctured the sternum of the victim and entered his heart, killing him instantly. The other attacker survived bullet wounds to his neck and chest. He was immediately charged with weapons possession and two counts of attempted murder. He was held under guard at the hospital until such time he would be stable enough to be transported to a criminal detention facility.

It was learned, through interviews, interrogations, and physical evidence, that the two attackers were members of the Jalil ul-Anmar group. The same group to which Dirk Conroy belonged. They were seeking revenge on Mac Taylor for his part in dismantling their plan to attack various cities and monuments across the U.S., the death of their comrades in the Meadowlands, and for—what they mistakenly believed—was his involvement in the murder of their leader, the Architect al-Satir.

Chapter Forty-Four

March 20, 2004

Aaron Ruger's chateau rested along a hillside not far from the Matterhorn on the outskirts of Zermatt. Surrounded by a ten-foot block wall, the grounds were patrolled by security guards and dogs. At 4:00 PM, Ruger's limousine passed through the wrought-iron gate and continued up the road to the main house.

"Be back at 6," Ruger said to his chauffeur. He then exited the black sedan.

"Good to see you again, sir." It was Ruger's housekeeper.

"Won't be here long, Randolph. I'll be leaving tomorrow."

"Tomorrow? Why so soon, sir?"

"Business."

"Well, I'll have the cook prepare your favorite dish tonight: bratwurst, sauerbraten, Metz, and a hearty Riesling."

"Not tonight. I'll be dining in town," Ruger said while brushing past Randolph. He then pushed open one of the two large entry doors of the chateau.

"Buon giorno, signore," said the maid dusting the grand piano in the entry hall as Ruger entered.

He stared at the young Italian woman. "Who are you? And where is Erika?"

"Mi chiamo Maria Sanantonio," said the young Italian woman.

"And?"

"Signore?"

"Again, where is Erika?"

"Dove Erika?"

"Do you speak German or English?"

"I speak English. No very much. Enough though."

"Why are you here? Where is Erika?"

"She no feeling good today. I sent by agency to prepare la casa per te."

"It doesn't matter. I'll only be here until tomorrow. And I won't be eating here tonight, so you can leave now. I expect Erika to be back tomorrow morning at 8 AM. Capisce?"

"Si, capito signore. E gracia. I leave now." Maria then left the chateau and met with the chauffeur by the garages.

"Where to?" he said.

"Take me to town," Maria Sanantonio said in perfect English.

The phone rang and Randolph answered it.

"Sir, it's for you. The gentleman said he is a friend of a person named Dirk Conroy."

"Who?!" Ruger cried out.

"A friend of Mr. Dirk Conroy."

"Give me that phone!"

Ruger placed the receiver to his ear. "Where did you get this number?"

"Is this Aaron Ruger?" asked the caller.

"Where did you get this number?!"

"Tell me if this is Aaron Ruger, and I'll tell you where I got your number."

"Yes, this is Aaron Ruger."

"Good" was all the caller said.

"What? Who is this? . . . Hello!"

Randolph saw a look of confusion on Ruger's face just before the telephone receiver exploded, blowing a large section of Ruger's head completely off his neck. Randolph stood there for what seemed an eternity with blood, bone, and brain matter dripping from his body.

Lamar Darcy's relationship with Mac Taylor came to an end back in February after the hardball interrogation. Darcy eventually paid him handsomely, though begrudgingly, for his services. His involvement with Mac and the FBI was kept under wraps, so Darcy continued working for Navesco Corp. He had recently been promoted to Chief Financial Officer at the company. Today, he stood motionless in the conference room overlooking the Hudson River by Battery Park on the south end of Manhattan Island. Looking out the window of the twentieth-floor Manhattan office building, he stared at the Statue of Liberty in the harbor. "Amazing country, America," he said to no one in particular. He then turned and addressed his staff.

"I have just received some sad news. The CEO of our parent company GNI, Mr. Aaron Ruger, has been killed, murdered at his home in Switzerland. The details on his death will be made public, I'm sure, in the next few days. For now, though, it would be best for us to wait and see what the funeral arrangements will be. In the meantime, let's strive to maintain the high standards associated with our company by continuing to find ways to minimize expenses and maximize profits. Mr. Ruger would have wanted it that way. From a business perspective, please know his death will not affect the solvency, structure, or employee base of Navesco. I suspect the same to hold true for GNI."

Darcy then went on to discuss company business. After he was finished with his meeting, he dismissed the group. He was pleased how everything worked out—well, except for the death of his dear friend Devin "Silky" Barrow and the rough treatment he received at the hands of Mac Taylor. He couldn't be too mad at Taylor, though. He did hire him, basically to protect him from harm and keep him informed. *Mac Taylor had kept those promises . . . and he protected my job for me. I even got a promotion*, Darcy quietly reminded himself. *There was one glitch, however, in this whole fiasco,* he thought. *Now I'm an informant for the FBI.*

"What will the king do?" asked Prince Amel.

"He knows nothing, Your Highness," said his counselor. "No one knows anything. Ahmed is dead and so I hear is Ruger. No one knows that you had any dealings with them."

"What about the flight Ahmed took to our country in the plane I chartered for him . . . or anything he might have had on him, in his apartment, or on his boat? How about my meeting with Ruger? I knew I shouldn't have met with him after Ahmed returned. And what about the money? Can it be traced back?"

"Please, sire, do not worry. There is a man outside who wishes to see you. He has assured me, you are not in any trouble."

"What man? What would he know? And who is he to assure you of anything! Unless you said something to him. Did you, against my orders not to mention my business with anyone, without my permission?"

"He called *us*, Your Highness. He knows something about what has been going on, that you are concerned for your safety and that of your family. I don't know how he knows that, but he does, and he wants to help."

"Who is this man?

"I'll send him in and let him explain."

The prince's counselor went to the door of the palatial study and opened it. In walked the gentleman.

"Do I know you?" asked the prince.

"No, sir, you don't," said the gentleman as he bowed to the prince. "I'm Mark Andrews. I run a company known as Security International. You may not have heard of us because we are very discrete in what we do. But, believe me, we are one of the largest, possibly *the* largest security company in the world."

"You are right, I have never heard of your company," said the prince. He then added, "I don't need you. I have my own security."

"And it's a good one at that, Your—."

The prince cut him off. "And what is it I hear that you think I might be in trouble? My family might be in trouble? Where did you get this information? Or is this your way of getting business from me?"

"I would not waste your time, Your Highness, if I didn't have concerns for your safety and the safety of your family. We're in the business of protection. We handle the safety and security of many major corporations and clients from around the globe. One of our functions is to gather information. We have many, many resources in that area. Recently, we have come across quite a bit of information involving you and, let's say, some unsavory persons. My company can make that all go away. We are a private enterprise. No governmental agency needs to know. There will be a fee for our services, of course, but that should not be a problem for you."

"Are you trying to extort money from me?"

"Certainly not. I'm only here to help you out of a very difficult situation. If any information gets out that you've been dealing with Ahmed Sal Mohammed, I think the king would not be terribly happy. Western governments dealing with the Royal Family would not be happy."

"I do not know anyone named Ahmed Sal Mohammed!"

"Aah, but you do, Your Highness. You know him very well."

"Then you must tell me what you know and what you plan on doing about it."

"We have information on a flight he took out of Canada in your chartered plane, a money trail from your accounts to his, business arrangements with a third-party financier in Switzerland who is tied to you, him, and terrorist activity. I have much more information, documented and undocumented that I can show or tell you about in time.

"You see, our business survives on information. I tell you what we know—for a fee, of course—and how to make it go away. And you will tell us what *you* know. That last bit of information about Ahmed was given as a courtesy. No charge. But as long as we maintain a free flow of information between us, I can assure you my company will do everything in its power to protect you and your family. It's your call, Your Highness."

The prince was quiet for several awkward moments. "Why should I not have you killed right here and now for threatening me?" he finally said.

Mark Andrews shrugged his shoulders. "Because all the information my company has gathered will be dispersed to your government, Western governments, and the media upon my death or disappearance. I think that would destroy your reputation, end your access to all the family's wealth, your personal dreams of jihad, and, in the end, your life. My company has a long memory. When the time is right—." He smiled. "Aah, we needn't go into that," he said. "I'd just give the idea of having me killed some real serious thought."

The prince began fidgeting. "Before I say 'yes', I need to know more."

Mark Andrews bowed again. "Fair enough. And I'll need a retainer, say 100,000 riyals."

The prince looked at his counselor and nodded. The counselor left the room.

"I've a feeling we'll be doing a great deal of business together from this point on," said Andrews.

"You must first tell me all you know, or think you know about my connections with this man you call Ahmed Sal Mohammed," said the prince.

"Why don't I sit down," said the Ukrainian. "We have much to talk about."

Epilogue

"Thou are hope in the day of evil."

Isaiah 17:17

Chapter Forty-Five

March 20, 2004

Father Polsani stood in front of the group in the hospital chapel. He reached out and offered his hand to Cheryl and her family sitting in the first row. Then stepping back, he said, "We are all here today to pray for the life of a good man, Mac Taylor. He dedicated his life fighting for justice, beating the bad guys, and saving lives. Our Lord places high value on those men and women who walk that path. He said, 'Blessed are the peacemakers for they shall be called the sons of God.' What greater honor is there?

"Most of you are not aware that Mac and I go back quite some time together. During the sixties we served in Vietnam. I was a helicopter pilot, Mac was a sniper. He saved my life on one occasion and he'd saved the lives of many of our brother soldiers during that time. Lives, unfortunately, had to be taken to protect ours. During that war, Mac had taken his share of those lives. And, in matters of self defense and in protecting others, he had continued to do so over the years. It's the world he lives in, protecting the people he loves. He's a warrior for good."

Father Polsani looked directly at Cheryl. "I know that his lifestyle, and his interpretation of the way to live that life, was and is a concern to many of you."

Agent Sara Dillon, standing in the back of the chapel with other representatives from the FBI and the Newark Police Department, nodded in agreement. Lieutenant Martin Presler cracked a smile remembering the many actions of his brother officer.

"It shouldn't be. He loves all of you. He spent his lifetime fighting evil, which comes in many forms. My mission and those in the Church are to fight it with the peace of the Cross. Those in the police and military choose to fight evil with physical resistance. Those defenders of God's realm, who have passed on, are now in the army of Michael the Archangel. Mac will someday be one of St. Michael's soldiers. But let's pray it won't be today. Let's pray that he'll live to see his newborn child, that he and Cheryl will have many wonderful years together, and that he'll continue to be a presence in our lives."

Father Polsani paused and looked back at the cross.

"But, if I am to be completely honest, and I know you, Lord, would want me to be, Mac needs Your help now. He is a soldier, always a soldier. Whether he served in the military, the police force, or as a private investigator, he was always a soldier for good in his heart and in his actions. Justice was his calling, but his method of seeking justice against evil sometimes spilled into other less virtuous areas. He'd tell me that there is a *just* vengeance in this world. And I would tell him Christian doctrine disagrees with that assessment. Nevertheless, he remained headstrong in his beliefs. He has his own special way of interpreting life's great mysteries. Right or wrong, he always acted out of love. We, here in this room, can attest to that. We trusted him with our lives and he was always there for us. Lord, You are infinite wisdom, mercy, and love. We ask for Your intercession, Your guiding hand for the doctors and nurses working on our brother Mac Taylor at this very moment. We ask this in Your name." He paused a moment, then added, "Let it not be our will, but Yours."

Father Polsani placed the Bible on the table next to the altar. He folded his hands. Looking at the family and friends seated and standing in the small chapel, he said, "Everyone, please bow your heads once more. I would like to offer a final prayer, one many of you know, on behalf of Mac Taylor, our brother in Christ. It's the 23rd Psalm of David . . . The Lord is my shepherd . . . ."

Doctor Mellone walked down the corridor from the operating room toward Cheryl, Jason, Ann, and Father Polsani. His operating mask was around his neck and he still had on his white surgical cap. Jason and Ann jumped to their feet. Father Polsani helped Cheryl as she struggled getting up.

"Mrs. Taylor."

"Yes, doctor," Cheryl replied nervously.

"Your husband is going to be fine. It was a bit touch and go there for a while. He had lost a lot of blood, and going into shock is always a factor. We were able to stabilize him and remove two of the three bullets. The third one, the one he took to his chest, fortunately hit a rib and exited his side. That one could have done a lot of internal damage, but it didn't. Believe it or not what could have been a much more serious wound was the one to his leg. An inch to the left and it would have severed his femoral artery. That would have resulted in profuse bleeding. Without immediate first aid, your husband would definitely have bled to death." Doctor Mellone looked at Father Polsani. "Someone's prayers have been answered."

"When can I see him?" Cheryl asked.

"He's still sedated. He'll probably be out until tomorrow morning. He has to be closely monitored. I suggest you go home and rest. Come back in the morning."

"I need to see him now," she said.

"I understand. He'll be in the recovery room shortly. You can see him there, but you must follow procedures: mask, hat, gown, gloves."

Cheryl thanked the doctor and waited until she was allowed to see Mac. He was hooked up to several monitors and he was on an IV drip. As the doctor said, Mac was still fully sedated.

"You are too much, Mac Taylor," Cheryl said to her unresponsive husband. "A normal person would get tired of the constant danger and insanity . . . but you don't. You actually like it. Maybe I should say love it. Now I know what your first wife must have gone through. You're a tough old bird. When you're able to hear me, we are going to talk. Our child will need a father who can throw him a ball or take her to dance class. Our child doesn't need a Rambo. So shape up, mister. I'll see you tomorrow." Cheryl leaned over as far as she could and kissed Mac through her mask.

Chapter Forty-Six

March 21, 2004—3 AM

Cheryl felt the contractions coming. She slid her legs over the side of the bed and stood up. Then, walking to the bedroom door, she opened it and called out, "It's time!"

Her brother, Jason, jumped from the living room couch. He was in his street clothes.

"Are you sure?" he said rubbing his eyes. "You're three weeks early."

"I think so."

Cheryl's sister-in-law, Ann, came running out of the guest bedroom.

"You sure they're not sympathy pains for Mac?"

"No. With all this stress I'm feeling and the trauma I've been through, I think my baby wants out."

"Okay, girl, let's get dressed," Ann said.

"I'll grab your bag and get the car ready," Jason said. "Annie, would you help Cheryl to the car?"

"Certainly, of course," came the response.

Within minutes, the three of them were barreling down the main highway in Jason's car, heading to the local hospital.

Cheryl didn't say a word during the entire trip.

"Here, take my phone," Jason said as he handed it to Ann who was sitting next to Cheryl in the back seat. "Call Father Polsani. Tell him we're on our way to University Hospital. I have his number on speed dial."

"Why are we calling him?" Ann asked.

"He made me promise. He wants to be there when Cheryl has the baby."

Ten minutes into the trip, Jason pulled his car next to a parked ambulance by the Emergency Room door. "Well, we're here," he said

As Ann helped Cheryl out of the back seat, Jason went into the Emergency Room and returned with a wheelchair. Ever vigilant, he looked around the lot as his sister eased her way into the chair. He then wheeled her into the hospital.

Not long afterwards, Father Polsani arrived at the Emergency Room where he was directed to Labor and Delivery.

"Father, we appreciate your coming," Jason said as the priest approached him in the hall. "Too bad Mac couldn't be with Cheryl."

"But he is. He's just a few floors away. He'll get to see the baby. If he's well enough, he'll even get to hold him or her. That's not the case with so many other fathers. Many of our servicemen never get that chance. They're overseas when their child is born."

"I guess so. As you know Father, Mac's one of a kind. He's been driving my sister nuts. Hopefully, he'll put his family first this time. He's got to let go of that notion of always being the first guy at a gunfight." Jason then added, "Sorry, Father. I know a lot of people don't like guns. You're probably one of them."

"No need to apologize. Yes, that is my position. But right now my concern is with Cheryl. We needn't worry as much about Mac. Doctor Mellone said he should be fine once he comes out of the anesthetic. Let's hope Cheryl will have a normal, healthy delivery."

"I hope so. Annie is in there with her. I thought it best to stay out of the way."

"I see. So how are *you* doing?"

"What do you mean, Father?"

"You've been through a lot lately, as has your wife, doing what you can to protect and be with your sister. How are you doing?"

"Fine, I guess. I'm just worried about my sister, about the baby, and about Mac. He's been through a lot. Danger always seems to follow that man. He can't separate himself from it."

"I know very well what you're saying. Battles are fought on many fronts. For some, like you and Mac, the answer to the world's problems is a gun. For others it's a pen. My answer goes back over 3,000 years. For me it's the Holy Bible. In my life I've seen what war has done to many men and women who have lived through it. Whether they shrink into a protective cocoon, decide to end their lives, or fight on aimlessly in a civil society they can't recognize anymore, they all share a common trait . . . or lack of one."

"What's that?"

"It's called hope. Without hope there's no recovery for most of them. I've chosen to help them find hope. I won't save lives with a gun, but I may save hearts, minds, souls, *and* lives by giving hope to those with whom I come in contact, when all else fails them. That's my mission in life."

Jason nodded his head and patted Father Polsani on the shoulder. "In that case, Father," he said with a smile, "let's *hope* everything goes well in there with Cheryl and the baby."

Chapter Forty-Seven

March 21, 2004—7:35 AM

"It's a girl!" Ann yelled as she came out of the delivery room and hugged Jason, then Father Polsani.

"How are they?" asked the priest.

"Cheryl's a bit worn out, but well. She's all smiles now that she has gotten to hold her baby. Her daughter is several weeks premature, she only weights 4 and a half pounds, so she needs to be placed in an incubator, but the doctor said all her vital signs are good. She's a beauty, just like her mom."

"Thanks Annie," said Jason. "I'm glad you were here for her."

"She's my sister, where else would I be."

"Actually, she's *my* sister," said Jason, "but I get your point."

"Can we see her and the baby?" asked Father Polsani.

"Yes, in a few minutes. They're cleaning up her little girl and doing their evaluations. The doctor should be coming out soon. I think we can see Cheryl and the baby before she's taken to natal care by the nurse. You'll have to wear those gowns and caps, though, once you enter the room."

March 21, 2004—8:30 AM

Mac opened his eyes and looked over at the digital screen showing his heartbeats and blood pressure. *I'm alive. I guess that's good.*

He reached for the clicker hanging from the side of the bed and pressed the button on it. Within a few seconds a nurse appeared.

"Glad to see you're awake, Mr. Taylor," said the young nurse.

"Thanks. Do you know where my family is? I don't want my wife to be upset. She's in her last month of pregnancy and I'm worried about her."

"I can tell you she's fine. She, your brother, and his wife have been waiting to see you. There is also a priest friend of yours who has stopped in to see you. I'll call and have them stop by now. I must tell you, though, that they have a wonderful surprise for you. I don't want to spoil anything for them, but I also don't want you getting too excited so soon after surgery. So, just be prepared to hear the good news. That's all I'm going to say."

"Well, that can only mean one thing. Is Cheryl all right? Is the baby all right? Is it a boy or a girl?"

"Yes, yes, and I'm not telling you. Let your wife tell you. And don't let them know that I gave you a heads up."

"Deal."

The nurse raised the head section of the bed so Mac was in an upright position.

"It'll be a few minutes before they'll get her ready to come down. In the meantime, I have an Agent Dillon outside the room who wanted to see you the moment you woke up. Would it be okay to send her in?"

"Sure, why not?" Mac said.

The nurse left the room. Thirty seconds later in walked Agent Dillon.

"I was told not to upset you. Why your nurse would think that, I have no idea."

"Well, Sara, I can't think of any reason either," Mac replied, tongue-in-cheek.

"I'm glad to hear you're going to live."

"That's what they say."

"You took three bullets, point blank range. Not easy to survive that. You are one tough old guy Mac Taylor."

"Did you find out what this shooting was all about?"

"It was the Jalil ul-Anmar group. An attempted revenge killing for the death of al-Satir and those guys in the Meadowlands. Your brother-in-law, Jason, killed one of the attackers, wounded the other. In time we'll take that group apart, piece by piece."

"Such confidence," Mac said. He then asked, "How did they know I was flying in from France, on that particular day, on that flight?"

"They didn't. They've been following your brother-in-law around these last two days hoping he'd take them to you . . . which he did."

"And Jason didn't pick up the tail. I'll have to have a good talk with that boy."

"Well, if it's any consolation, he did take care of your wife for you while you were gallivanting all over Paris. Not to mention, he put enough lead into those two perps to send one to the hospital and the other to the morgue. I suggest you go easy on him."

"You're right, Sara. He's a good guy. We've been through a lot together. I only wish I had my Glock with me at the time. I wouldn't be lying here right now if I did."

Mac rolled slowly onto his side and reached for the glass of water on the tray next to his bed.

Sara reached the glass first and handed it to him.

"Thanks," he said, then took a long drink from it. He handed the glass back to her. She returned it to the tray.

"So, did you finally put all the pieces together on this case?" he asked.

"Done. Case closed. The Austrian killed in Scotland was Ruger's guy. He was the connection between Darcy, Barrow, Ortez, al-Satir, and Ruger. His death broke that connection. The Saudi murdered in Italy was the middleman for Prince Amel. He was the connection between Darcy, Barrow, Ortez, al-Satir, and the Prince. His death broke that connection. As for Barrow, he was Darcy's friend. He was needed for the two letter and money exchanges abroad with Conroy, which he—Barrow—later delivered to Ortez. He was also needed here to transfer the map and documents to Conroy, which were subsequently given to al-Satir. Once that transaction in Fort Lee took place, Barrow's usefulness was over. He had to go. And so went his connection with Ortez and the Prince."

"What happened to Burkner?"

"The attorneys are plea bargaining for him right now. We found a map of Newark Bay and security documents for that area in al-Satir's Bayonne condo. The lab boys, using one of their ultraviolet techniques, found a partial print of Burkner on one of those documents. We also have a statement from Detective Grossman acknowledging that he had given the maps and documents to Burkner. Telephone records and a statement from John Thomlin connect Burkner to Ortez. Ortez's connection with al-Satir completes the circle. Burkner's only hope is to plea out to a shorter prison sentence."

"What about Darcy? Why wasn't he killed after the transaction in Fort Lee?"

"Your boy finally gave up his complete involvement in this whole scheme. He was a money man. Darcy told us he dropped off $100,000 in the Bayonne park Dumpster for Burkner. That solidifies our case against Burkner. The deputy attorney general wants to keep Darcy's statement under wraps, though, for homeland security reasons. He's going to work for us now."

"He's going to be a CI, what, to bring down GNI?"

"Sorry, I can't discuss it."

"Sambogna," Mac said under his breath.

"What?"

"Nothing."

"Did he set up Barrow?"

"No, as a matter of fact, he told us Barrow recognized Burkner from the old neighborhood when he picked up the map and documents from him. He was nervous to go on the last exchange because he feared *that alone* would be a good reason to have him killed. Darcy further stated the reason he went to you and not the police was because Burkner, a deputy chief of Newark, was involved in the scheme. He didn't know anyone in the department he felt he could trust."

"So Darcy was to pay Barrow after the exchange with Conroy?" Mac asked.

"Yes. He insists that he believed the exchange would go well and Barrow would get the money he needed to get out of debt. Once Barrow was killed and he received the telephone call telling him to use the money to make a profit in the currency market, he knew his days were numbered. Another reason he came to you."

"So, he was involved in the transactions all along."

"Darcy was not only involved in supervising the exchanges in the U.S., but also in the trading of dollars for euros and for acting as a liaison between GNI slash Navesco and ul-Anmar. His main contacts were Conroy and al-Satir. He swears he didn't know Barrow and Ortez were going to be killed, or that Conroy was planning to kill you or your wife. He even passed the polygraph on those points."

"I was his last, or only, resort, it seemed."

"Yep. He knew Barrow was murdered—not a suicide—and that it was only a matter of time before he'd be eliminated. He hired you to protect him. He didn't lie to you about that. What he didn't tell you was that he was still doing the bidding for Ortez, al-Satir, Ruger, and Amel in the hope that they still needed him, so he could buy some time to figure out how not to get killed after this whole plan shaked out. He convinced them he hired you to gather information from the police on their investigation, in order to cover their—the company, Ruger and the Prince's—back. He was playing both sides against the middle. A very tricky place to be."

"Ortez's murder must have really put the fear of God into him," Mac said. "He had to think Ortez was a fair-haired boy in the organization, that he would never be targeted for elimination."

"This operation was so big, Ruger and the Prince were to gain so much money and power that no one in the organization was safe."

"Even Darcy. It took him a while, but he finally realized it," Mac said.

"That's when Ruger and Amel feared Darcy might go to the police. They not only had Conroy kill Ortez, they had him cut up the body to send a message to Darcy."

"What message?"

"You will be tortured, killed, and dismembered if you think about turning coat at this time. They even ordered Conroy to kill you . . . twice, once almost resulting in the death of your wife. They didn't know how much he might have told you about the operation, but they weren't going to take any chances. You were expendable. Killing you would render what, if anything you were told, mute. They still needed him, though, to handle the currency trades and to keep up his contact with Conroy and al-Satir. When he learned that Conroy planned to kill you in the swamp, he knew he'd better come clean on the whole operation. Still, he felt trapped. I know you used gentle persuasion to extract some of the information from him at that time."

"You know me, 'Mr. Kind and Gentle.' But why did that bunch try to kill a sitting senator?"

"Two reasons. One, as a diversion. While we're spending most of our time gathering intelligence on international terrorist groups, they wanted us to shift our focus to homegrown survivalist organizations. They thought an attack on a senator would force us to be re-active, instead of pro-active; that we'd be looking more within than without. So crossing into the country might not attract much attention. They must have a dim view of our security measures, particularly our lax border controls. Contrary to what they might think, though, we *can* chew gum and walk at the same time."

"You said there were two reasons to shoot the Senator. What's the second?"

"To create chaos and instill an elevated level of terroristic fear across the country. Not good for the dollar, but good for Ruger and his cohorts."

Mac shook his head. "So, in a nutshell, Ruger wanted the dollar to drop like a rock so he could make a ton of money; the Prince wanted money, too, but more importantly, he wanted greater political and religious powers; and they both wanted all conduits between them and the operation eliminated. Is that it?"

"Pretty much."

"Well, it's been one hellava case," Mac said.

"And you've done one hellava job," Agent Dillon replied

"My next one should be a bit more demanding."

"More demanding than this one?!"

"I've heard a rumor that I may be a dad."

"I've heard that rumor, too, but I wasn't going to say anything. I was sworn to secrecy."

"But of course you were. I know how you people operate—it's all on a need to know basis."

Agent Dillon cracked a smile. "I'm going to miss you, Investigator Mac Taylor."

Five minutes after Agent Dillon thanked him for his service to the country and said goodbye, Cheryl was wheeled into the room by the nurse. Ann, Jason and Father Polsani followed closely behind.

"Well look at you," Mac said upon seeing Cheryl. "You get a queen's entrance. And I like your entourage. Being an investigator, I draw from the evidence—you being in a wheelchair in a hospital—that there is a strong possibility you have given birth. Is that true dear?"

"Why yes, dear, I have," Cheryl said rather smugly. Then, as she was rolled to his side by the nurse, she grabbed hold of his hand.

The others gathered around the bed and exchanged greetings and well wishes. After which, Mac turned his attention back on Cheryl.

"How are you feeling?" he asked.

"I'm fine," she said.

"And the baby? How's the baby?"

"Good, good," she replied patting his hand. "She will have to be placed in an incubator for a few days, but you can see her once you're able to get in a wheelchair yourself. You have to be taken up to Maternity."

"You said 'her.' I have a little girl?"

"Yes, and she's beautiful."

"Daddy's little girl. That's wonderful! Daughters are wonderful. Have you given her a name?"

"Yes, I have. We had discussed both boy and girl names. I know you weren't crazy about most of the latest names. You just wanted it to be special and you wanted me to pick it. Well, I did. I picked a name that I thought was pretty, appropriate, and *very, very* special."

Mac tightened his grip ever so slightly on Cheryl's hand. "Well Mom, you have me in suspense. Pray tell, what is this glorious name you've given my daughter?"

A warm glow crossed Cheryl's face. "I named her Hope."

Jason snapped his head toward Father Polsani. The priest just smiled.

Glancing at his war buddy, Mac said. "Now that's one righteous name, eh, Father?"

Nick Polsani took Cheryl's other hand in his. He shook his head and replied, "Can I have an Amen to that?"

They all laughed, and answered the call in unison.

About the Dedication

I dedicated this book to my son, Staff Sergeant Joseph D'Augustine, who was killed on March 27, 2012 in the Sangin Province of Afghanistan while defusing an Improvised Explosive Device. Joe was a U.S. Marine for 11 years. He served two combat tours in Iraq and two combat tours in Afghanistan, as well as tours in the Pacific which included South Korea, Okinawa, Indonesia, and Australia. One of his missions in the Pacific was to work with the Fiji and Australian militaries in providing stability and humanitarian aid to the island of East Timor, where the locals were involved in a civil war. His Military Occupational Specialties included Military Police, Infantry, and Explosive Ordnance. His personal awards included the Bronze Star with Valor, the Purple Heart, the Navy and Marine Corps Commendation Medal, the Navy and Marine Corps Achievement Medal, Combat Action Ribbon, Good Conduct Medal (third award), National Defense Service Medal, Afghanistan Campaign Medal, Iraqi Campaign Medal, Global War on Terrorism Medal, Global War on Terrorism Service Medal, Korean Defense Service Medal, Humanitarian Service Medal, and the NATO-International Security Assistance Medal.

Mac Taylor, Cheryl Taylor, and Father Nick Polsani are fictional heroes. Men and women like Joe, who have fought the good fight and have passed on, are the real heroes. There is a mural on the wall of a building at Omaha Beach in Normandy, France which reads

"Les vrais heros ne meurent jamais!" The true heroes never die! And so, Joe lives on in the hearts and minds of his family, friends, and in all those his warm smile and sacrifice have touched. Thank you, son, for those precious moments we shared together and for your service to our country. 'Til we meet again on the other side, Semper Fi!

CPSIA information can be obtained at www.ICGtesting.com
Printed in the USA
BVOW08*0800170316

440307BV00018B/4/P

9 781478 763611